The Night of

A gripping psych

Max China

First published by skinnybirdproductions: September 2015

The right of Max China to be identified as the author of this work has been asserted by him in accordance with the Copyright, Designs, and Patents Act 1988.

All rights reserved. No part of this publication may be reproduced, stored in or introduced into a retrieval system, or transmitted in any form, or by any means (electronic, mechanical, photocopying, recording or otherwise) without the prior written permission of the author.

This work is entirely a product of the author's imagination, and is therefore a work of fiction.

A CIP catalogue record for this title is available from the British Library.

Copyright © 2015 Max China
All rights reserved.
ISBN: 978-0-9571312-5-5 Paperback
Also available in e-book/Kindle format

Cover by Akiragraphicz

DEDICATION

In memory of my late father, Stefan.
In time, Dad, we'll meet again.

ACKNOWLEDGMENTS

I'd like to thank everyone involved in the creation of this book, but most especially the talented author of The Trilogy of Noor, Chloe McDonald for her much-valued advice and continuing encouragement. I'm extremely grateful.

Contents

Cover Page
Copyright
Dedication
Acknowledgements

Prologue
Chapter 1
Chapter 2
Chapter 3
Chapter 4
Chapter 5
Chapter 6
Chapter 7
Chapter 8
Chapter 9
Chapter 10
Chapter 11
Chapter 12
Chapter 13
Chapter 14
Chapter 15
Chapter 16
Chapter 17
Chapter 18
Chapter 19
Chapter 20
Chapter 21
Chapter 22
Chapter 23
Chapter 24
Chapter 25
Chapter 26
Chapter 27
Chapter 28
Chapter 29
Chapter 30

[Chapter 31](#)
[Chapter 32](#)
[Chapter 33](#)
[Chapter 34](#)
[Chapter 35](#)
[Chapter 36](#)
[Chapter 37](#)
[Chapter 38](#)
[Chapter 39](#)
[Chapter 40](#)
[Chapter 41](#)
[Chapter 42](#)
[Chapter 43](#)
[Chapter 44](#)
[Chapter 45](#)
[Chapter 46](#)
[Chapter 47](#)
[Chapter 48](#)
[Chapter 49](#)
[Chapter 50](#)
[Chapter 51](#)
[Chapter 52](#)
[Chapter 53](#)
[Chapter 54](#)
[Epilogue](#)

[A message from the author](#)

Prologue

Churchend, Bristol. Monday, August 10, 1987. 7:57 a.m.

Dragged over uneven ground between the gravestones of the churchyard next to St. Michael's Orphanage, five-year-old Timothy Salter stumbled, almost falling. 'Stop it. You're hurting my hand,' he squealed.

Ahead of him, the girl's blonde pigtails swished from side to side as she ran. She didn't turn round. 'Quiet, Timmy,' she said, in low tones. 'Do you want us to get caught?'

He pulled against her, digging in with his heels.

Six years older and twice his size, his sister had little trouble jerking him back into a slow trot.

'Sarah, where are we going?' the little boy asked.

'We can't stay. We have to get as far away from here as we can.'

'But why?' He tried snatching his hand from her grasp.

Sarah tightened her grip. 'Stop that,' she said, her voice harsh, yet barely above a whisper.

Tears brimmed in Timothy's eyes. His lips trembled. 'But why?'

Sarah's face crumpled. *Oh, Mum. Dad. Wherever you are. How can I tell him?* Her mother spoke softly, as if she were right next to her, and not just in her mind. *He's too young to understand.* 'When you're older, Timmy,' Sarah said, 'I'll explain.'

'I'm scared,' he sobbed.

'So am I,' she said. 'Now, come on.'

A hundred yards further, where the churchyard met the lane, they reached a low stone wall and stopped, both of them panting. Sarah released him, placed both hands, palms down, on top of the smooth coping, and swinging her leg up, she straddled it. 'Give me your hand, Timmy.'

He held it out. She took it. Bracing herself, she hauled him up next to her. 'Everything will be all right,' she said, jumping to the ground. Reaching up, she helped him down.

The caretaker stood in the boiler house doorway and watched the children clear the wall. A simple man, he'd done what he thought best. He knew the men who came to the home in the dead of night were powerful, untouchable. He'd seen what had happened to the new girl the night before, and he knew it wouldn't be long before they went into the little boy's wing. If he blew the whistle, they'd destroy him. The magistrate would have him put away in prison.

He would give the children a few more minutes, and then report that he'd mislaid his keys.

In the dry and dusty country lane, tall trees leaned over the fleeing children. Up ahead by the crossroads, alert to their approach, a crow hopped, reluctant to leave the remains of his meal behind. Sarah stared at the carrion with disgust as they ran past. The head was flattened against the road; she recognised what the dead animal was by its ears.

'Yuck,' the little boy said. 'What is it?'

'A rabbit, I think. Come on, Timmy, you'll have to run faster than this,' she urged. 'We have to hurry. Any minute now, they'll find out we're gone and come after us.'

Sarah stopped at the crossroads. The little boy fell in behind her. 'Oh, God, Timothy. Which way do we go?'

'That way,' he said without hesitation, pointing to a lane that ran downhill. With barely enough room for a car to pass between its high tree-lined banks, it seemed the safest option. Overhead, the canopy of leaves gave the appearance of a long, dark tunnel. 'All right,' she said. 'Let's go. I don't think they'd expect us to go down there.'

Sarah hadn't a clue where they were. They'd passed only one house in the last five minutes. She'd almost knocked for help, but the cottage being so close to the orphanage worried her. She needed to get them to a police station. Running downhill gave them a brief respite. At the bottom of the lane, there was a level crossing. The barriers were down. 'There's a telephone box, Timmy,' she said, excited. Then she remembered they had no money. You don't need to pay for a 999 call, she recalled her mum had once told her. 'Timmy, over here.'

She heaved on the door and squeezed through the gap as quick as she could before the door closed on her. She stared in disbelief. The handset was missing. Pushing her way out backwards, she took Timothy's hand and approached the railway track. She looked both ways and saw nothing. She listened intently. A car! Coming down the lane. She shot round the end of the barrier, pulling her brother alongside. 'Come on, Timmy, we have to go!' Beside her, the rails hummed. She looked down the track. A train approached in the distance. The car's engine grew louder as the driver changed down through the gears.

'Let's go,' she cried. 'We've got enough time to make it!' She ran forward. Timothy pulled back. Dragging him forward, she tripped. Her foot wedged behind the rail. She tugged at it to free herself, screaming, 'Go, Timmy! Go! I'll follow.' Metal screeching against metal, sparks flew from the beneath the wheels. Through the glass of the cab, Sarah could see the driver's face, his mouth open and his eyes wide, full of horror. *It isn't going to stop!* Her little brother's feet skidded, scrabbling for purchase as he held onto her hand, desperately trying to pull her clear. The train sped towards them. Sarah screamed and let go of his hand. Timothy fell backwards out of the path of the train.

He would never speak again.

Chapter 1

Ashmore Top Security Hospital. August 10, 2014. 8:07 a.m.

Blood. Warm. Sweet. Saline. The man named Wolfe acknowledged the contradiction. Salt has a sweetness all of its own. A sweet taboo. He sighed. The taste of his own blood could not compare. Hunger consumed him. Forbidden fruit. Fresh meat.

Salivating, becoming erect, he touched himself, cursing the devil. *You promised me the Earth for my soul and delivered nothing.*

Biting down hard on his lower lip, he closed his eyes and then swallowed. The flavour, vile, tainted by hospital diet, revolted him.

They were moving him. On a bloody Sunday. Somewhere, he'd been told, better equipped to deal with him. From the angle of the sun, he knew it was almost time. *Will I go quietly?* He grinned. A trickle of bloody saliva escaped the corner of his mouth. Wiping it on the back of his hand, he examined it before licking it clean. *Lull them into a false sense of security. That's what I'll do.*

The tramp of heavy boots announced the approach of a squad of guards. They paused while steel doors were opened and banged shut.

More men than before. After the last time, it was to be expected. He'd got a taste of meat before they'd overpowered him, before tenderizing his six-foot-ten-inch frame to a bloody pulp.

The footsteps resumed and then came to a halt outside his cell. He jack-knifed from the bed and crossed the room, ready.

Guard Chisolm peered through the observation panel in the steel door. From the other side, Wolfe glowered at him.

'Stand away from the door,' Chisolm said.

'You coming in?'

'Step back, Wolfe.'

Instinct dictated he should stay where he was, defiant. And then he changed his mind. *Lull them into a false sense of security . . .* Wolfe took a backward step.

The outer skin of the medication hatch grated as it slid open. At just a couple of inches short of Wolfe's great height, Chisolm stooped with some discomfort and put the plastic cup he carried on the flat surface. 'Drink this,' he growled, and slamming the steel plate shut, peered through the viewer to watch the giant patient's approach.

'Got anything good in it?'

'Something to help you relax. That's all.'

Wolfe shrugged, took a step forward, and collected the cup.

'You know how this works,' Chisolm said. 'Easy or hard. Now, let me see you drink it.'

The patient swallowed it like a fine whisky.

'Best get on the bunk, Wolfman. That little cocktail's going to hit you hard. We don't want any accidents, do we? And you know what they say, the bigger you are, the harder—'

'You'd know better than me about taking a fall, Chisolm,' Wolfe sneered.

'Is that right?' the guard said. 'Now get on the bed.'

Chapter 2

Hilltop Cottage, Churchend. 8:12 a.m.

Michael Anderson carried a silver breakfast tray, laden with toast, marmalade, and coffee through the open French doors and onto the timber patio deck. He checked the position of the sun, and satisfied the shadow he cast was conducive to glare-free reading, he put the tray on the open slats of the hexagonal table and went back inside to collect his latest reading material.

He thought about his trip to Brighton, wandering the lanes as he'd so often done with Margot. *Did I really go there yesterday?* If it wasn't for the book, the whole thing could have been a dream. He'd browsed as if she were still with him, peering into stores that held no interest for him out of a habit that hadn't existed in years. He did a double-take as he walked past the front of a second-hand bookstore called Fortunes. Intrigued, he entered the store. The shop had been decorated in gipsy themes, the centrepiece an old vardo. At the base of the steps to the caravan, he'd spotted a bargain bucket. Anderson wasn't usually given to rummaging for cut-price deals, but a book, its title poking out from one side, caught his attention. *Problem Child*, by Stella Bird. The author wasn't anyone familiar to him. He extracted it from the piled-up contents of the wicker basket and purchased it on a whim without looking at the pitch on the back cover.

It was after nine o'clock when he arrived home, the evening all but gone. Stuck in traffic, he'd chewed on mints to stave off hunger, and now that he'd made a cheese sandwich, it tasted of cardboard. After two bites, he threw what was left in the bin and climbed the stairs to run a bath. He turned the taps on and then stood by the washbasin while it filled, staring at his reflection in the mirrored cabinet. A familiar debate started inside his head. *You're tired. You don't need those. But I sleep so much better when I've had them.* He opened the cabinet, took out a box of Nytol, and automatically popped two of them through the foil. He no longer took the pills to help him sleep; he'd acquired a psychological dependency on them. He swallowed them and then got undressed. He lowered himself into the water.

Half an hour later, already in the grip of the pills he'd taken, his initial glance at the back-page pitch stirred long-forgotten memories. The author stated that the book was a tribute to a psychiatrist who hadn't been afraid to experiment with new ideas. That she'd assembled the book based on the notes and diaries of Dr Ryan. *My old friend Ryan? Couldn't be.* A sense of jubilance had risen in him. How right he'd been to purchase the book! Stella Bird's introduction ran to several pages. She apologised for not using his Christian name and explained that she'd only learned it after his death. Out of respect, she'd refer to him by his surname, the way he'd preferred in life.

Ryan, he mused, such a character. Although a friend, he never knew his first name either. Once, when Anderson had asked him for it, he'd said, "Just call me Ryan. Shall I call you Mick?"

Anderson's smile broadened, lifting his spirits as he recalled his answer. 'No, call me Michael.'

Ryan never did address him by his first name.

Anderson retrieved the book from the coffee table in the conservatory. He relished the idea of reading for a couple of hours with nothing to disturb him but chirping birds and the lazy buzz of fat bumblebees. He strode through the house and returned outside with the book tucked under his arm.

The chair's legs juddered as he dragged it back, preparing to sit. The desktop magnifying glass and book set down, he sat and shuffled himself into position, arranging the magnifier to straddle the page he'd bookmarked the night before.

After spreading jam on a piece of toast, he poured himself a coffee. A final adjustment to the layout of the book, and he lifted his cup and sipped before taking a bite, savouring the taste. He leant forwards and peered through the convex glass.

With no clear recollection of what he'd already read, beyond a fuzzy memory, Anderson flicked through the book and realised he'd only completed two pages. Beginning again, he skipped through the author introduction until he reached the section's last page. His eyes locked momentarily on her justification for releasing the book.

"I was with Dr Ryan in his last hours and he'd been remarkably lucid. Although I was only a secretary, he'd treated me like a confidante for much of the time I worked for him. He told me of his great interest in the supernatural, and how he'd hoped to one day use his notes to write a book, something he never got around to doing. He had no children. His wife had died some years before. I'm not sure why, but he decided to bequeath me his personal notes and files. I believe his hope was that I'd find a way to publish them." Stella concluded with the legend, 'Patients' names have been changed to protect their identities.'

Will I recognise any of them? How long ago did Ryan and I part company? Anderson sat back in his chair and squinted at the walls of the house made brilliant by the sun, as if caught in a spell. His mind rolled back through the many milestones carved from joy and pain. *Thirty-five years.* His life as it was then danced before him. He smiled wistfully. Finally, he blinked and turned away.

He resumed reading.

When I was a young doctor working in Ireland in the late sixties, I met a girl who would change the course of my life. She was little more than fifteen. I had attended her following a report from her aunt that she was sick. Her family doctor could not be summoned. I was his stand-in. From the moment she told me, "Doctor David's not coming," and then whispered, word for word, the contents of a note later found with David's body, I knew she was something special. How had she known? I'd already begun to develop an interest in the paranormal, and here I was in the presence of a child who, without doubt, had been blessed with powers of clairvoyance. I wanted to study her further, an opportunity that was to be denied, but she triggered an interest that became a lifetime obsession. If I'd never met her, would I have become a child psychiatrist? Would I have tried alternative treatments where conventional methods had failed? If it hadn't been for her, I'd have never dreamed of it. And I certainly wouldn't have become involved with some of the most interesting events imaginable.

Fully engrossed, and with Ryan's voice in his head like he'd last heard it yesterday, Anderson didn't notice the shadow encroaching on his peripheral vision. Instead, a strange sensation drew his focus. Numbed pain. Dull and insistent, at the soft corner of his left eyelid. *What the?* He cuffed himself as he swatted the thing away. *Some kind of insect.*

Anderson drew a finger across the affected area; a bump was already forming. *Leave it alone, or it'll start to itch.* If it did, he'd call in at the chemist and buy some antihistamines. *Damned mosquitoes.* He'd never been bitten there before. He swivelled his eyeballs left. The swelling, a skin-coloured blur, irritated him like a smear on a pair of reading glasses. *Damn.* He pushed back in his chair and as he stood, he glanced through the magnifier at the page beneath. *What the hell?* Peering closer, against the background of a two-line break – between scenes, apparently dead, lay the biggest and blackest mosquito he'd ever seen. The magnified image held him fascinated.

The creature had come to rest on its side. In profile, it looked like a grotesque parody of an ostrich. Attached to a tiny head, the petrol-tank body was fuelled by means of an enormous proboscis. The hind legs, disproportionate in size, intrigued him. Designed for walking? *No, more like landing gear.*

His eyelid began to itch.
The irritation too much, he decided he'd find some lotion to relieve it temporarily. He turned away, got up, and went inside.

Chapter 3

St. Michael's Church. 8:21 a.m.

A silent scream parting his lips, Timothy Salter jolted upright in bed and pitched himself forwards, eyes wide, hands outstretched, snatching at empty air; his first thought, always his sister. Crushed by nightmares as surely as Sarah had been under the wheels of the train, his shoulders slumped. He fell backwards onto the dishevelled bedding.

Arrows of light beamed through the boarded-up slats of the presbytery window and stabbed at the darkness of the squalid room. His eyes adjusted. On top of the bushel crate he'd turned onto its end to use as a makeshift bedside table, was a photograph of him and Sarah taken by his father in the garden of their home. It was a tenuous link to the only happiness he'd ever known. His gaze lingered over her. Only ten, wisdom beyond her years already apparent on a face now faded by exposure to daylight. She stood with one hand on his shoulder and a wan smile at her lips. Her hair was swept from her face by the breeze blowing that day. Blonder than he was, she seemed to be staring right back at him. For an instant, he saw through his father's eyes, saw himself dressed in a black and white cowboy outfit, wearing a too-big Stetson, sat astride a tricycle, aiming a toy gun at his dad, while Sarah, grinning at his antics, looked straight ahead. He imagined the touch of her hand on his shoulder. He always thought of her hands. They seemed too big for a little girl. He remembered his mother's words. "Smile for the camera, my lovely angels."

He smiled.

A flashbulb went off in his mind.

Long lost voices came back to him. His mother and father. He'd already been alive longer than they had lived.

'Are you sure it'll be all right to leave the children with your sister, Russ?' His mother saw him watching, and she moved with his father out of earshot. Though he couldn't hear them, Timothy read their lips, a talent he'd picked up from a deaf boy at the nursery. 'She isn't really old enough.'

'Don't be daft,' his father replied. 'She's eighteen next month, and she's lived with us long enough to know what's what.'

'I know. I just worry Jane isn't mature enough to look after them without us around.' She sighed. 'I wish Mum and Dad hadn't gone to live in Australia.'

'And I wish mine weren't dead. Look, it's just for the weekend,' his father said, embracing her. 'Don't worry. They'll be fine. We'll have fun.'

Timothy lifted the photograph and began the ritual he repeated every day. He scrutinised the shiny surfaces in the background of the picture. A dark garage window had caught the shadowy image of his parents, their faces obscured behind the brilliant star-shaped flash from the camera. *What happened to you?* Even today, he didn't know for sure. He knew they'd been killed, but there had been some reluctance on the part of the authorities to explain exactly how. On the day his parents were due home, the police arrived with a man and woman he didn't know. Social workers. Despite Jane's protests – 'I'll call Nan and Grandad,' she'd yelled – he and Sarah had been taken away and placed into care.

If Sarah had only known their grandparents had left Australia almost straight away, to come for them, she might have been able to hang on. *No, she wouldn't – we ran because she wanted to save me.*

After the accident, he'd been returned to the home. The same night, the men came and took him out of the dormitory to another room. He shook his head violently, but the experience remained. The men were fascinated by his apparent refusal to cry out. They drank, laughed and took photographs.

When it was over, and he'd been returned to bed, the caretaker came. 'Come on, boy. I'm getting you out of here.' Snatches of what the man had said in the car journey came back to him. 'One day, Timothy, you'll see what I did was right. I'm taking you to a woman I know. She couldn't have a kid of her own. She'll see you right. Her people are rough and ready, but they'll not allow any harm to come your way.'

He lived with the woman among travelling people for twelve years, always moving. There wasn't a part of the country he hadn't seen. They'd accepted his refusal to speak, assuming he was mute. He learned to work the land using only basic tools, earning his keep doing odd jobs; he became a skilled gardener.

One night, sitting around the fire somewhere in the wilds outside Scotland, a wandering woman came by the camp. She stayed for just one night. He listened enthralled as she told stories, but one in particular struck him. The woman's eyes burned into him as she related the tale. It was his story. The story of him and Sarah, right down to what happened with the train. The old woman concluded by saying the little girl's ghost would find no rest until her brother returned to the lanes she haunted.

As soon as he had the chance, he returned to Churchend. The orphanage had been closed for years. The old priest had accepted his offer to work on the grounds; he'd seen how destitute the boy appeared.

'Where are you staying?' the priest asked.

Timothy took a pad from his pocket, scribbled on it with a pencil, and held it out.

Father Raymond took it. 'I'll not see you sleeping under the stars – not while there's room under God's roof.' The old man had never discovered Timothy's true identity. Over the years, he revealed snippets of information to his guest, usually when in drink. 'My predecessor, he knew what was going on. How could he not have?' He'd scrutinised Timothy. 'If that's what you're thinking, you'd be right. The drunken pervert kept a diary. I found it over there.' His hand indicated the altar. 'There, of all places. Brazen. No shame. Died of a heart attack when he heard the caretaker had gone to the police. And then the whole sorry tale came out.' The priest took a sip of his whisky, swilled it around the glass and then drained the last of it. He wiped his mouth with the back of his hand. 'It took a while for the authorities to close the place down. They never found the little boy. His grandparents had come all the way from Australia to apply for adoption. Heartbroken, they were. That family was cursed, I tell you. The caretaker stood before the courts and testified, but I think he knew more about what had happened with the children than he let on. With the men involved convicted and jailed, it didn't take long for the stain to spread over the church. People began to stay away.' He stood and swayed, gripping the edge of the table. 'Pass me the bottle, would you?'

Timothy obliged.

Father Raymond poured himself another and offered the open neck to his guest. Timothy shook his head.

The priest lowered his voice, and holding the back of his hand to his mouth, spoke with theatrical discretion. 'You'll probably think I'm crazy, but I swear I've seen a little girl running among the graves.' Distracted by his recollections, he failed to see Timothy sit up, more attentive. 'I always think there's more to ghosts than we can fathom. You know, there's a reason for everything on God's Earth. Life has a way of negating evil things. Did you ever wonder why you always find a dock plant among nettles? The cure for our ills is never far away if you know where to look for it.' After that conversation, Timothy took to walking the lanes, the tracks, the graveyard, endlessly searching. But he never saw Sarah.

His reverie over, he picked up the tear-off calendar. August 9. The words of wisdom beneath the date were attributed to Abraham Lincoln: "The best thing about the future is that it comes one day at a time."

Twenty-seven years had passed exactly like that, but nothing had changed. He caught a glimpse of himself in the mirror on the wall. Gaunt. Deep-set eyes stared back at him. He saw nothing in them other than a bleak wilderness and ever-lasting guilt. He touched them, expecting to feel pain. He'd lost weight. He had to eat. If his death was judged self-inflicted, that would be suicide, and he'd be consigned to purgatory, never to see his loved ones again. He hesitated, and then, ripping the page clear, crumpled it into a ball and placed the calendar back by his bed.

He got dressed, slipped his Bible into the top pocket of his boiler suit and prepared for what he had to do.

Chapter 4

Ashmore Top Security Hospital. 8:25 a.m.

The guard pushing the wheelchair bearing the oversized prisoner along the corridor glanced down at Wolfe. The giant's head, dipping lower with each stride, slumped and came to rest on his shoulder.

'He's gone,' the guard said, like a parent who'd succeeded in getting a wayward child to sleep, and continued towards the lift.

Although the patient was strapped in and flanked by a contingent of ten men, Chisolm eyed him warily. 'Do not assume for one moment he's less dangerous because he's doped up,' he said, without breaking stride. 'I heard he came up like a jack-in-a-box last time he was moved. Doctors underestimated the dose needed to keep him under. Took a bite out of someone's arm, right through the shirtsleeve, swallowed it before anyone could stop him. He knew he wasn't going anywhere. Did it for pure devilment.'

'I heard that, too.' The guard steered the wheelchair round a corner. 'No one knew what he was like back then, did they? To be honest, I'd gladly finish him if I had the chance. Do society a big favour.'

'I think that goes for all of us,' Chisolm replied. A chorus of grunts signalled the squad's approval.

Impassive, if Wolfe had heard their words, he gave no sign. His face pressed close to his exposed upper arm, a trickle of fluid oozed from the corner of his mouth, staining the high-cut sleeve of the blue gown he wore. Wolfe had long ago perfected the art of swallowing and sly regurgitation after studying early twentieth-century magicians and escape artists, particularly Houdini. The cocktail was strong enough to fell an elephant; Chisolm had told him that once he'd drunk it. The effects, though diminished by his slow expulsion, were enough to dull his senses. He wondered absently if they'd deliberately overdosed him. He needed to be sick, and fast. But not yet. Outside, that's when he'd do it – if he was still conscious. He focused on the whisper of rubber wheels against the hard vinyl floor, on the stopping and starting, as he was reversed into the sterile security zones between doors; one banged shut and locked before the other unlocked and opened.

The last of the liquid expelled, Wolfe's tongue felt huge, rubbery. He bit into it, focusing on the pain. Sheer force of will prevented him from falling under the spell of the residual chemicals.

Another door. Fresh air on his skin. The sun shone through his eyelids; blood orange, the colour of tomato soup. He was outside. The August warmth soothed him. Suddenly spun around, he was being hauled in reverse. The wheelchair bumped up something with a metallic clang. A ramp. The whine of an electric lift. He daren't peep beneath his eyelashes – Chisolm would see. The motor stopped. More manoeuvring. He was in a vehicle. His concentration lapsed, and he slipped into the dark streets he inhabited in his dreams, lurking in the shadows, away from the gas-lit pools of light that gleamed off wet cobblestones in the midnight mist, looking for prey.

His body sagged.

'Finally,' Chisolm said, checking his watch. *Eight twenty-eight a.m.* 'Now he's *really* under.'

Chapter 5

Copse Hall. 8:31 a.m.

George Kotlas turned into the visitor's car park and pulled up close to the reception building. He looked around as he opened the back door and unhooked his suit jacket from the holder above the window. The tarmac and white-lining was obviously new. Only one other car was parked there. A mixture of excitement and anticipation fluttered in his stomach. He recalled the letter Dr Rubenstein had sent three weeks ago. It had contained a brief introduction, together with an invitation to call him, but it was the title – Director of Forensic Psychiatry, Proof and Experimental Unit – that drew Kotlas in.

'Dr Rubenstein? It's George Kotlas. You wrote to me—'
'Dr Kotlas.' Rubenstein cleared his throat. 'Yes, I did. I take it you're interested?'
'At this stage, I'd say I'm more curious. Why approach me?'
'Haven't you heard, Kotlas? There's an acute shortage of psychiatrists per se. And practitioners with your provenance are rarer still. I sent a non-disclosure form with the letter. Sign and return it to me. Until then I'm not at liberty to discuss anything further.'

Kotlas complied. A flurry of correspondence followed; a formal interview was arranged and confirmed in writing, along with a list of procedures to be followed on his arrival at the hospital. It occurred to him that Sunday was an odd day to ask him to come in, but it was his day off. It suited him. He still didn't know exactly what his new role, if successful, would entail. He patted his pocket to check his passport hadn't fallen out, locked the car, and then followed the directional signs for Reception.

Once Kotlas had completed his security induction, he sat examining his knuckles, comparing one hand to the other. When he'd finished that, he turned to his palms. Unsurprisingly, the calluses on his right were harder and thicker than those on his left. The security guard that had recorded his fingertip biometrics had remarked on them. 'Are you sure you're a doctor? Your hands look like you lay bricks in your spare time.'

Kotlas had grinned. 'I do a lot of work with my hands.'

The door in front of him opened. A bespectacled middle-aged man stepped through and locked it behind him. 'Dr Kotlas, I presume?' He closed the space between them with surprising speed and held out his hand. 'I'm Dr Rubenstein. Philip, but we use last names around here. Welcome. I'm sorry about the delay. Control Room protocol, I'm afraid. Come on through.' He unlocked the door again. 'I'll escort you up to my office.'

Rubenstein used his keys to open and close the numerous doors that barred their way. Finally, he led the younger man into a long passage around the corner.

'I've lost my bearings a little bit,' Kotlas said, and paused in the middle of the corridor. 'Is this new? It's just that I noticed a large, older building close behind where Reception would be.'

'Keep moving, Kotlas.' Rubenstein glanced at the CCTV monitors projecting from the ceiling. 'You'll make security nervous. To answer your question, it's a blend of new construction and the adaptation of the existing. This institution is the first of its kind in the country. Aside from those who work here, few are aware of its existence. Copse Hall is a private enterprise, located on a vast country estate, well away from prying eyes. Here, we hope to gain greater insight into the minds of some of the worst former juvenile killers in the world. What goes on here is not for discussion beyond these walls,' Rubenstein said. 'You know, I'm envious of you, Kotlas. At your age, the possibilities of being on the cutting edge, the opportunities that will present themselves . . .'

'We'll see.' Kotlas nodded thoughtfully. 'Very quiet, isn't it?'

'We have just a few patients at the moment, and the staffing levels are commensurate with that. I'll explain further when we get to my office. Right. Here we are.' Rubenstein stopped by a passenger lift. He placed his fingertips on the reader control, and the steel sleeves of the doors slid open. They stepped inside. The doors automatically closed and they began to ascend.

Rubenstein unlocked his office door and ushered Kotlas through. 'There's another reason for the facility appearing quiet. We've sent ten guards out to collect our star patient, from Ashmore.'

'Ashmore? That's where I work,' Kotlas said.

'I must confess, it's part of why I approached you.'

'So, not so much about shortage, more about provenance.' Kotlas' eyes narrowed. 'Ten-man security detail? Not many warrant that. I think I know the answer to my next question. What's his name?'

Rubenstein indicated the vacant chair. 'Take a seat,' he said, walking around his desk. 'First things first. I already know a lot about you. Let's fill in the blanks.'

'No. Wait. How can you have arranged to do that without me knowing?' Kotlas shook his head.

Rubenstein peered over the top of his spectacles. 'Patience, dear boy. We'll come back to that in a few moments.'

Ten minutes later, Rubenstein pushed away from the desk and walked to the window. He turned, and leaning against the window board, faced Kotlas. 'Look, as far as I'm concerned, based on what we've discussed, the job's yours.'

Kotlas smiled. 'That's great, but you haven't explained exactly what my role is . . . if I accept. Or how you managed to find out so much about me. You said this is a private company?'

Rubenstein rubbed his lower lip with a forefinger. 'Yes, I did.'

'So tell me, who leaked the information?'

Rubenstein strode back to his seat, sat down, propped his elbows on the desk, and clasped his hands together. 'I want you to continue your work with Wolfe.'

Kotlas leaned back in his chair. 'And the leak?'

'There's no leak. All this may seem presumptuous, but if you accept, you're cleared to begin working with us right away.'

Kotlas pulled on the lobe of his left ear. 'Forgive me. I just have to be sure of a few things . . .'

'I told you, this establishment is top-secret. We're in partnership with the government. It's an arm's-length arrangement.'

'In case things go wrong,' Kotlas said, tight-lipped. 'And if I don't accept?'

'Someone else will. But you are our preferred option. What do you say?'

'I get to continue working with Wolfe?'

'Under my stewardship, yes.' Rubenstein paused. 'Do you accept?'

Kotlas reached for a sheet of paper. 'Can I?'

'Of course.' Rubenstein watched, puzzled, as Kotlas took a pen from his inside pocket and scribbled a list of notes. He pushed the paper across the desk. 'Subject to these terms.'

The older man took the sheet and read. 'I can live with those things. We'll get a contract drawn up. Now, tell me what you know about the man.'

'I'm sure you know most of this already, but this is my resume. Wolfe weighed in at twenty-three pounds when he was born.'

Rubenstein raised his eyebrows.

'You didn't know that?'

'Of course I did, but hearing of such an abnormality never fails to stagger me,' the older man said. 'Carry on.'

'I think it's obvious he was delivered by Caesarean section. His parents were both six-footers, but neither side of the family had had a child that big before. Destined for greatness, some might say, but he was never going to have a normal life. He outgrew his parents by the time he was nine years old. He claims he first killed when he was ten, but there's nothing to substantiate that. By the age of thirteen, he was uncontrollable. Killed two girls that year, and despite a massive police hunt, went on to kill five more before they caught him. Bad, isn't it? The savagery of the killings shocked even hardened detectives. The method used was pretty much the same in each case. They all had something in common: He ate bits of them. Took different parts from each. Trying different things on the menu, he told me. As you're aware, he's been in the system ever since.'

'You've worked with him for the last two years. How do you see him? Mad or bad?'

'What do you think?'

'Kotlas, I'm asking you,' Rubenstein said.

'He's had dozens of psychiatric assessments, and not one of them agrees. To me, he's both. He sees himself as a victim of his genes.'

'He does? That one is news to me,' Rubenstein said. 'Elaborate.'

'Wolfe,' Kotlas said softly. 'What's in a name, eh? It comes from his mother's side. As you probably know, he adopted it when his father died.'

'Yes, I found that strange. You'd have thought he'd want to keep his father's name alive.'

'Maybe. You also know he claims a psychic link to Jack the Ripper?'

'That wasn't taken seriously.' Rubenstein, perhaps sensing a change in tack, viewed Kotlas with suspicion. 'Why do you bring it up?'

'Wolfe became more difficult to deal with, complaining that no one listened to him. He went berserk during a routine transfer. Bit one of the staff. He almost overpowered eight burly nurses, all of them highly trained. He ended up in seclusion for a long time. It took me ages to get through to him again.' Kotlas moistened his lips. 'Can I have a glass of water?'

'Over there,' Rubenstein pointed at the water cooler. 'Help yourself.'

The young candidate got to his feet, continuing to speak as he approached the machine. 'I told him there was only one way to prove what he was saying was true.' He filled a clear plastic cup and took a sip. 'Submit to a DNA test.'

'They went along with that at Ashmore?' Rubenstein seemed incredulous. 'For that to work, you'd have needed a sample from the Ripper.'

'There is genetic material,' Kotlas said. 'It was recently recovered from historic samples found at the scene of one of the murders.'

'I heard about that, but honestly, that semen could have come from anyone.'

'That's what they said at Ashmore, but I wanted to take it further, if only to get Wolfe to see that what he was experiencing had no basis in fact.'

'Did they relent?'

'No. I took some of Wolfe's hair. It wasn't hard; he consented. I sent it for independent testing.'

'I'm going to stop you there, Kotlas. What you did is in contravention—'

'Hear me out, Rubenstein,' he said harshly.

The older man reddened, unaccustomed to being addressed in such a manner.

'I'm sorry. But guess what? It was a match. He's related. Now, you can argue till you're blue in the face that it may not be the Ripper's DNA, but even if it isn't, what are the odds of Wolfe's sample coming up positive? Answer me that. And what is even more bizarre, I read somewhere that the Ripper had a taste for blood, and that certain body parts were missing from his victims. The official line from those days was that he'd taken them as trophies, but I now believe he ate them. Maybe blood-thirst runs in the genes, and if we accept that, it could be where Wolfe gets it from.'

Rubenstein stared, measuring the younger man. 'It seems you're not above a little experimentation yourself, Kotlas.' He stood abruptly and strode around the desk, offering his hand. 'Welcome aboard.'

Chapter 6

St Michael's Church. 8:36 a.m.

Timothy Salter looped a piece of string around the stems of the wildflowers he'd collected and tied it. Every year he performed the same ritual, increasing the number of species collected by one. He had to find twenty-seven this time.

Kneeling on the grass by the grave, he put them in the vase he'd filled with water earlier. He teased the spray of multi-coloured blooms to best effect, the delicate reds of Burning Love fashioned into a heart-shaped centrepiece, then placed the vase on the weathered Yorkstone slab at the foot of the headstone. He shuffled in close and ran his outstretched fingertips over the letters carved in the light riven face.

Russell Timothy Salter July 8, 1955 – Aug. 9, 1987
May Marie Salter May 31, 1956 – Aug. 9, 1987
Sarah Grace Salter Feb. 29, 1976 – Aug. 10, 1987

Tragically taken . . .

On a tour of the graveyard, soon after Father Raymond had provided him with shelter, the priest had told him how the grandparents of the little girl had arrived from Australia to bury their daughter, only to discover Sarah, too, had died tragically while they were enroute, and their grandson was missing.

'It was a hell of a thing, Timothy,' the priest had said. 'Can you imagine the upset? The children's parents were murdered in the early hours of the Sunday morning on their way home from a night out. That poor family. They laid the three of them to rest in the same grave. The grandparents stayed a good long while, hoping the little boy would turn up, but despite a nationwide search, he was never seen again. They paid for an extra deep plot just in case the worst happened, though the grandmother wouldn't accept he was dead. She said she hoped he'd find out where they'd been buried one day. And if he chose, when his time came, he could be buried there, too.'

Timothy marked the anniversary each year, only on the day Sarah had died. He carried her more in his heart than his parents. Head bowed, he crossed himself and prayed in silence, remembering her and what he could of his mum and dad.

'Why were you screaming in your sleep last night, Timmy?' Sarah asked.
'I can't remember,' he'd replied.
The two of them were laid alongside each other outside, in the garden at home, on the lawn. Sarah plucked a blade of grass and carefully stood it between her thumbs, holding it firm. She blew over it gently, producing a low, reedy sound.
He'd plucked a blade for himself and tried it, but only succeeded in dribbling.
'Here, Timmy,' Sarah said, 'let me show you.'
And he'd watched her and he'd learned. Soon, they played a chorus of screeching notes before falling about, overcome by laughter. Sarah lay on her back. 'Timmy,' she said.
'What?'
Sarah rolled over towards him and blew a devastating shriek close to his face. Timothy retaliated, trying to match it for loudness. And on and on they went.

Five minutes later, their mother came out. 'What's all that awful noise?'
The children giggled.
'Pack it in, before the neighbours complain.'

In the quiet moments that followed, remembering his nightmare, Timothy became sombre.

'What is it, Timmy?'

'I just remembered what I dreamt about.' He began to wail. 'I got lost and I couldn't find any of you.'

Sarah sidled up close and put her arm around his shoulders. 'Timmy, if you ever get lost, just do this.' She blew between her thumbs. The blade of grass screamed its song into the air. 'And no matter where you are, if I hear it, I'll find you.' She smiled. 'Better now?'

'Oi, you two.' Their father stood, hands on hips in the doorway. 'Your mum says, stop making that racket and get inside for your supper.'

Timothy plucked a blade of grass, clamped it top and bottom between his thumbs the way Sarah had shown him years ago, and replicated the sound he'd heard her blow.

No one came.

Chapter 7

Hilltop Cottage. 8:42 a.m.

Anderson looked in the mirror. The eye the mosquito had bitten had not only swelled, it itched him like a nest of tiny vipers. He couldn't find anything in the bathroom cabinet to provide relief other than calamine lotion. He dabbed it over the affected area before returning downstairs to the kitchen.

He filled the kettle and switched it on. A brief silence followed as the element heated to optimum temperature. The water began to fizz, pop and rumble. Anderson swilled his cup clean under the tap, drying the outside and bottom surface only before placing it ready on the worktop. He turned to pick up the teaspoon he'd left on the drainer earlier and paused. *Something's wrong.* The light outside grew brighter and flashed with brilliant intensity. Instantly, every shadow was scoured from the walls and ceilings. Plugs exploded. The burglar alarm signalled power failure, its stand-by battery beeping a warning. He smelled burning. The smoke alarm kicked in. The pulsing pitch pierced his ears. He covered them. *Shit! I'm going to need an electrician.*

Unholstering his mobile, he took it from his hip. Looking at it, he frowned. The screen was blank. Turning it off and on made no difference. Lightning flashed. Thunder grumbled. *My book!* He dashed outside as it started to rain. The pages seemed to have changed from white to yellow. He blinked, convinced the brightness of the light he'd just witnessed had affected his vision – and then he noticed the mosquito had vanished. He snatched the book out from under the shelter provided by the magnifier, checking to see if the creature had definitely gone before closing it. Puzzled, he scanned the table top looking for the insect. His brow furrowed. *Did I really kill it? If so, where is it now?* Great splats of water – two, three, a dozen – machine-gunned him, chasing him inside.

Clifton Bridge.

The cellular, purpose-built Ford Transit was, in effect, a mobile prison. Once Wolfe was secured in the wheelchair within one of the two cells, Chisolm split eight of the guards between the escort cars.

The vehicle cleared security and departed the exit gates. Confident he'd hear nothing from his prisoner for the duration of the journey, Chisolm stretched the length of the bench seat and closed his eyes.

The driver saw the simultaneous failure register on the instrumentation panel a split second before a brilliant surge of light blinded him. Instinctively he hit the brakes. The servo system cut out. No longer power-assisted, the steering wheel pulled left. The driver's arms heaving, he hauled right to compensate for the unexpected drift.

Ahead, the lead vehicle screeched, braking hard. It collided with the back of a line of cars that had also stopped suddenly.

Desperate not to crash, the driver half stood, his body weight pushing down on the brake pedal, his face a mask of terror.

BANG. The bus slammed into the rear end of the escort.

Behind, the second car skidded and struck the transport vehicle, adding momentum to its superior weight. Unstoppable, it crushed the car in front, jamming it further up the line and compressing it to half its normal size. Metal creaked and crumpled. Tyres exploded.

Thrown from his seat, Chisolm leapt to his feet. 'What the fuck's going on?' he shouted above the noise. 'A hijack?' Oblivious to the dazzling light outside, he anchored himself, feet planted square, hands clamped firm around two of the handcuff straps fitted to the wall. The van banked. Rose swiftly to forty-five degrees. Chisolm braced himself. The vehicle flipped, rising sharply on the driver's side like it had hit a stunt ramp, smashed through a brick wall and left the road. Chisholm's body twisted; his feet left the floor. Desperately gripping onto the straps, legs flailing, he was flung upward.

BOOM. He realised they'd hit something – hard. The vehicle's trajectory changed; it spun in the opposite direction. His weight, combined with forces greater than he could handle, snapped his arm. He screamed, eyes bulging in disbelief as bone, piercing skin, dug through his sleeve. Unable to hold on one-handed, Chisolm tumbled end over end, smashing into the van walls, ceiling and seats, cracking ribs, battering his head, hips and thighs. He cried out in agony, helpless as a shirt in a washing machine, trying to make sense of the feeling of weightlessness that followed. Airborne, he thought he'd caught a fleeting glimpse of Wolfe looking out of the cell door at him. Long seconds later, the vehicle crashed down, the impact buckled the roof, twisting the chassis out of shape. Doors, bursting their locks, exploded open.

What's that smell? Something alight? He clutched at his arm. Useless. Wincing, ribs on fire and crippled by pain, he dragged himself outside, clear of the van. He passed out.

Copse Hall.

Kotlas shielded his eyes at the sudden glare. 'What the hell was that?'

Rubenstein squinted, stood and approached the window. 'I don't know. Can you feel that heat?' He stopped short of the glass. 'I'm no expert, but the only thing I can think of that would do that is some kind of detonation or a solar flare. Either way, wouldn't we have had a warning?'

'It wasn't a bomb. If it were, we'd have heard an explosion or felt an aftershock. I don't think you'd see a solar flare with the naked eye. I read something a while ago about sunspots being a precursor. As for predictability, I happen to know that the utility companies were supposed to redesign the power grids and so on to withstand a surge.'

'Okay, so we agree.' Rubenstein jerked a thumb in the direction of the sun. 'And if we're right, that has to be a solar flare like we've never seen before. Imagine what it would be like if the glass wasn't tinted?' He pressed the blackout blind control. It failed to work. 'What's wrong with this thing?' He pushed the switch again. 'Kotlas, do me a favour and turn the lights on.'

The younger man rose and flipped the switch. 'They're not working either,' he said. 'And I hate to say this, but your computer is off as well.'

Rubenstein sat down heavily. 'Oh, God. I hope auto-save kicked in.'

'If you're connected to the server, you'll be fine.'

The look on Rubenstein's face told him he wasn't. 'I was working offline; we've had an IT problem. Contractors are coming in to fix it later.'

'Had you done much since your last backup?' Kotlas asked.

'Some theory I wanted to test before going live, that's all, and no, I haven't backed up since last night. So much for you saying the grid's been redesigned.' He glared at Kotlas and flushed with anger as if he held him responsible.

'I once lost a whole day's work like that—'

'Fucking hell.' Rubenstein slammed the desktop with the flat of his hand.

Kotlas stared, uncomfortable with his senior's display of anger.

'Okay, so if it's gone, I'll just have to do it again. Shit.' Rubenstein cocked his head. 'Can you hear that?'

Kotlas opened the soundproofed door. Cacophonous noise poured through the gap. People running, shouting. Screaming. He grabbed at and caught the shirtsleeve of a maintenance worker as he ran past, stopping him. 'What's happening?'

'It's chaos,' the man yelled to make himself heard. 'Power's out. Auxiliary has failed. There's been a surge. The generators are working, but the juice isn't getting through.' He looked at Kotlas' hand still holding onto his sleeve. 'Doctor, I have to go.'

'Hang on. Are the patients secure?'

'I think so, but with the cameras down there's no co-ordination. Head of security is downstairs now, but I did hear one had escaped,' the worker said, and pulling free, he made for the stairs.

'Get that door shut, Kotlas, and lock it. I can't believe we spent millions on a place like this and failed to protect the delicate circuit boards. And now someone's escaped? That's fucking unbelievable.'

'I wonder if anyone's called the police?'

'No one could get out beyond the footprint of the building. Impossible. But call them just in case.'

Kotlas picked up the phone, transferred hands, and lifting it to his ear, listened. 'Dead,' he said.

Chapter 8

Avon Gorge. 8:47 p.m.

Chisolm floated in an unfamiliar realm of consciousness. Searing heat from the burning van scorched his skin. His body was battered beyond the threshold of pain. Chest tight. Arms and legs numb. Awareness slowly returning, he opened his eyes and stared in disbelief at the height of the cliff. *How the hell did I survive falling from that?* Flashes of recollection played out. His attempt to get up failed. Confused, he looked down at himself, expecting to see his legs broken and skewed at crazy angles. His gaze wandered across wide straps. He was strapped into a wheelchair and dressed in a blue gown. Blood dripped from his face.

Wolfe stepped into his line of sight and grinned. 'That was some fall you took, big man. You should've worn a seatbelt.' He dusted off his newly acquired uniform. 'One good thing about you and me, we're about the same size.'

The effort of drawing breath contorted Chisolm's features. 'You won't get far,' he gasped, 'before they catch you, Wolfe.'

He stared up at the cliff face. 'Is that right? Maybe. But I'm going further than you.' He knelt by the stricken man, grabbed his head and ran his tongue along his chin, savouring the taste. 'You know something?' Wolfe licked his lips. 'You're sweeter than you look.'

For the first time, Chisolm seemed to comprehend the nightmare he faced. Wide-eyed fear and apprehension spurring him, he rocked violently against his bonds in a futile effort to break free.

Wolfe stood and unzipped his fly. His cock sprang out. Hard. Proud. Expectant.

'Oh Christ,' Chisolm croaked, pain no longer of primary concern. 'I'm a married man, got kids. You don't want to do that. I know you don't.'

'You don't know anything about me. You see this?' he said, his hand wrapped around the thick stalk. 'This is what it does to me, and it won't go away until it's satisfied.'

'C'mon, Wolfe, you'd best be going.' Chisolm stared at the ground, afraid to meet the other man's gaze.

'You have no idea how this makes me feel,' Wolfe whispered, moving closer.

'The police will be here any minute,' Chisolm wheezed. 'The transponder will bring them.'

'Right now, do you think I care?' he said, stroking himself.

'I'd sooner you killed me than do that.'

Wolfe laughed, then growled, 'You think I want to drill you? What kind of a man do you think I am, huh?' He shook his head in disapproval, straddled the other man's lap, twisted his head to one side, and whispered, 'Shush.' Relishing Chisolm's desperate screams, he mumbled, 'Sing for me, baby,' and bit into the flesh of his victim's neck.

At the water's edge, fully clothed, Wolfe eased himself into the river. It was colder than he'd expected; a shiver of delight ran through him. He rinsed his face and hands, scrubbing the clothes he wore, fully expecting a helicopter to appear overhead, or the sound of dogs and men at any moment. He didn't care about losing his chance of escape. There were limits to how much a man of his size could disguise himself. Whatever happened, freedom would be short-lived. Might as well make the most of it.

Clambering out, he crossed the rocky shoreline, unsure which direction to take. In the distance he heard bells tolling. He turned and loped off along the valley, making for the sound.

Chapter 9

Copse Hall. 8:48 a.m.

Executive director Fleur Tadier had rushed into the ladies' washroom and spent the last ten minutes on her knees, dry-retching until finally, she'd purged herself of the breakfast she'd eaten. She hadn't paid much attention when the lights went out, but ten seconds later when the extract fan whirred to a halt, it registered with her that something was wrong. *It could be something to do with the glitch in the computer system.*

In the relative gloom of the cubicle, she pressed the flush button and then unlocked the door. She glanced up at the sun pipe. At least someone had thought to put one of those in. The daylight transference into the room wasn't great, but enough for her to admonish her reflection in the mirror. *Two weeks into the job and you're pregnant, eh?* Fleur forced a smile. It came back grimmer than she'd intended. She ran the tap, and cupping cold water into her hands, splashed some onto her face and then pulled a length of paper towelling from the dispenser. Drying herself, she checked her watch. *Best get going. The IT contractors will be turning up at Reception asking for me any moment now.*

The door swung open. An inmate dressed in a blue treatment gown stepped inside, brandishing a long, flat-headed screwdriver. It was bloodstained. His eyes darted from hers to the implement and back again. He put it out of sight behind his back. His tone unconvincing, he said, 'Don't worry, miss, we won't hurt you.'

Stay calm. Fleur moved her hand discreetly and activated her personal attack alarm. Although trained to a high degree, she'd never found herself in such a perilous situation before. 'What's your name?' she said.

'My name is Fisher.'

'Go and wait outside, Fisher. You shouldn't be in here.' Fleur fought to keep a rising sense of panic from her voice. 'Where's your escort?'

A gleeful look spread over his face. 'They're dead.'

A rush of bile caught in her throat. She choked it down. *Help will be here any second.*

Fisher thrust the tip of the screwdriver to within an inch of her left eye. 'Get your fucking clothes off.' He drooled in expectation. 'Go on. What the fuck you waiting for? DO IT.'

Her hands trembling, Fleur began to undress.

Chapter 10

Copse Hall. 9:07 a.m.

Rubenstein sharpened a pencil over a sheet of paper on his desk, testing the point for sharpness several times before he was satisfied with it. 'It shouldn't take long to get everything switched back on,' he said, tipping the shavings into the wastepaper bin beside his chair.

'It might be an appropriate time to discuss some of the things I wrote on the list I gave you.'

'That you are to be his primary carer? Without question.'

'And his medication?'

Rubenstein laid the pencil down on the blotter in front of him. 'You know, Kotlas, a big part of our funding comes from drug companies. It's an important part of our development to test new products—'

'Not on Wolfe. Not unless I test them first.'

'That's admirable, Kotlas, but impractical. I need you fully functional and fit to carry out your duties.'

'Have you ever tried any of the drugs we dispense as a matter of course?'

'No.' Rubenstein frowned. 'Have you?'

'In the interest of further understanding, yes, I have.'

Rubenstein nodded. 'We're about proof and experimentation, but our immediate aim, Kotlas, is not to cure these patients.' The creases on his forehead deepened. 'You do understand that, don't you? Our aim is to discover what factors created them. If we can isolate and trace the triggers far enough back, it's possible we can take pre-emptive steps, in the earliest stages of development.'

'You do mean mental development?' Rubinstein's fixed expression told him otherwise. 'Surely not in the womb?'

'Why not? That's where it all begins.'

'Termination will be next.'

'In the case of Wolfe and the others we have here, that wouldn't be a bad thing.'

'I disagree.'

Rubenstein sighed. 'On what grounds? Traditionalism? You know how technology has come along, Kotlas? What we could only dream of doing just a few years ago, is now a reality. We have smart drugs which we can use to target individual areas of the brain. We can modify how cells behave.'

'I understand all that, Rubenstein. However, in your enthusiasm, you forget something.'

'What's that?'

'We're human.'

'Exactly,' Rubenstein said, as if the thought had never left his mind. 'And we err. Let's agree to differ for a moment. Also on your list was that you wanted to pursue an avenue of investigation you'd already started. I assume you refer to the Ripper thing.'

'I do indeed,' Kotlas said. 'You spoke of preventative steps being taken early to avoid the propensity for violence or whatever, to iron it out?'

Rubenstein raised an eyebrow. 'What's this, an about turn?'

'Not at all. I'd like to trace Wolfe's lineage, in the light of what I found out.'

'Wait. What possible benefit can that have for this establishment?'

'Imagine, since others have tried and failed, if we were to discover the true identity of Jack the Ripper.'

Rubenstein sat forwards. 'Go on.'

'I'd imagine the drugs companies would fall over themselves for a share of the publicity.'

'We're a secret establishment. We couldn't go public. As far as the world outside is concerned, these premises are part of the Ministry of Defence.'

'Is that so?' Kotlas shook his head. 'God, can you imagine how the neighbours would react if they learned the truth about this place?'

'I'm not sure what you're getting at, Kotlas.'

'Let me continue my experiment with Wolfe. He has lucid dreams. I've been working to find out what it is his mind is churning up. If we give him drugs, we might lose not only a key insight into how his mind works, but also the chance to tap into his memories.'

'Have you made any progress with that side of it?'

'I've discovered that his father forced his mother to take psychotropic drugs while she was pregnant.'

'That's interesting.'

'So you see, potentially, it isn't just about DNA,' the younger man said. 'But the taste for blood—'

Rubenstein raised a hand. 'Hold on. The assumption the Ripper ate body parts isn't proven.'

'I know that. Let me just ask you this. Did you ever come across a Dr Ryan?'

'In my age group, there are few who aren't aware of him. But you, how did you get to hear about him?'

Kotlas ignored the question and continued. 'Wasn't he discredited?'

'Not officially,' Rubenstein said. 'Interesting you should bring him up. His early studies in chemical imbalance and the effects on children were quite an eye-opener, but I have to say, I always considered him on the fringe.'

'Because he believed in the supernatural order of things?'

'Frankly, yes.'

'And yet he got results. You only have to look at what he did achieve. He understood the link between these imbalances and adolescent suicide, perhaps better than anyone.'

'We've gone off topic, somewhat,' Rubenstein said, shifting in his chair. He craned his neck to look out of the window.

'Not really,' Kotlas said. 'We were talking about genetic makeup and a taste for blood. What if something in the blood addresses the imbalance, and makes Wolfe feel better?'

Rubenstein raised his eyebrows, considering the point. 'Could be. Or maybe he's just plain evil.' He looked at his watch. 'Wolfe should have been here by now.'

'I'm beginning to wonder if the power problem isn't just confined to here,' Kotlas said.

'Yes, I think you may be right,' Rubenstein said. He stood, walked to the window, and stared down into the courtyard. 'People are running around in the rain. I don't like it. Not one bit.'

The door handle rattled up and down. Startled, they exchanged apprehensive looks.

A sharp rap on the door followed.

'Whoever you are in there,' a muffled voice cried, 'you're to come out immediately. The building's on fire.'

'I don't like this,' Kotlas whispered.

'There's no need to whisper. No one outside can hear us. See who it is,' Rubenstein said. 'But don't open the door.'

Chapter 11

Copse Hall. 9:19 a.m.

Kotlas pressed an ear to the door. The sounds reminiscent of being submerged underwater, he slowly rotated the control knob for the Venetian blind set between two skins of glass. The blades parted, revealing a man's face pressed up against the vision panel. 'There you are,' he shouted, his voice muted. 'If you don't want to die, you'd better come with me right away.'

'What do you mean, die?' Kotlas yelled.

The man turned away to face away from him.

'Don't open the door,' Rubenstein shouted. Getting up from his desk, he crossed the room to peer through the glazed slot. 'I can't see his face. There's something going on I don't like.'

Kotlas listened intently. 'I can't hear what he's saying.' His hand hovered over the locking snib. 'Block the door with your foot, Rubenstein, if you're concerned. There are only a few inmates in here and how many staff? You didn't say. I don't believe anyone could get out and still be on the loose.'

'I think we should sit tight.'

'What are you afraid of? Exactly who else is locked up behind these walls?'

'We needn't concern ourselves with that at this moment.'

'Really? I'm not so sure. We need to find out what's happening. This problem with communications and power failure is widespread, not just local.' He gestured at the window. 'I haven't seen a single aircraft. Before the cut, I noticed one every few minutes.'

'Maybe you're right,' Rubenstein said, and then moved, taking position just to the right of his colleague, foot cocked, ready, hands flat, pressing against the door. 'Okay, do it.'

Kotlas quietly unlocked the snib, and opened the door a crack. 'Who are you?' he demanded.

The other man wheeled around. 'Dennis. That's my name. It's all right; I'm a cleaner here.'

'No uniform?' Kotlas ran his eyes over the boiler suit he wore.

'Where have you come from?' Dennis said. 'Here, only the guards wear uniforms.'

Kotlas glanced at Rubenstein for confirmation. The older man nodded. 'Where's everyone else?' Kotlas asked.

'Someone's escaped,' Dennis said.

'We heard. So where is everyone else?'

Dennis shrugged, smiling uneasily. 'Downstairs.'

Reading the other man's thin face, Kotlas concluded he was of a simple disposition. 'You say there's a fire?'

'There is,' Dennis nodded. 'Someone escaped and started it.'

'Shut the door,' Rubenstein whispered, leaning, directing his weight through his hands.

Kotlas joined him in pushing. Stuck. He looked down. The cleaner had his foot against it.

'Come out and look.' He gestured, crooking a finger. 'Come on. You can't see it from in there.'

'I can't smell anything. Can't hear any urgent shouts. Who's dealing with it?'

Dennis' blank expression turned to one of wicked glee. 'I am. I'm getting you out before it spreads to your office.'

Kotlas shouldered the door. 'Dennis, you have to move your foot. We can't come out unless the door's fully shut, and then opened again. It's the way the mechanism works.'

'You think I'm stupid, don't you. Well, let me tell you something. If I don't get you two downstairs, people are going to start dying. We already have that Frenchwoman naked, tied up like a starfish on the table-tennis table. She's embarrassed, but so far, she's okay. We've got everyone except you. So come on, boys, come on down. Join the party.'

'Your foot?'

Dennis grabbed the door, his shoulder slamming once, twice against it, forcing it open another few inches.

'Shut it!' Rubenstein cried, twisting around, his back buttressed against it using his legs for maximum leverage.

Dennis' foot denied closure. If he felt any pain, he gave no sign. The fingers of his other hand, white-knuckled, tightened around the frame. His face, a bony masked wedge, pushed into the gap, forcing it wider.

'He's too strong. I can't hold him off,' Kotlas wailed.

Determined, the man twisted his head, scraping both sides until his face poked clear into the room.

'Christ. It's Bales.' Rubenstein snatched a Bic from his shirt pocket and leapt into position, levelling the biro at the inmate's eye. 'Out! Or I swear I'll blind you.'

Bales crashed forward, knocking Kotlas aside.

Rubenstein jabbed with the pen and missed. He stepped back, alarmed at the ease with which the patient had forced his way through.

Hands flailing, Bales grabbed at Rubenstein as he pitched forward into the room, followed by the substantial form of a uniformed guard wielding a baton. He clubbed the back of the inmate's head.

'Edwards!' Rubenstein's tongue flicked the dry corners of his mouth. 'Are we glad to see you. How did he get out?'

'They're all out.' The guard squatted by the prone body and checked his neck for a pulse. 'They're busy playing games downstairs with the hostages they've taken. In the confusion between shifts swapping over – night leaving, day arriving – and the power cut, not sure exactly how. Fisher got out and threatened to kill a female hostage. She's still alive, but for how much longer?'

'Fleur Tadier?'

He nodded, gazing at the dark pool of blood spreading from the smashed skull. 'Well, this one's dead. One less horror to deal with.'

'How many hostages?' Kotlas asked.

'We're the only ones free, apart from Barker. I left him holed up in the Control Room.'

'Thank God we'll have reinforcements arriving in a while,' Rubenstein said.

Edwards frowned. 'How so?'

'A ten-guard detail went out to collect another guest. They'll be back any time now.'

'Ten guards? No wonder we were short,' Edwards said. 'Did you say guest?' His eyes narrowed. 'Not guests?'

'No. Singular is what I meant.'

'As if this lot isn't bad enough,' he said, fixing Rubenstein with a glare. 'Who the fuck is it we've got coming here now?'

'My name's Kotlas,' the young psychiatrist said, holding out a hand. The guard swiped it with his fingertips, avoiding prolonged contact. 'What's the plan, Edwards?' Kotlas said.

The guard met his gaze. 'To stay alive.' He jerked a thumb at Bales. 'They might miss him, but somehow I doubt it. One of my colleagues had a soft spot for Fleur; he caved in when he saw what that vicious bastard Fisher was doing to her, what he said he'd go on to do. He promised to let her go, as long as the rest of them were released. Wouldn't have happened if I'd been there.'

'Surely there's a fail-safe system in place to prevent—'

'If there's a power failure, batteries cover the system until the generators kick in. In the event of everything failing, we revert to Victorian times. Maintenance might have been able to fix the generator problem, but when they came inside to check it out . . .' He shook his head. 'We now have a situation where eight violent and unstable inmates are effectively controlling the whole place, armed with our batons, electrical tools and anything else they can make a weapon out of. Murderers, rapists and torturers. We are truly in the shit.'

'But where are the remaining guards?' Rubenstein said.

'Locked in the inmates' cells. I was in Control, which is on a separate locking suite. The inmates couldn't get to me. For now, I think our best bet is to stay calm, and hope the power comes back soon.' He took his radio from its holster, and pushed the controls. 'Still not working. What time did you say this other inmate is expected?'

Rubenstein glanced at his watch. 'They should have been here forty minutes ago.'

'Well, with an extra ten men, we might have a chance to turn the tables.'

'Whatever we do, we have to keep it in-house,' Rubenstein said gravely. 'If we seek outside intervention, our cover will be blown and our license to operate revoked. The government will throw us to the wolves, close us down.'

'That's what should happen,' Edwards said. 'You don't really think you can cure these people?'

'You think I don't know that?' Rubenstein said. 'We're here to work on how to prevent others suffering the same way.'

'With respect, Dr Rubenstein, I've worked in places like this for years. No two of these patients, or whatever you want to call them, are the same. Their lives are chaos. They attract it, embrace it, and if it doesn't seek them, they look for it. There's no cure. No smart drug you can manufacture to put things right—'

A woman's agonised scream pierced the air, followed by maniacal laughter.

'I think we should shut the door,' Rubenstein said.

The three men stared at one another as each descended further into hell.

'Leave it for a moment,' Edwards said. 'I need to hear what's going on. Besides, I'll be going back through it at any minute.'

Kotlas and Rubenstein knelt by Bales' body. Rubenstein pointed out the ratio of his narrow face to its height. 'The levels of aggression normally associated with a man like Bales are usually accompanied by a much wider face. It was just one of the mould-breaking anomalies I encountered when I first met him. From his point of view, it was a wonderful disguise, but most unfortunate for his victims—'

'I can't just sit by and listen to that screaming,' Edwards suddenly announced, standing up.

'You can't do anything. You said earlier—'

'Neither can I do nothing, Rubenstein. You two stay put. Man the phone in case the power comes back on.'

'What are you going to do?' said Kotlas.

'Break a few heads. If I'm lucky, I've got a fighting chance.'

'And if you're not?'

'You'll hear me screaming.'

'I'm coming with you,' Kotlas said.

Edwards measured him. 'You'll get in the way. Your job is to fix heads, not break 'em.'

The young psychiatrist stared defiantly. 'I might be able to talk to them.'

Rubenstein laughed. 'Stay here; you'll live longer.'

'You got a spare truncheon, Edwards?' Kotlas said.

Edwards approached the door. 'For your own good, you'd best stick with Rubenstein's advice.' He checked the corridor in both directions and then stepped out. 'Lock it,' he said over his shoulder, and marched south towards the stairs.

Chapter 12

Hilltop Cottage. 9:27 a.m.

Michael Anderson peered through the window. The rain had eased. He ventured outside. The sky had taken on an odd silvery gleam, and he guessed it was the sun trying to burn its way back through, the high moisture content creating the strange glow. Taking his car key from his pocket, he pointed it at the Land Rover and pressed the unlock fob. Nothing. Frowning, he tried again. He withdrew the key from within its electronic housing and opened the door manually. Once inside, he attempted to start the engine. Nothing. Frustrated, he smacked the steering wheel with both hands. *Shit. No car. No phone. What should I do?*

He was in two minds. *Is it worth the effort of cycling to the nearest town for something so insignificant? Why do you always make a big thing out of something, when there's no need? Okay, calm it.* He breathed long and hard, blowing out, counting. Leaning forward in his seat, he peered into the rearview mirror, examining his swollen eyelid. The bite hadn't responded to the lotion, and now he could see, quite clearly, the hole the insect had drilled precisely at the centre of the swelling.

Think, Michael, think. What's good for mosquito bites? He racked his brain. Vinegar? No, that's for wasps. Antihistamines were all he could think of. *Hang on.* He remembered his Nytol tablets. Didn't they have something like that in them? If the irritation became too bad, he'd take them later. At least he'd be able to sleep.

Removing his key from the ignition, he opened the door and clambered down from the driver's seat.

Anderson pumped air into both semi-flat tyres of his bicycle, and then rode down to the unmanned railway crossing. Dismounting, he waited, looking at his watch. The barrier lights were off. Were they always off? He couldn't think. The train that usually rattled past at 9:37 a.m. didn't show. He got back on his mountain bike and cycled home, deep in thought.

Whatever had caused the failure wasn't limited to his house.

Laying the bike down outside, he collected the things he'd left on the table before the rain and carried them inside. He placed the tray in the sink, and muttering to himself, dried the chromium that surrounded the magnifier, polished the lens, and then checked his phone.

Still nothing.

He'd reset the switches on the fuse board before he went out, ready for the power coming back on. It was quite safe, he convinced himself. If there were a problem with the circuitry, it would trip out. His efforts to trace the source of the odour that had permeated every room had proved impossible. *It's going to be all right,* he told himself. *Relax.* Anderson picked up his book, tucked it under his arm, and wandering into the conservatory, immersed himself in Ryan's words once more.

What fascinated me, over and above Vera's clairvoyance, was what I'd gleaned from her medical notes. Born on April 16, 1954, it was a Good Friday. I attach no particular significance to it, other than to note that according to folklore, children born on that day are considered unlucky. She was the thirteenth child. The last of seven to survive. The six previous children had died, either at birth, or a short time afterwards. A sickly baby, she'd been baptized on Easter Sunday, a measure taken by her parents that perhaps led the fates to smile on her.

At age thirteen, she'd almost succumbed to a fever. The family doctor had recorded extremely high temperatures. Her mother had refused hospital treatment, under the notion that, if it were God's will, she would survive. The girl pulled through. But she was never the same again, developing what David had assumed was a psychosomatic illness. However, it was at that time her clairvoyant episodes began. Her family tragically perished in a fire. The girl had left the house earlier in the night. Suspicions were raised. Now an orphan, her aunt took her in. The episodes continued. The predictions she made came true. Her aunt began to fear her.

Deep in thought, Anderson fingered the lump on his eyelid. He'd started to put things together. Ryan had already said she changed the course of his life. How many others? Intrigued, he checked his watch and read on.

Her aunt thwarted my plans to study her, handing her over to the Catholic Church, who had her whisked off to Rome. They'd seen something in her they wanted for themselves.

Part of me knew I was destined to see her again. She'd told me so, and unlikely as it might seem, when we crossed paths a few years later, in Brighton, it only served to confirm my earlier thoughts. She was the real McCoy.

Anderson checked the light switch, flipped it on and off. Still no electricity. Outside, the sky had turned dull. He could have done with the power coming back. For the past hour, distant bells had rung out a continuous clanging loop of sound. The pattern permeated his consciousness. The church at St Michael's. The place had been closed for years, the bell tower crumbling. Who would risk their lives to ring them? He shrugged and continued to read. Darkness gathered outside; he screwed his eyes tight, trying to focus. There's going to be another storm. The pages. Something's wrong. Cream, yellow, green, shades of blue. You're hallucinating, old boy. He glanced up at the dark skies. Phantasms of green shimmering light rippled in the vastness as if unseen hands flicked gigantic silken sheets, teasing the folds and creases from them. Northern Lights? During the day, and this far south?

'Christ,' he said aloud. 'The bells. Someone's ringing out a warning.'

Chapter 13

Copse Hall. 9:36 a.m.

Kotlas paced up and down the room. 'How long has Edwards been gone?'

Rubenstein glanced at his watch. 'I'd say about seven minutes.'

'You know,' Kotlas said as he approached the door, 'I shouldn't have let him go on his own.'

'Keep the door shut. He knows what he's doing. You don't. You're acting like a fool—''

'What kind of men are we?' Kotlas said, passion rising in his voice. 'Prepared to sit and do nothing, while one man risks all?'

'We're psychiatrists, not guards.' Rubenstein realised the younger man had made up his mind, but still tried to dissuade him. He shrugged, spreading his arms wide. 'What can we do? Besides, if Fisher has Fleur at his mercy, I fear it's already too late to help her.'

Kotlas picked up the telephone and listened. 'Still not working.' He replaced the receiver. 'If there's the slightest chance, it has to be taken. I'm going after Edwards.' Turning the snib, he unlocked the door, checking left and right before stepping out.

'Good luck,' Rubenstein said.

Kotlas, hearing the bolt ram home, glanced behind him. Through the slats inside the glass panel, already closing to break visual contact, he saw the older man watching, an expression of deep concern on his face. 'Thanks,' he muttered, and then dashed off in the direction the guard had taken.

Minutes. Only minutes separated him and Edwards. A demented howl in the distance unnerved him. He looked out of the quadrangle windows to his right, and down through the atrium covering the ground floor, but could see no sign of movement.

At the end of the long corridor, he turned right. The lifts wouldn't be working. A fire exit sign hung over the stair doors. *Exit, but only if you have a key*, he thought. *Shit*. With the power out, the fingerprint sensor wouldn't work. He slammed his fist against the toughened glass panel in frustration. Spinning around, he back-heeled it for good measure.

'Looks like you're on your own after all, Edwards,' he said grimly. Faint sounds reached him, coming up the stairwell from below. Pressing an ear to the glass, he screwed his face in concentration. Why had no other inmates come upstairs? Of course. They didn't have keys. But the man lying on Rubenstein's office floor had one. To have accessed the floor above, he had to have.

I need those keys.

Sprinting back the way he'd come, he skidded around the corner and halted. What was that? Kotlas backtracked a couple of paces and peeked around it. The staircase door had opened.

He froze. Adrenaline surged. Breath held. He was about to run for the sanctuary of Rubenstein's office, when Edwards came into view.

'Edwards, thank God it's you.' Relief washed over him. 'What happened? Did you change your mind?'

'No,' the guard said. 'I'd taken off my stab vest and left it in the stairwell. I thought, this is shit or bust. Without it, I've got greater mobility, but once I'd gone into the airlock between the doors down there, I saw Fisher brandishing a bloody great screwdriver. When I weighed it all up, I decided I'd need the vest. That's when I heard banging. I knew all the inmates were confined to the ground floor, so I came back up. I thought it might be you.'

Noting the officer's grim expression, the young psychiatrist said, 'It's bad, isn't it? Or you'd have gone in.'

'It's a suicide mission,' Edwards said, his voice matter-of-fact.

'Well, I've come to join you. Is there a weapon I can use?'

'No, but,' he began to undo the straps securing the stab vest, 'you can have this.'

'Keep it,' Kotlas said. 'I won't wear it. I'm a lot smaller; it'll slow me down far more than it will you.'

Edwards scowled. 'You're either brave or stupid.' He held the stair door open. 'Come on. Let's go.' He locked it after Kotlas entered the lobby. 'Here, take these.'

The psychiatrist looked at the cuffs offered.

'Go on, take them,' the guard urged. 'They're better than nothing.'

'You want me to cuff one of them?'

'If you get the chance, but use your imagination. Swing them around your head; hit 'em, cuff 'em, whatever you can do. They're picking off the staff one by one. Not a pretty sight, and poor Fleur. She's covered in bite marks and bruises, so it looks like she's been repeatedly raped. I don't know if she's in shock, doped or even dead. Fisher, the Norfolk Cannibal, won't leave her alone. Softening her up, working himself into a frenzy.'

'What is it with all these cannibal killers lately?' Kotlas said.

'They've always been around, but now it seems to have become fashionable.'

'Are you sure we're the only ones free?'

'Like I said earlier, only the gatehouse is still manned. The problem is, without communication, Barker hasn't a clue what's going on, but one thing's for sure. He won't come out of there. Everyone else must be in the basement. That sick bastard Brody is down there with them. I think he has two of the other inmates with him. Heaven help those poor bastards they've taken hostage. At least three are already dead in the recreation area alone. We need an edge, Kotlas, or we're all fucked.'

'Brody?'

'You not heard about him?'

Kotlas shook his head. 'No. I've never been here before, but I had a general chat with Rubenstein. I hear they're all kept isolated from each other.'

'Apart from two or three of them,' Edwards said. 'Policy. Something to do with Rubenstein's work as much as health and safety.'

The young psychiatrist looked thoughtful. He narrowed his eyes, the glimmer of an idea shining. 'This is the first time they've all been out together?'

Edwards caught on to the other man's expression. 'You got something in mind?'

'Divide and rule,' he said. 'Now, quickly, tell me what you know about the inmates controlling the recreation area.'

'I told you about Fisher—'

'I don't need to know what they are. Mum and dad alive? Brothers, sisters? Signs of remorse? Religion?'

'Christ, I don't know all that. I know Fisher was fostered, brought up in shocking conditions, kept prisoner under the stairs and subjected to sexual abuse. Apparently, the woman liked to watch while her husband tortured him.' Edwards' face and voice conveyed his disgust. 'When Fisher was fifteen, he snapped in the middle of a session and killed the man. Then he tied up the woman, spread-eagled like a starfish, as he put it, and then spent the next couple of days giving her a dose of her own medicine. He force-fed her with the husband's body parts while doing all kinds of things you don't want to know about. The pathology report said they found his semen in every orifice of her body—'

'Enough about him,' Kotlas snapped. 'Has he mixed with any of the others?'

'Only Vanner,' Edwards said. 'He was kidnapped as a child along with three others. Kept for months; he was the only survivor. Of the four, he was the only one who sensed that if he were to survive, he needed to do more than just cooperate. It worked. Trouble was, when he was twelve – he caught four little boys—'

Kotlas spat on the floor. 'I take it his parents disowned him?'

Edwards, surprised at the doctor's reaction, said, 'Only the father did. The mother stayed loyal to him.'

'Does she visit?'

'No, he barred her a couple of years ago. Every month she puts in a request and he refuses to see her.'

The wrinkles on Kotlas' forehead deepened. 'Any idea why?'

'He heard that Fisher fantasised about starfishing her.'

'Really? Who told him that?'

Edwards shrugged. 'I think it was Rubenstein.'

Kotlas frowned. No time to think about the reason now. 'This is what I propose. We go in quietly; let me do the talking. If my plan works, we neutralize the ones upstairs and then take the others as they come to investigate.'

'You've been watching too many movies, Kotlas. We don't have a prayer of that working.'

'Oh, ye of little faith,' the young psychiatrist said. 'I didn't tell you, but if need be, I can handle myself.'

The guard grabbed his bicep and squeezed, surprised at the firmness of the muscle. 'You'll need more than experience of pumping iron to deal with those animals. You're like a poodle going in with a pitbull. That's what catches people off-guard: the craziness. Murderers like them don't think twice about going for the kill. By the time you've realized that, you're dead.'

'Tell me about it,' Kotlas said. 'I've seen a few make that mistake.'

'So you've worked with people like these before? Where have you come from?'

'Ashmore.'

'Christ,' Edwards said, 'that is a rough place.'

You do realise that we're damned whatever we do.'

'I know,' Edwards said, 'but I've made up my mind.'

'So have I.' Kotlas was grim-faced. 'Couldn't live with myself if I didn't at least try.'

A heart-rending scream, muted, unmistakably female, pierced the silence. The men looked at each other in dismay and then rushed down the stairs.

Chapter 14

Copse Hall. 9:46 a.m.

Crazed laughter reaching fever pitch, spurred the two men on towards the door at the foot of the stairs, a portal into a world of insanity.

A look of consternation appeared on Kotlas' face. 'Why has she stopped screaming?'

'Fleur,' Edwards said, 'her name is Fleur.' His hands trembling, haste, not fear caused Edwards to miss the keyhole. One hand steadying the other, he guided the key home and opened the first airlocked door, and secured it after they'd stepped into the space between.

'I know you could point them out to me, but I want to do it this way. As soon as we go through, I'll say Vanner's name,' Kotlas said, dry-mouthed. 'Then, I'll know which one he is. Fisher, if he still has the screwdriver, will be obvious.'

'As soon as we go in, I'm busting heads,' the guard said, his eyes scanned the monitor out of habit, despite it being blank. He drew his baton, and pressing close to the vision panel, checked that no inmates were lurking immediately on the other side. The key slid home. He twisted it and took a deep breath. 'Remember, don't give them a chance. Fight dirty.' His fingers wrapped around the door handle.

Kotlas grabbed his wrist. 'We agreed I'm going in first. You open it, but fall in behind me.'

'Are you fucking mad?' Edwards said, glaring, surprised at the strength of the smaller man's grip. 'Didn't you hear what I said just now? What do you think you're going to do? Talk them out of it? They'll tear you apart—'

Calm and self-assured, the psychiatrist returned his gaze. 'No time to explain. Give me a few seconds before you go wading in. Do I have your agreement?'

'If it was just your funeral, I wouldn't care. Now, take your hand off me.'

'Your way is suicide. You said it yourself.'

'At least I'll go down fighting.'

The younger man didn't waver. His confidence and resolve unmistakable, he convinced Edwards, who looked down at the hand restraining his wrist. 'All right. Let's try it your way.'

Kotlas released him.

'You ready?' the guard said, turning the handle. The heavy-duty lock drew back with an ominous clunk.

Kotlas stepped through the open door.

Naked, spread-eagled on top of a table-tennis table, her limbs tied to its legs, the Frenchwoman lay motionless, either dead or passed out. Like doctors in conference around an operating table, four inmates in varying stages of undress, two of them barefoot, were too busy molesting her to notice the intrusion. Fisher – trouserless, crazed, his tongue protruding – withdrew a long, flat-headed screwdriver from her body. Fluid, predominantly blood, smeared its otherwise shiny length. 'Mmm,' he crooned, licking it.

Kotlas, sideways on and without a clear view of Fleur, hardly dared imagine the tortures inflicted to make her scream the way she had. One man, Kotlas saw, wore an officer's trousers. The fly gaped open, revealing a semi-flaccid penis. Semen stained the fabric of the upper left thigh.

'Vanner?' he said, loud enough to get their attention without alerting the inmates in the basement.

A head shot up. Wild-eyed, his face remarkably lined for an eighteen-year-old, Vanner wiped saliva from his chin. 'Who's asking?'

'My name is Kotlas. I'm a doctor.' Eye contact established, he continued, 'I'm new. We haven't met. I've just been running through Dr Rubenstein's notes with him, and I have to say, I'm pleased you and Fisher are getting along.'

'Been talking to Rubenstein?' Fisher said, measuring him. 'Where is he? And where the fuck is Bales?' He levelled the screwdriver at Edwards, and jerking his head, signalled the two men adjacent to him. 'Bring that fucker over here. To me.'

Grim-faced, but with laughter dancing in their eyes, they separated and moved towards the guard. Nonchalant grins on their faces, they manoeuvred themselves instinctively, angling wide, then coming in left and right, knowing the officer would be hard-pushed to counter a simultaneous attack.

Edwards' feet moved apart. His stance lowering, the baton rested on his shoulder, ready to strike.

'You know, Vanner,' Kotlas said, without taking his eyes from him. 'I thought there might have been some animosity between the two of you, especially after Fisher told Rubenstein that he knew why you banned your mother from visiting.'

The youth stared, his silence inviting the psychiatrist to continue.

'He told him that once you heard about starfishing, you fantasized about doing it to her with him.' Kotlas jabbed an accusing finger in the other man's direction. 'Isn't that right, Fisher?'

Vanner spun around. 'What's this, you two-faced cunt?'

'He's lying. Can't you see?' Fisher said, waggling the glistening steel shaft. 'Get him over here and we'll soon have him squealing the truth. I'll screw it out of him with this.'

'How did he know about that, then, if you never said it?' Vanner raged, pointing at the woman on the table-tennis table. 'You've just fuckin' done it to her.'

'So did you,' Fisher sneered.

Vanner lunged at him.

Distracted by the confrontation, the bare-footed men closing on Edwards hesitated.

The guard seized his chance. Exploding into action, he brought his baton down with great force onto the skull of the patient to his left. The man dropped, as instantly as if the tendons behind his knees had been severed. Spinning to face the second assailant, the guard raised his weapon to deliver another blow. Fuelled by desperation, the second man snatched at Edwards' wrist with his right hand, and catching it, yanked down, his left elbow driving into the hapless officer's face.

Kotlas shot forward, pushing the inmate sharply, causing his follow-up blow to miss. At the sound of footsteps thundering along the corridor downstairs, he spun on his heels. In seconds, he realised, reinforcements from the basement would arrive. Heart thumping, he swept his gaze around the room, taking in Fisher and the teenager locked in combat and grappling at arm's length. Vanner held the screwdriver at bay, his fist wrapped around the fluid-slicked shaft. Fisher wrenched it left and right in a vain attempt to snatch it away from him. He saw Edwards, down on one knee, lashing out with his baton, ineffectively, struggling under a rain of blows as he fought to stand up.

Kotlas thought quickly. He had to even the odds. The rings of the cuffs given him earlier grasped in both fists, he rushed at the fallen guard's attacker. In one fluid move, he dropped both hands over the inmate's head, yanking the chain back, strangling him.

Edwards lurched to his feet.

'Quick,' Kotlas cried, 'get the door!' The patient's hands found his, struggling to relieve the pressure on his airway. They shuffled around full-circle, grunting with exertion. Saliva bubbled from the man's lips, his head thrashing from side to side, desperately trying to escape the metal links crushing his windpipe. The psychiatrist tightened his grip, and forcing the man to his knees, finished him.

Fisher bit down into Vanner's wrist. The youth screamed.

Edwards reached the door. The first inmate slammed into it, driving him back. The guard, off-balance for an instant, regained his footing and used his superior bulk to narrow the gap. *If I can just get it shut, the latch will secure it – unless they have keys.* Bracing himself, he shifted his weight and rammed forwards with both hands.

Fisher's teeth tore through flesh; blood flowed. Vanner relinquished the tenuous hold he had on the slippery steel spike and clawed at the other man's face. Triumphant, the implement free, Fisher drove it into his opponent's belly, forcing it upwards. Vanner's eyes bulged. His hands flying downwards, he made a futile effort to prevent the steel from going deeper. He gasped and slid sideways, crumpling to the floor.

Fisher circled the table with blood dripping from the carpenter's flat-headed tool. 'Don't matter what you do. You two are fucked when Brody gets here.'

'Kotlas, quick,' Edwards yelled, leaning back. He lowered himself, and bending his knees for more leverage, desperately tried to hold his position.

'One more move,' Fisher yelled, 'and she's dead.' The tip of the screwdriver touched Fleur's closed eyelid.

'If you've not killed her already, she'd probably welcome it,' Kotlas said.

'Rawrrr!' A deep-throated bellow filled the room.

Edwards' feet scrabbled for purchase, sliding backwards across the floor as the movement of the door began to reverse.

Fisher howled with delight. 'Now you're *really* fucked.'

Chapter 15

Copse Hall. 9:51 a.m.

Brody forced his hand through the gap and gripped the edge of the door. From the size of the fist, and the meaty forearm now visible, Kotlas judged its owner had a bull-like physique. Only moments remained before he barged his way in, and once that happened, he knew, with the two men following behind, and Fisher, he'd be unstoppable.

Kotlas eyed the door leading to the stairs. It was ajar. Had Edwards been thinking about a quick getaway when he left it like that? With Fleur dead and the situation deteriorating fast, their efforts had been in vain. He gauged the distance. Fifteen paces. If he and the guard bolted for it now, could they make it?

'Quick, grab my baton!' Edwards yelled, shrinking away from Brody's fingers. 'Come on. Use it to smash his hand away from the door. If he gets through, we're dead.'

Kotlas dashed forward, but Fisher cut him off, manoeuvring into a point midway between the guard and psychiatrist. 'Not so fast,' he said, adopting the engarde position, the tip of his screwdriver cutting small circles in the air. His gaze fixed first on Kotlas' chest, and then flicked between the two men, the flat-headed tool conducting a silent eeny-meeny-miny-moe. It was obvious who he'd attack first. Edwards was a sitting target.

Kotlas, knew he had to do something. He attacked. The unexpected move wrong-footed the madman, who struck out with the weapon an instant too late.

Handcuffs flashed with blinding speed. Adrenaline raced as Kotlas, his body a blur, parried the blow with the cuff in his right hand. Striking bone, the force of impact so fierce, the sudden inertia snapped the metal jaws shut around Fisher's wrist. The doctor shifted grip, his thumb digging into the back of the captive hand, turning it up, twisting and locking it back against itself. Fisher's mouth gaped, at first in silent agony, then he screamed pain as Kotlas, applying more pressure, rendered him helpless. His left hand reaching over the immobilized inmate, he plucked the weapon from Fisher and dropped it. Fluid, without relinquishing the controlling hold, he sidestepped, kicked the back of Fisher's knee, and took him down.

Edwards, red-faced with exertion, his feet skidding backwards inch by inch, lowered his stance, struggling for purchase. He glanced at Kotlas, unmasked desperation in his eyes. 'Leave him,' he shouted. 'Get back upstairs. Save yourself!'

Kotlas didn't speak. His expression was grim; both hands clamped around those of his prisoner, his fingers knotted and tightening, applying tendon-tearing force to ensure continued compliance. He had no need for words as he steered Fisher, who, cursing and growling, could do nothing but follow meekly where he was led.

Now only two feet from his objective, Kotlas jerked him closer to the door. Brody wedged his arm and shoulder into the growing gap, forcing them through.

Drained by his efforts, and with sweat pouring down his face, Edwards avoided eye contact with the young doctor. 'Go,' he said, through gritted teeth. 'I can't hold on any longer—'

Kotlas responded swiftly. Fisher's hands yanked up; he released his grip. The free end of the cuff struck Brody's exposed arm. For an awful moment, the doctor thought the serrated teeth of the steel ring wouldn't catch.

Brody roared outrage.

Edwards released the door, scrambling clear.

The sudden action caught the giant unaware. He hurtled forwards, the other two inmates stumbled in close behind. Brody took several steps before regaining his balance.

Kotlas weighed the odds. The guard was exhausted and vulnerable. He doubted he could make it to the door in time and secure it behind them.

Brody stood erect, puffed out his barrel chest, and looked in disgust at the metal bracelet linking him to the trouserless Fisher. His tattooed face quivered with rage. 'Get this piece of shit away from me. Right now. Unlock these,' he snarled, jerking the cuffs, 'or I'll tear his fuckin' arm off.'

'Wait, wait,' Fisher begged, cringing. 'The key's over there, on the floor by the table.'

Brody scowled at the blood-soaked body of the naked Frenchwoman. 'Did you do that? You sick fuck.'

'I swear it wasn't me,' Fisher whimpered. 'It was the others.'

'And you just watched?'

'They made me do it; I had no choice—'

'That why you got no trousers on, is it?' Brody spat, jerking the cuffs with such force, he swung Fisher off his feet. Oblivious to his own pain, the Goliath snapped back on the links coupling them together. Fisher's shoulder popped. 'Fuck,' he cried, sprawling to the ground. 'Why would you do that? Aren't I the one who let you out?' Breathing heavily, he struggled to his knees and wheedled, 'The others didn't want to—'

Brody, placing a foot on his chest, slammed him to the floor.

His calves trapped beneath him, Fisher could do nothing as his fellow inmate twisted and wrenched, pulling his arm upwards. The veins in his neck standing out, his eyes wide with terror, he screamed, 'Don't! Please, Brody, don't.'

In awe of the hulking brute's strength, no one did a thing to help his victim. 'Go on, Brody,' one of his companions yelled, 'pull that fucker off.'

Sinew tore like rotting fabric. Fisher writhed from side to side trying to hook Brody with a leg; his eyes bulged with horror while pain screwed his features. 'Not my arm'' he sobbed. 'No. Please, they made me do it. I'm sorry.'

A bloodcurdling scream pierced the room.

The harrowing sound pinned everyone in place. It hadn't come from Fisher. Kotlas swivelled in the direction of the table-tennis table. 'Fleur's alive,' he bellowed.

'Now we'll find out who did what to who,' Brody growled. 'We'll ask her.' He dragged Fisher over to the violated woman. His voice almost tender, he said, 'Stop that crying. It's all right, luv, it's gonna get sorted.'

'I need a doctor,' Fleur whimpered.

Brody glowered at Kotlas. 'Get me the keys, you skinny fuck, or I swear I'll finish the job and batter you with the stump, woman or no woman present.'

'She needs treatment, Brody,' Kotlas said.

'Somebody get me the keys before I lose my fuckin' rag.'

The other two inmates exchanged glances and spread out. The doctor edged nearer to Edwards.

The tallest inmate stepped forward. A guard's baton slapped against his palm and he sneered, 'Do as he says, skinny fuck.'

Kotlas scooped up the screwdriver.

'Don't make me laugh. You're a doctor,' he scoffed. 'There's no way you'll use that. Hippo-somebody's oath. You ain't allowed.'

'Stop fuckin' about. Do him,' Brody yelled.

'You're right,' Kotlas said, discarding the tool. 'I don't need it.' He tilted his head at Brody. 'Won't be long and there's only going to be three of you.'

'Three? You mean four. I might be crazy, but I can add up,' the other man said, inching closer.

Kotlas snatched at the baton, grabbing it. Meeting resistance, he stepped in close, his other hand sliding up the man's elbow. Raising the arm as if to pirouette, he ducked beneath it, and whipped the limb round in a short arc, causing his adversary's feet to leave the ground, his body spinning in a compact somersault. He seized the weapon, and clubbed the man behind the ear as he hit the ground.

'You wait till I get hold of you. I'll tear you apart,' Brody raged, resuming his murderous attack on Fisher.

Brody's shoulders hunched. He wrapped his hands around the cuff on Fisher's wrist, and jamming his foot into the other man's armpit, dropped into a half-crouch. Bending his arms at the elbows, he took up the slack on the chain and then with a roar, exploded upright. Fisher's arm, already dislocated, stretched, brute force tearing sinew and skin. Brody ripped it off. Blood sprayed, spattering across the room. His mouth twisted in shock, Fisher howled agony and writhed on the ground.

Freed from his encumbrance, Brody examined the dripping end of the disembodied arm. 'Didn't I fuckin' tell you,' he said, eyes bulging, triumphant. He loomed over his stricken victim. 'What's all that noise, you piece of shit?' He stamped hard on Fisher's anguished face, caving in flesh and bone. 'You hear that, boys? Sounded like a fuckin' dropped melon, didn't it?' In the deathly silence, Brody grinned, fascinated by the dark halo spreading around the dead man's head.

'Then there were three,' Kotlas said.

Brody glared from Kotlas to Edwards, and wielding the bloodied appendage, growled, 'Like predictions, do you? Well, how about this?' A curt nod to his cronies a cue to attack, he stormed forwards. 'Then there was none.'

'Wait!' Kotlas held his hands up, making eye contact with the other two inmates. 'All of you. What about poor Fleur? She's in a bad way.' Blood oozed from the table, pooling on the floor underneath. 'Fisher's done something to her insides.'

'And now he's dead,' Brody tipped his head towards Fleur, who whimpered softly. 'Even if she survives, her head's fucked beyond help. Best thing, when we get done, is put her out of her misery.'

'Please . . .' she whispered.

Kotlas' gaze slipped over her mutilated body, appraising her injuries from a distance. Fisher and the others had bitten her breasts and thighs, semen evident on her face and in her hair. He lingered over her neatly trimmed pubic area before looking away. 'If you did that, Brody, you'd be no better than they were.'

Brody's eyes flicked left and right and then bored into the psychiatrist. 'Do you think I give a shit?' He shifted his grip on the wrist of the severed arm. 'Why do you think I'm in here, eh? Because I give a fuck about people?'

Kotlas detected movement. Slow, deliberate, moving low, approaching the inmates from behind. A glimmer of recognition froze in his eyes. His face impassive, he said, 'It's never too late to do something good.'

'Do you know who you're talking to?' Brody's expression grew colder. 'Do you know what I've done? There's no good in me.'

'I used to think that about me,' Kotlas replied.

'Bullshit!' Brody thundered. Taking two short paces, he held Fisher's arm like a club. With a jerk of his head, he signalled the others to join the fray.

Kotlas' feet shifted, his upper body leaning back. He avoided the blow, snatched the chain, and whirled it around in a tight circle. His timing was out, the intended grip missed, but he instantly improvised. Brody's head cannoned towards his. Kotlas dodged, delivering an elbow strike hard into the big man's temple. Brody sneered.

No effect. Dismayed, Kotlas saw Edwards fell one of his attackers, the crack of wood on head registering with him only afterwards. *You're out of sync. Focus.* Distraction now his primary aim, he peppered Brody with a flurry of light blows, looking for an opening. *Get him off-balance, take him down.* Noting the deep laceration the big man had inflicted on his own wrist with his dismembering of Fisher, Kotlas knew attempting to control him through pain would be a problem. To one side of him, Edwards grappled with the last of the cronies who, despite blood flowing freely down his face, attempted to wrestle the guard's baton from him. He paid for his momentary inattention as Brody clamped a hand around his testicles and squeezed. Kotlas jammed his hand down, fingers hooking, thumb levering, and forced Brody's digits back. Brody would not relinquish his grip. One of the goliath's fingers snapped. He squeezed Kotlas harder.

'Jesus!' Kotlas cried and jabbed a thumb into Brody's eye socket.

'Fucker!' the big man yelled, one hand covering his injury.

Rubenstein broke from around the corner he'd hidden behind. Kotlas saw something flash in his hand as he covered the distance between himself and the big man. He jabbed a syringe into Brody's neck, his thumb slipping off as he pressed the plunger home. In the ensuing melee, the cylinder still attached to his neck Brody went wild, slamming Rubenstein with a bone-crunching fist. The older man crashed to the floor. Kotlas held on in desperation as he was swung through the air. Edwards rained blow after meat-thwacking blow down onto the huge head. Too late, Brody switched attention to Edwards' murderous assault. Released from the iron grip, Kotlas sailed through the air. Twisting and turning like a cat finding its feet, he landed upright in time to see Edwards grabbed and hauled into a spine-crushing bear hug.

Adrenalin numbing his pain, Kotlas focused on the back of Brody's head. He took three short steps and delivered a blow, driving his fist upwards into the point where the big man's neck connected with his skull.

Brody staggered around, out on his feet, still locked on to the guard.

Kotlas kicked the back of his knee.

Brody toppled, bringing Edwards down on top of him.

The young psychiatrist surveyed the carnage. 'We need to check for surviving inmates and get them locked up, quick.' He glanced from the dormant body of Rubenstein to Fleur and then to Edwards. 'Where's the hospital wing?'

Chapter 16

Avon Gorge. 9:52 a.m.

Wolfe climbed the wooded cliffs, drawn to the sound of bells ringing in the distance. Halfway up, he switched from the punishing direct ascent he'd taken to a less arduous one, after discovering a zigzag series of pathways that ran all the way to the top. Panting from exertion, he paused, bent over, hands resting on knees. Two thousand press-ups a day while incarcerated had done nothing for his leg muscles. *What's with those bells? A wedding going on? Could be in line for a piece of bridal cake.* Staying close to the treeline, he resumed walking, focused on no other thing or destination.

He scanned the landscape. His eyes swept the sky, confused as much by the pink and green colouration he saw shimmering in the gaps between the clouds as he was the fact that no one appeared to be searching for him. No helicopters, no dogs. Apart from the rhythmic clanging, the world was strangely silent. He breathed deep; the intermittent rain had released a cocktail of earthy smells. A strange kind of energy pulsed in his brain. The climb had cleared the remnants of the drug he'd partially absorbed. Turning his head in the direction of the ringing, he saw the bell tower through a gap in the trees. He gauged the distance. *No more than two miles.* The thought of champagne amused him. Joining in the celebrations, he'd tell them a maniac was on the loose, to add an element of chaos to the proceedings.

The church appeared deserted, the high-low peals the only sign of life. He loved and hated the sound, and therein lay the attraction. The closer he got to divisions and boundaries, the more he liked it.

The building was medieval, stone-built, under a red clay-tile roof. At one end, louvres had been installed at the top of a three-story crumbling tower to keep birds and bats out. He wondered if the small door on the north elevation was unlocked. The devil's door. He smiled, gripped the iron ring and turned. Open. He ducked inside and made his way to the tower, the peal of bells ringing in his ears.

Chapter 17

Hilltop Cottage. 9:54 a.m.

The pain in Anderson's eyelid had transferred into his eyeball, making further reading intolerable. With some reluctance, he postponed finishing the chapter. He'd go for a lie-down until he felt better. Clinging to the balustrade, he trudged upstairs. In the bathroom, he peered at his reflection in the mirror over the sink, running a finger around the extent of the swollen bite. Far worse than any he'd had before. He scowled, and wetting a flannel with cold water, opened his medicine cabinet. He popped out two Nytol tablets from a half-empty sachet. They'd make him woozy, but he positively welcomed the idea of closing his eyes and waking in a couple of hours, the swelling down, the antihistamine having done its stuff.

He dry-swallowed the tablets and grimaced as one lodged in his throat. *When will I learn?* He turned on the tap, and bending towards it, scooped a palmful of water into his mouth and swallowed. *That's better.*

He made his way to the bedroom and lay down. With the cool flannel over his eyes, he contemplated what he'd read in *Problem Child* so far.

Anderson came to the conclusion that the clairvoyant girl was in many ways just like some of the other disturbed children he and Ryan had treated. Circumstances were one thing, learned behaviour another, but Ryan had become convinced there was a genetic blueprint at work, something programmed in at the start, behaviour patterns transferred through the DNA. A forgotten irritation elbowed itself into his thoughts, turning the sweet chemical taste on his palate sour. Ryan hadn't trusted him enough to confide in him. *He kept me out and I'd just accepted it like it was meant to be.* His eye throbbed as he struggled to recall details; he traced the swelling to determine if it had spread.

Thoughts from long ago crept into his mind. *What's wrong with your eye?* It was a question he'd once asked Ryan, and not long after, the psychiatrist had gone blind in it.

A sense of dread fell upon him.

Words strung out like festoons emerging from the depths of his memories. *What you were, you will be again.* The words repeated over and over. Anderson wrestled with understanding, and on the cusp of victory, he remembered that Ryan had once hypnotised him without his consent.

Chapter 18

St Michael's Church. 9:55 a.m.

Wolfe ascended the stairs to the first floor and watched unseen from the doorway into the rope room, amazed at the efforts of the ringers. A man and woman in their fifties, surprisingly agile for their age, managed a rope in each of their hands, pulling the padded length, snatching at and catching the looped ends secured to their wrists, ringing four bells between them. *Look at them,* he thought, *they look like a pair of chimpanzees wandering through the vines high up in the canopy, swinging without travelling.*

Sweat poured from the man's reddened face; the woman was pink, aglow with a light sheen of perspiration.

Wolfe licked his lips. He relished her saltiness.

Up, down, heaving the dirty grey ropes, blackened, almost polished at the ends. He noticed knots tied at intervals. Daylight, penetrating through two vertical cracks at the southeast corner, slashed the worn timber floor and formed a ragged T-shape, illuminating dust and falling detritus.

Wolfe looked up. The beams rocked and creaked an accompanying beat between each note.

'No one's coming,' the man yelled, breathless. 'I wish Timothy were here; he could jump in and share some duties, be less of a strain.'

'Are you sure he still lives here?' the woman shouted.

'He still sleeps here, I know that much,' he said. 'I can't keep this up much longer.'

'But we must. How else can we draw attention to what's happening?'

'The place is falling down, that's what's happening,' Wolfe shouted, brushing dust from each shoulder as he stepped from the shadows.

The woman, petite and just over five feet tall, watched him warily, but didn't stop pulling. Wolfe grabbed her rope. The bell's momentum yanked at his arm. Holding it firm, he stopped it from rising again.

'What do you think you're doing?' her companion said. 'We must warn everyone.'

He grinned. 'You knew I was coming?'

'Not you,' the man snorted. 'The Antichrist. The world has been plunged into darkness. The work of modern man has ceased to function. Have you not seen the signs?'

'I was in a dark place, set free to walk in the light.'

The man stopped hauling on the ropes. He stood open-mouthed, registering the gleeful visage framed by long dark hair, the rugged growth of beard and the sheer size of the man before him as if under a spell.

Wolfe sprang forwards and grabbed him by the throat with one hand, hoisting him high. Aware of the woman's screams, he laughed. Pulling the rope down, he looped it around his victim's neck twice and yanked towards the floor, simultaneously releasing his captive, who struggled frantically to remove the coils from the base of his skull. The bell rang out. An instant later, the rope's upward travel snapped the ringer's neck.

A trickle of urine stained the dead man's trousers.

'My God,' the woman gasped. 'You've killed him!'

Wolfe dragged his attention from the twitching legs of the corpse and turned towards her.

Terrified, she backed up towards the stairs. Wolfe leapt at her. Fear crumpled her legs. She dropped to her knees and prayed.

'That's right, pray to your Saviour. Ask him where he is in your hour of need.'

'Jesus, save me,' she implored, anguished tears streaking her face.

Wolfe clawed his hand into her fine silvery-blonde hair, twisting a hank of it around his fingers. He lifted her up. Tiny hands sought his, trying to relieve the pressure on her scalp. Holding her firm, his other hand slid down the front of her blouse, into the cup of her bra, pinching the nipple.

'Don't,' she sobbed.

He forced her head back, and staring directly into her eyes, ran his hand down, over the curve of her belly, the buttons of her top popping under the strain. She pleaded, 'No, please.'

His fingers slid under the waistband of her jeans, down into the front of her pants, over the sweat-moistened tuft of hair. Tears coursing, she whimpered as he probed, slipping his fingers between fleshy lips and plunging them into her dry warmth.

'You see?' he leered. 'It's not all bad.'

Less than a mile away, Anderson, hovering in the state between sleep and alertness, noticed the bells had stopped ringing.

'Thank God,' he muttered, and drifted into a world where dull pain ruled and a giant mosquito stalked the land.

Chapter 19

Priestley police station. 10:15 a.m.

Newly promoted Inspector Tom Emerson strode out of his office and along the corridor, taking the last door on the right into Reception. Sergeant Adams had his back to him, talking with two elderly women. 'I'm sure the electricity board is working on it even as we speak, ladies. The best thing I can suggest is to keep calm. Go home and put your feet up. You live far from each other?'

'We're sisters,' the tallest one said. 'We live together.'

'That's all right then,' Adams said. 'At least you can keep each other company.'

'We don't want to miss the *EastEnders* omnibus; that's what I'm worried about,' the shorter sister said.

Emerson cleared his throat theatrically. 'Any news on this power cut, Sergeant?'

'Can't even record it with no electricity,' one of the women said as they shuffled away from the counter.

Adams watched them leave.

Emerson glowered at him, impatient for an answer. 'Well?'

'Not as yet, sir, but I'll tell you something. If it carries on much longer, we're going to have problems.'

'I've already got problems.' Emerson moaned. 'I've only come in today to get a head start on tomorrow. I've done all I can that doesn't involve technology and now I can't do a thing. Where's Williams?'

'I assume he's either been delayed or he can't get in. Everyone else turned up before all this happened.' A rapid series of car horn blasts sounded.

'The trouble with drivers these days,' Emerson said. 'They've got no patience.'

'Have you looked outside, lately, sir?'

Emerson stepped around Adams and peered through the window. 'There shouldn't be that many vehicles queuing on a Sunday. What's with all the traffic?'

'I'm not sure. I've heard a hell of a lot of cars broke down earlier and they're jamming the streets, preventing those that are still running from getting through.'

'Can't even call a breakdown service,' Emerson observed drily. 'Do we know why?'

Adams shrugged. 'No, sir.'

'But you think it's related?'

'How can it not be? We had that brilliance in the sky. Then it rained straight after. Now it looks like someone's playing rainbow-coloured searchlights all over it.'

'Christ,' Emerson said. 'How did I not notice that before?'

Because you've got your head up your arse? Adams thought.

'Do you think it's to do with global warming?'

'It isn't a subject I know much about, sir,' Adams said, turning his attention to the front door as it opened. 'But I'll bet this man coming in now does.' He leant closer to the hatch. 'Morning, Professor Young. To what do we owe the pleasure?'

The old man entered the circulation area in front of the station desk, nodded, returning the greeting, and held the door open for a younger man and a woman with a baby in her arms to follow him inside.

'I've got it,' the young man said, taking hold of the door.

Professor Young walked up, rested an elbow on the counter, and whispered through the glass, 'There's something out of the ordinary about this power failure, Mike.'

'Let the Sergeant deal with the people behind you, professor, and then we can talk,' Emerson said.

The street door opened again. Four Chinese tourists walked in laden with camera equipment. The leader, a woman in her late twenties, said, 'You know when next bus for town centre coming?'

Emerson turned through one-hundred-and-eighty degrees, to face away from the desk. *Shit!* he mouthed. The day before starting his new role at the station was turning into a disaster. He walked out of reception, turned right into the corridor, and opening the secure lobby door, invited Professor Young inside.

The professor sat across the desk from Emerson, in the inspector's office. 'I used to teach the Sergeant, you know.'

'You don't look old enough,' Emerson remarked truthfully.

'So you're the new inspector. Tom, isn't it? I've heard all about you.'

'Really?' Emerson replied, his irritation undisguised. 'From Adams?'

'Good Lord, no.' He smiled knowingly. 'Not much love lost there, eh? My grandson is a reporter. Nick Summer. Works freelance.'

'Well, that's all very nice, but shall we get to the point? You seem to know something about this power cut. If you do, I'd like you to enlighten me.'

Professor Young inhaled. 'All right,' he said. 'The Earth has been hit by a solar wind. I can't tell, in the absence of communications, how widespread the problem is, but I think that given that we have daytime aurorae – that's Northern Lights – on display here in Bristol, the chances are the whole of the country is affected. Maybe the entire Northern Hemisphere. In a nutshell, the problem isn't going to disappear in a matter of hours, Tom. We should be making plans for the long haul. Far be it for me to say, but I have to tell you, you're going to need to get some plans in place to manage the civil unrest that will surely come.'

'Hang on. I know this station doesn't have an emergency generator, but the bigger ones do. We'll transfer from here to there.'

'It isn't as straightforward as that. Yes, if their backup power management doesn't fail, they'll have a supply of electricity for a few days, but communications have been knocked out with all that that entails, and that has nothing to do with power. I suspect the storm has damaged satellites. Within hours, people will realise that as well as having no power or telephone, they can't withdraw money, can't pay with plastic. Those lucky enough to have vehicles unaffected won't be able to buy petrol even if they have cash because the pumps won't be able to deliver. I'm sure I don't have explain further.'

'I hope you're wrong,' Emerson said.

'I don't want to be right.' The professor watched Emerson's face closely. He wondered how he would shape up in a crisis. 'You saw the young woman with the child who followed me in. Why do you think she's here?' He didn't wait for an answer. 'I heard her talking as we came down the road. She needs to feed her child. I gave her enough cash to tide her over for today. She's one of the lucky ones. But what about tomorrow? She's in here because she's scared.' The professor paused, listening. 'Can you hear that, Tom? It's the sound of more and more people arriving with grievances. This is only the beginning.'

Adams appeared in the doorway. 'I've just had a street robbery victim come in to report she'd had her bicycle and handbag stolen.'

Emerson glanced at the professor. 'I only came in to get a head start on my first day tomorrow.'

'I'll leave you to it,' the old man said, rising from the chair.

Constable Williams walked up the front entrance ramp to the station's main entrance. A dozen members of the public gathered by the door pounced with a barrage of questions.

'How much longer is this power cut going on?'

'Why aren't our phones working?'

'Can you explain to me why so many cars have broken down all at once?'

Williams fielded the queries politely. 'I don't know any more than anyone else here does. All I can say is, keep calm, go back to your homes. I'm sure the power will be up and running soon. No, I don't know why the telephones aren't working, or why none of your cars will start.'

A soft baritone voice lilted over the general noise. 'I'm Professor Young; I think most of you fromaround here know me. What we've been affected by is a solar flare of some description.'

'A solar flare?' a young woman gasped. 'Isn't that what's supposed to happen at the end of the world?' Concerned voices rose. Words took flight. Omen. Prophecy. Antichrist.

'Never mind all that bollocks,' the professor countered. 'I don't know about any of that, but the aftereffects we're seeing are consistent with such an event.'

'What would you know about it, old man?' wheezed an elderly woman gripping a Zimmer-frame. Professor Young spread his hands as if indicating the size of a fish he'd caught, and shrugged.

'Let the professor speak,' Williams said. 'If anyone knows anything about what could have happened, it's him.'

'You say it's something to do with the sun, but that's ninety bloody million miles away,' a man with an Italian accent said. 'So how's that knocked out our electricity supplies?'

'Yeah, and why won't our cars start?' a youth shouted.

'One at a time,' the professor said, his voice projecting without apparent effort. 'Older cars and motorcycles will almost certainly be able to keep running. We've just experienced something which last occurred on a similar scale in Quebec in 1989. That one shut down the entire supply grid. Communications, everything. A solar flare is one thing, but it's the geomagnetic storm that follows that does the damage. Put simply, a massive surge of power trips out circuit breakers all the way back to generator stations and everywhere else in between.' He stared directly at the youth. 'To answer your question, young man, sensitive circuit boards in cars, alarm systems and so on are particularly vulnerable. Not good news, but replacing the boards should sort the problem out.'

A rumble thundered in the distance, growing louder. A classic Enfield motorcycle roared up onto the pavement outside. 'Look at that beauty,' someone shouted above the noise.

'That's your theory up the wall, prof,' the young man sneered.

'Not at all,' the old man said, peering through the open door. 'Older cars and motorcycles with traditional distributors and carburettors will almost certainly still run. The more modern the vehicle, the more dependence on circuit boards, the more chance of problems.'

A uniformed officer stepped back from the pillion, removed the helmet he wore and handed it to the black-clad rider with a curt nod of thanks. The motorcyclist strapped it to the rear seat with bungee clips and rode away, keeping to the footpath.

The officer dusted himself down and strode purposefully through the gathering who parted unbidden, allowing him unhindered access to the entrance.

'You,' he said, pointing to Williams. 'I need to speak to the officer in charge. It's urgent.'

In the absence of an emergency plan, or anyone to consult with, Emerson sat in his office considering his options. Leaning his elbows on the desk, he cradled his head in his hands. At the sound of raised voices, he sat up straight. He heard someone asking for the inspector. He sat up, knowing whoever it was outside would be directed in to him at any moment.

The door opened. Emerson looked up. 'About time, Williams. Where have you been?'

'The roads are chaos. I couldn't get anywhere. It's gridlocked. So many broken-down vehicles. I just walked back from the approach road to Clifton Bridge.'

'Who's that with you?'

'This is a prison officer. He wants to talk to the person in charge. I know you don't start until tomorrow . . .'

'Who are you and what's this about?' Emerson said. 'Seeing as you're here, Williams, take notes for me.'

The escort confirmed his name as Jordan. Wet and dishevelled, he appeared to be in a state of shock. Glassy-eyed, chewing on his lower lip, he explained what had happened.

'How long ago was this?'

Jordan glanced up at the clock. 'About an hour and three-quarters ago.'

'Ten of you.' The inspector pushed himself back in his chair away from the desk. 'And only four survived?'

'The car in front was crushed. We were in the car behind. How none of us were injured, I'll never know.' Noting the inspector's raised eyebrows, he said, 'I left the others at the scene, doing what they can.'

'Let's be clear on this. You saw the bus explode at the bottom of the ravine?'

'That's what I saw.'

'Christ. Imagine how many would be dead if it had landed on the other side of the water, where the road runs below? Stupid question, but have you been in contact with your drop-off? Where were you taking the prisoner, by the way?'

'That information is need-to-know only.'

'I need to know,' Emerson growled.

'We didn't know ourselves. Officers from the final destination were meeting us and we were under instructions to hand him over and then they were taking him the rest of the way in another vehicle.'

The inspector shook his head, incredulous. 'All very secretive. Where were you meeting?'

'I don't know. We were just following the guys in front.'

'And you're not sure, but you think the prisoner's name was Wolfe. Since when did it become usual practice, transferring prisoners in transit?'

'There's a purpose-built secure compound near Bristol Airport. Some of my colleagues have done transfers there before, so it isn't that unusual.'

'Interesting,' said Williams. 'Near the airport, you say? I can't think where that would be.'

'Someone's missing a human cargo.' Emerson said. 'It won't be long before they're drawn out of the woodwork.'

Lights flickered and came on. The desktop fan hummed, rotated on its pedestal, and blasted mechanical breath over each man in turn.

Emerson grinned, jubilant. 'Now we're getting somewhere.'

His joy was short-lived. A minute later, the supply cut out again.

Chapter 20

Five miles southwest of Clifton, Bristol. 10:40 a.m.

The sudden simultaneous breakdown of the escort cars and prisoner transport vehicle from Copse Hall had put the detail on high alert. Unable to communicate via radio or telephone, the guards got out and gathered by the roadside.

The men, all in their early thirties, began to speculate.

'It's sabotage,' Soames said.

'It can't be.' Davis, the bus driver replied, looking thoughtful. 'How could anyone rig all three vehicles to fail at the same time? Bang, bang, bang. One after the other. No radio. No phone. Unless it was an inside job?'

The men looked at each other. Senior Prison Officer Styles shook his head. 'No,' he said, 'even if it was, why would anyone go that far to free a giant bloody cannibal? It doesn't make sense. No, it's got something to do with the bright light that flared up earlier. See the sky, those shimmering colours?' The other men glanced up, fear and fascination mixed in their expressions. 'Whatever caused it hasn't finished yet.'

'What do you reckon it is?' Davis asked.

'I don't know,' Styles said. 'Anyone got any ideas?' The question was met with blank stares, shaking heads and shrugs. 'Come on, Soames, you're always reading the *National Geographic*—'

'Twice a year!' the young guard exclaimed. 'At the bloody dentist's, and even then I just look at the pictures. I'll tell you what, though. A few years ago I spent Christmas in Norway. One night, everyone rushed outside from the lounge to look at the sky. I only followed to see what all the fuss was about. What's going on up there now looks similar to what I saw then.'

'The Northern Lights? It can't be that,' Styles said dismissively. 'Davis, you used to be a mechanic, didn't you?'

The driver finished checking the connections under the bonnet of the crippled prison bus. 'Completely dead. This is really weird,' Davis said. 'A vague smell of burning around the engine like the others, but I can't see anything actually burnt.' He reached up and pulled the bonnet lid down, allowing it to slam shut. 'We can't just sit here indefinitely.'

'You're right,' Styles agreed. 'You lot wait here. Soames, you come with me.'

An hour later, Styles stopped, and wiping his brow with his forearm, surveyed the surrounding countryside. 'You don't appreciate how far a few miles is until you're walking them.'

The young guard chipped a large egg-shaped stone from the baked mud of the verge with the tip of his steel-capped boot and dribbled it onto the surface of the road. He crouched and balanced it with the pointed end skywards, lining it up like a rugby ball. He kicked it. The smooth piece of rock took off in a low arc. It came down in the centre of the road thirty yards away, bouncing several times before coming to rest at the crown of the hill they'd just climbed. Soames turned to face Styles. 'Maybe they turned back?'

'No,' the older man said. 'Even though it's Sunday, I haven't seen any other traffic since we broke down. They're stranded, just like us.'

'What are we doing? I mean, what does this achieve even if we find the bus?'

'If we find it, apart from being stuck, we know everything's fine. If we don't—'

'Wait a minute,' Soames said. Approaching the stone, he stooped, positioning it for another kick. 'We left at twenty-five past eight. They did too. It's only forty miles. About three quarters of an hour taking the country route into account. Halve that because we were converging on each other—'

Styles cut in. 'Stop fucking about with that stone. I did all that in my head ages ago.'

'Not like this you didn't, sir. I mean, work it out. That's around twenty five minutes to our rendezvous point'

'And we'd been driving less than twenty minutes.'

'Exactly.'

'Assuming they stuck to the route, it means we can only be six miles apart. We've walked for an hour and not passed them,' Styles said. 'Something's wrong.'

'No doubt about that,' Soames said, 'but to cover six miles we probably have to walk for another hour.'

Styles scowled. 'Let's get a bloody wiggle on then, shall we?'

'Sir, I can see a pub down the road. I need a glass of water.'

The barmaid, blonde and in her forties, eyed the men as they entered the bar.

'Morning,' Styles said, peering into the dark corners. 'You've got no lights on.'

The woman lifted the bar flap and met them on their approach. Dressed in a too-tight black dress and frilly white blouse, she was heavily made up, the gash of red lipstick creating a focal point for Soames as she spoke. 'There's a power cut, and before you ask, the phone's not working either. I'm sorry, luvs, but we're closed. I would've locked the door, but didn't expect anyone.'

'Just a glass of water, that's all we want. We're parched, been walking for miles,' Soames said.

She frowned. 'What are those uniforms?'

'We're private nurses,' Styles said.

'Look at the size of the pair of you.' Her lips parted and she bit the tip of her tongue playfully. 'I'll bet you are. You can nurse me any time. All right,' she said. 'A glass of water it is.' She turned and walked, hips swaying, back behind the bar, and taking two glasses from the shelf, went to the tap over the sink. 'I don't suppose you know how long this cut will go on for, do you?'

'No,' Styles said. 'Has anyone else been in?'

'I haven't even seen the postman this morning,' she said, turning the water on. 'I think it was something to do that that big flash earlier. Did you see it?' She finished pouring and brought the drinks over. 'Two pounds, please.'

'You couldn't miss it.' Soames turned to look over his shoulder, orienting himself. 'The airport, that's nearby, isn't it?'

'Yes, not ten miles away.'

'Have you heard any planes at all? We've walked for over an hour and not seen hide nor hair of one.'

The barmaid frowned. 'Now that you mention it, I haven't heard an aeroplane for a couple of hours.'

'Come on, Soames,' Stiles said, draining his glass. 'Finish your drink and pay the lady. We haven't got all day.'

Three-quarters of an hour later, they crested the top of another hill. 'Look,' Soames said, pointing. 'See there in the distance. That's the bridge. Surely they'd have crossed it? They must be stuck by the roadside a little further on.'

Styles squinted at the vehicles strung out along the Victorian structure. 'I can't see anything resembling a prison bus.'

'I'm not being funny, sir, but there won't be. There's a weight limit. They'd have had to come in something smaller.'

Styles lowered his gaze. Wisps of smoke curled from the gorge below. He could just about see people were out of their cars looking over the side of the bridge. 'Shit,' he said.

The two guards scrambled down through the wooded cliff, and sweating from their efforts, arrived at the base of the gorge. The smoking wreck, a scorched white minibus, looked as if it had driven over a landmine. A small crowd had encircled the vehicle, keeping at a safe distance.

'Let us through,' Soames cried.

Once people saw the men's uniforms, they parted to allow them through.

'When did this happen?' Styles asked one of the onlookers.

'Must have been over two hours ago now. Lucky it didn't happen on the other side.' The officers followed the man's gaze to the line of traffic stuck on the road beneath the bridge. 'If it had landed on top of the tunnel....'

Styles stared at the in-car fire extinguishers scattered close by.

'The fire,' a soot-faced man explained, his voice thick with emotion. 'We got down here as quick as we could. We tried putting it out, but couldn't get close.'

'I should think the impact killed them, not the fire, mercifully,' Styles said. 'You should all go home; there's nothing to be done here.' He inched forwards, shielding his face behind his arm, the heat from the twisted metal of the burnt-out bus still intense enough to keep him at bay. 'Look at that,' he said, his voice hoarse from the fumes given off by seared plastic, rubber and charred flesh. 'The impact burst the doors open at the back.' He moved his head to get a better view of the inside, looking at the seats, denuded of their coverings, reduced to wire springs. Squinting through the dense plumes of smoke, he couldn't make out any bodies.

'They're dead,' Soames said. 'All of them. Doesn't take a genius to work that one out.'

Styles got as close as he could and circled the wreckage. His eyes drawn to two parallel furrows in the shale, he croaked, 'Wait up.'

Soames rushed to his side. 'What is it?'

'Looks like someone got out. Two people.'

'That's impossible.'

'Is it? Look,' he pointed at the drag marks on the ground.

They exchanged glances, and began to follow the trail. Skirting a row of huge boulders, they reached the other side, out of sight of the bridge above.

'Shit!' Soames shouted, spotting the back of an unmoving figure slumped to one side in a wheelchair. 'From the size of him, it has to be Wolfe.'

His senses heightened, Styles crept up cautiously from behind, noting the heavily blood-stained blue gown. Just inches away, he slipped in something wet, and grabbing the wheelchair to break his fall, knocked it off-balance, tipping it to the floor. The body spilled from the seat, tumbled to the ground and came to rest facing away from them.

'Thank God, he's unconscious,' Soames yelled.

'No, I think he's dead,' Styles said.

Soames approached the cadaver, dropped to his knees and rolled it over. 'Christ,' he yelped, 'What's happened to Wolfe's face?'

'It isn't him,' Styles said in horrified awe. 'Wolfe – he did that. Fuck! There's only one other man I know anywhere near his size who'd have been around here, and that's Chisolm.'

'But how did they survive the fall?'

Styles puffed out his cheeks. 'Because of their size? How the fuck would I know? What I do know is a killer's on the loose. We have to warn people.'

'Sir,' Soames examined the corpse, 'These marks on Chisolm's face . . . ?'

'What about them?'

'Wolfe chewed it off, didn't he . . . ?'

'Well of course he fucking did. He's a cannibal, isn't he? Get back to the bus,' Styles said, wiping his mouth in disgust, 'and tell the others, while I go on to the nearest police station to report this, and warn them the devil is at large.'

Chapter 21

Priestley police station. 10:45 a.m.

'Traffic Officer Williams, I want you to gather everyone who made it into the station this morning for a meeting in the briefing room,' Emerson said. 'No, on second thoughts, make it the canteen. You as well, Jordan. Now.'

'Right away, sir.' Williams wanted to take his superior to task. He'd only applied for his new position to get away from Emerson's oppressive regime, but he said nothing as he slid from the corner of the desk. 'Feet are killing me,' he quipped to Jordan. 'Not used to all this walking.'

The inspector looked over the small group. Three constables, including female officer Croft. A sergeant, plus Williams and a prison officer. Emerson settled his eyes on Croft's chest. 'Who's going to get the phone if it rings, Lara?' he said, his voice edged with sarcasm.

Croft shifted uncomfortably.

'I was joking, Lara,' Emerson said. 'Right, we can't just sit on our hands waiting for the power to come back on. We need to think about what happens if it doesn't.'

'Are there contingency plans in place for a situation like this?' Jordan asked, sauntering over to the drinks machine. 'Don't tell me this doesn't work without electricity.'

'That only keeps it cool,' Croft said. 'It should work.'

Jordan parted the slats at the window and looked out. 'Have you seen how many people you've got queuing up outside?' He pulled a plastic cup from the stack. 'There's been a lot of talk about cyber terrorist attacks lately, but no clear direction on how we'd cope if there were one. In a prison environment, we can still turn locks with keys. But what about the emergency services? How can they run?' He filled the cup. 'No answers? Okay, where's the nearest army base?'

Emerson inwardly seethed at the lead taken by the prison officer. With no immediate answers, he diverted their attention to the foyer. 'The electronic keep on reception won't be working. Has anyone thought to physically lock the door with a key?'

A series of exchanged looks and shrugs followed, but no one answered.

'Who was the last one in?' Emerson scowled. 'It was you, Williams, wasn't it? Get down there and secure it. Otherwise we're relying on good behaviour to keep that bloody crowd out, for Christ's sake. Speaking of which.' Emerson paused, listening intently. 'It's too quiet. I don't like it. What are they up to?'

Williams leaned out into the corridor. 'I can hear Professor Young talking,' Williams said. 'He must have their attention.'

'I thought he left half an hour ago.' Emerson's brows knitted together. 'What can he still be talking about? Let's go and have a listen.'

The professor had hit his stride. He stood in the open doorway to the entrance ramp, in what had become an extended alfresco lecture theatre. 'Some of you may have noticed the behaviour of birds earlier on this morning, wheeling in great flocks in the sky. I wondered if they were trying to realign themselves to the Earth's magnetic field, en masse.' He searched the sky. 'Migratory birds mostly. None out there at the moment,' he said. A dozen pairs of eyes switched their focus from looking up, fixing on the professor as he continued. 'Think of it like synchronising watches. Insects too, I should imagine, especially bees, wasps and the like. It's going to be a while yet, I suspect, before normality returns.'

'But what does it all mean for us, professor?' a young woman said, shifting her child higher in her arms.

'Now, that's hard to predict. Aurorae displaying in daylight? It's unprecedented. It could be days or even weeks before we start getting back to where we were before.'

'Why haven't we been affected like the birds?'

'We're not wired up in the same way.' He laughed. 'Though the bushmen among us claim to feel it through the soles of their feet. Seriously, we've been around a long time, living under our closest star. Our atmosphere protects us, always has. And that's the thing. Throughout the years, we'd have noticed bright skies, coloured lights and so on, but beyond that, we were largely unaffected.' The sky darkened, lowering the light levels still further. A faint green glow ghosted the features of those present. A low murmur burbled among them. 'See that,' he pointed enthusiastically. 'That shimmer of emerald light.' His eyes shone. 'Never heard of that in daytime, let alone seen it.'

'This is like the end of the world.' The Italian crossed himself.

'Or the beginning of a new one,' a voice cried.

'It isn't anything like that,' the professor's smooth baritone assured them. 'In the past, we weren't heavily reliant on technology; we had no communications to speak of. The last major flare before technology really got going was 1859. And at that time, it knocked out telegraphy. The strange thing was, because it overloaded circuits and wires caught fire, we discovered that some gadgets carried on working even after being unplugged, running on what became known as the celestial battery. That's what we're seeing out there. Geomagnetic waves.'

From the doorway, Emerson interrupted and addressed the crowd in a loud voice, 'We appreciate your patience,' he said. 'As soon as we hear anything meaningful, we'll let you know.' He opened the door wider. 'Professor, seeing as you're still here, a word if I may?'

The old man nodded. He moved backwards, adding, for the benefit of the mass of people now gathered. 'According to some, ancient aboriginal art seems to indicate they saw the skies lit up much as we have here today. In other words, it's nothing new.'

Five minutes later, in the corridor by reception, Professor Young surveyed his meagre audience. 'I was asked earlier, how it was that no one knew about this, event. Well, let me tell you,' he said. 'This storm *was* predicted. NASA calculated it would miss us, but the size of it was clearly far bigger than anything previously recorded.'

'I didn't hear any warnings—' Emerson said.

'They don't generally filter through to the public. So many predicted events amount to nothing. There's no point in causing needless widespread panic. If I can finish outlining the scenario we're facing, we can then base our response on what we know so far.'

Williams shook his head, addressing Emerson. 'I can't believe that other than following routine emergency guidelines, nothing definite has been laid down.'

'It's fucking ridiculous when the officer in charge doesn't know what to do.' Sergeant Mike Adams, nearing retirement, wasn't known for his tolerance.

'Okay, Adams,' Emerson said. 'If I weren't here, it would be down to you. So come on. What would you do, eh?'

Adams flushed, eyes blazing.

The professor's smooth voice cut in. 'I don't think anyone took it seriously until a few years ago. Some countries strengthened their power grids. Others spoke of shutting down before the storm arrived to protect them, thus switching back on once the threat had passed. Scientists have long been able to predict a big storm beforehand. They spot a flare, followed by a coronary mass ejection. I heard about it yesterday, read about it on the Internet, and even before it arrived, I noticed birds and insects behaving strangely. Swarming. Aggressive even. Of course, I didn't put two and two together at the time; never seen it before, not like that. I have to say, I don't think anybody had pre-planned for a total wipe-out of communications.'

'You were talking out front about us having them before?' Williams said.

'That's right. The last big one, Quebec, in 1989, took a couple of days after it was first observed to reach Earth's magnetic field. As I was saying to the people outside, our atmosphere protects us, but geomagnetic current transfers into the ground and overloads the grid. Anyway, from what we know, if it's as bad as the one known as the Carrington event in 1859, then we can expect at least two days of disruption, followed by however long it takes to rebuild. The difference between now and then is we've created a vast infrastructure that is vulnerable. Fail-safe devices work within calculated parameters, but until tested by an actual event, they only work in theory.'

'And they didn't work,' Emerson said. 'That's obvious. From where I'm standing, that means we're fucked. If we don't get the power up by tonight, there's going to be anarchy in the streets and there isn't a thing we can do about it.'

Adams, taut-faced, slow-clapped his hands.

'Don't, Mike. He's doing his best,' Croft said.

'That's right. I don't know what it is with you two, but let's keep personal scores out of it,' Jordan said. 'When I came from the bridge on the back of a motorbike, there were already queues forming outside food shops. Fights breaking out between the owners and people trying to pay with plastic. All the main roads are jammed—'

'How can we be sure our partners are safe while we're here? My missus was going to the shops,' another officer said.

'My little girl,' Croft said. 'I've left her with a babysitter. If things aren't back to normal by lunchtime, I'm going home.'

The agitation spread beyond the confines of the corridor. In the foyer, fear and anxiety grew. The men at the head of the queue listened, their ears pressed against the doors, relaying what was being said. Dissent soared. 'What's going on in there? Open up. We've a right to know what's going on!'

Someone hammered on the door. Unsecured as it was, the repeated blows swung it an inch into the corridor.

'For Christ's sake Williams, didn't you lock it?' Emerson yelled.

The crowd surged forward. Adams reached for his truncheon.

The professor held Adams' forearm down. His voice had natural calming qualities. A Welshman, he'd sung in choirs throughout his youth. Until he'd given it up a few years before, he'd been well known on the local karaoke circuit, often winning prizes; he had the respect of the community.

'Simmer down. All of you.' He shot Adams a glance and released him. 'Don't worry. Together we'll get through; no falling apart now. The strong must look out for the weak. The officers here will do their best. Nothing like this has happened to us before, so it's all new, see?'

'What if it goes on for days – won't we run out of food?' a young woman with a small child said.

'Look, so far as I know, Powergen or whoever it is responsible has a mountain of transformer spares stockpiled for just such an event. Could be the engineers are working even as we speak—'

'A few minutes ago, the lights flickered and then went out again,' Emerson said.

The professor sighed. 'There you are. It isn't all doom and gloom. Someone's onto it already.' He scanned the faces around him; they looked less anxious. He continued, 'The army has older vehicles at their disposal which should work. Any equipment that wasn't turned on should function once the power's restored. Only certain components are vulnerable, so not all modern cars are useless, but mobile phones need satellites to work. Worst case scenario, we could be looking at a day or two for the storm to die down enough to get signals again. Radios, similar – though some wavelengths could still work.' He turned to Emerson. 'Where are your spare radios?'

'On charge from last night.'

'They could be okay. We'll scroll the frequencies, establish a connection. If not, we can try CB. Thinking about it; that should work. Once we're in contact with each other, we can make inroads. Are we all clear?' Noting most heads nodding, he continued. 'The roads. We must get out to other police stations. We can do this. Can we count on you lot cooperating?'

A walking stick waggled in the air at the back. 'I'm with you,' an elderly man shouted.

Zimmer-frame woman added her voice. 'And me.' This was followed by a reluctant grunt from the youth.

'Include me in,' the Italian yelled.

The professor smiled. It seemed all agreed.

The inspector picked up an officer's cap. 'You'd better put this on, professor,' he said. 'You didn't say how you know all this stuff.'

'No, I didn't. I graduated in physics at Cardiff University, and then later became a lecturer at Cambridge University.' He grinned. 'You'd be surprised what us academic folk talk about.'

'Right,' said Emerson. 'Let's get all our radios together and see if any are working. Then we get ourselves out there, reassuring people on the streets. We've got bicycles. What we need are some older cars. Use our emergency powers to commandeer them. Do we know anyone with an older car?'

'I have one,' the professor said. 'But I suspect you'll be better off getting around through the snarl-ups on a motorcycle. I have two of those: a Norton 500 and a Triumph Bonneville 250. They still run. My grandson looks after them for me. I'm going to use the Norton. Nick will be livid, but if pushed, you can take the Bonneville.'

Chapter 22

St Michael's Church. 10:55 a.m.

Wolfe lay on his back staring at the slots in the ceiling through which the bell ropes travelled. The room above had been part dismantled – open joists and unboarded, apart from a few new-looking boards around the head of the stairs and leading across to the pulley wheels. The work had long since been abandoned.

Unconcerned about capture, he'd taken his time with the victims. Satiated and woozy, he wondered why no one searched for him. An hour had passed since the last bells had rung and pigeons had slowly returned to roost. The birds, lined up on a rotten beam, shuffled nervously, their eyes shifting from Wolfe to the motionless woman beside him and then on to the broken-necked cadaver, which twisted, suspended from a creaking rope.

Wolfe traced a downy white feather falling on a lazy spiralled course, picked out individual flecks of dust floating in the bars of light let through the cracks in walls and louvres. Content, he closed his eyes. His mind drifting like the feather, he felt a part of himself shift. He slipped into another world.

Footsteps and drunken laughter echoed down a narrow passageway in the dark. A woman, dressed in a filthy white bonnet and drab skirts that dragged the ground, led a man deeper into darkness. Both stumbled over cobbles slicked with rain. Away from the main thoroughfare, save for the moon dusting silhouettes, there was no light.

'This'll do,' the woman said, stopping so abruptly, her companion staggered into her. She giggled as he leaned into her, pawing at her clothes. She drew him further into shadow, back against a door. It rattled. Fumbling, his fingers succeeded in freeing one of her breasts. 'Yes,' he announced triumphantly, before lowering his mouth over the dark flesh of her nipple. 'Mmm,' he mumbled, nibbling and sucking greedily. She writhed against the door, expert fingers finding his cock while she hoisted her dress with the other. Parting her legs, she stroked and pulled, milking him. 'Come on, I ain't got all night.'

'On the floor, girl,' he said.

'But it's all fucking wet.'

'The wetter the better.'

She shrieked, the door clattering in its frame as he wrestled her. 'Awright, awright,' she whispered. 'Before you wake everyone banging against the door.' She took the shawl from around her shoulders and laid it down. They sank onto it.

'Don't you shoot your load inside me.'

'Fuck off,' he snarled through gritted teeth, 'can't stop now.'

With the frenzied thrusting of his hips and open-mouthed panting, she knew he wouldn't stop. Timed to perfection, she jerked up and rolled away, breaking contact as he ejaculated. 'Bitch,' he growled, his fist coaxing the last drops of semen from a rapidly subsiding cock.

'Come on, up,' she said, getting to her knees. 'You're on me shawl.' She stuck out her hand. 'And where's me tuppence?'

'For that?' His fingers balled. Lurching at her from a half-crouch, his fist exploded from the darkness, smashing her jaw. 'You can 'ave five.'

The man staggered to his feet, adjusted his clothing and lumbered down the alleyway towards the gas-lit street.

No sooner had the drunkard disappeared into the night than a tall man, dressed in dark clothes and carrying a polished black leather bag, stepped from the shadows.

The woman groaned, rolled off her back and struggled onto all fours before pausing to collect her scattered wits. She stood up, one hand against a wall to steady her, and became aware of another customer. Her exposed breast popped back under her clothing, she said, 'I've shut up shop for the night.'

'You appear to be hurt.'

She focused on him, saw his bag. 'I'm awright, doctor, 'ad worse.'

'Let me see,' he said, grasping her chin as she turned away.

'Honest, I'm awright.'

His hand slid around the back of her neck, holding her firm.

He stared into her eyes, his desire unmistakable.

'Oh, awright,' she said. 'Cost you sixpence.'

'Will you do something extra for me?' He held up a shilling in the space between them.

She snatched it from his fingers. 'For that, you can 'ave me upside down in a wheelbarrow.'

The bargain struck, he tightened his grip and pulled her in for a kiss. His mouth enveloped hers. A finger and thumb closing her nostrils, the woman's eyes bulged. He bit down hard. Blood burst through her mangled lips. He sucked.

Minutes later, the woman lay dead, sliced ear to ear, cunt to collarbone. He took a moment to survey his handiwork, grunted satisfaction and then scurried away through the alley. He carried a trophy, wrapped in a fine silk handkerchief. Mouth watering, he felt his cock stand up at the thought of devouring her heart in the privacy of home.

Wolfe awoke, disoriented, and blinked his eyes. Next to him, the woman, and above, her silent witness. Running his finger from her collarbone, he traced the line of the cut he'd just seen in his dream. 'Nothing to slice you with,' he said. 'Shame, I fancied a takeaway.'

He stood and stretched.

Where to now?

Outside, the contrast in light stung his eyes. The sky, colours morphing from greens to pinks and back again. Not right. Still no one searched for him. It occurred to him there was more fun to be had while he remained free. On the other side of the untended graveyard, a dense copse of trees beckoned. The hand of an internal compass swept around in his head, confirming the way. It was impossible to tell how long he'd slept or what time of day it was. He weaved among the uneven tombstones and stepped over the wall. Avoiding the road, Wolfe reached the treeline. He entered the woods and stumbled down the gradient, dropping through undergrowth until he arrived at a steep embankment.

A railway cutting. No sign of life. He paused, looked both ways, and then, turning right, followed the tracks.

Chapter 23

Priestley police station. 11:05 a.m.

Adams, the longest serving officer and most familiar face, was chosen to guard the entrance to the station, while Trent, the youngest, was assigned to provide him with backup.

Everyone else adjourned to the briefing room.

'All these are working, but I can't send or receive on any wavelength,' Emerson sighed, replacing the last of the radios on the desktop. 'Can't even reach Adams down the corridor.'

'With daytime aurorae as powerful as those out there, it's hardly surprising,' the professor said, observing the sky through one of the windows. 'When they dissipate, electromagnetic interference will have dropped to a level where some communications will be restored.'

Williams raised his eyebrows hopefully. 'And I don't suppose you can say how long that will be?'

'I can't,' he said, rubbing the bridge of his nose. 'This is, as I said earlier, unprecedented. Quebec was down power-wise for around nine or ten hours, radio disrupted for perhaps only a few . . .'

'So, in other words,' Emerson said, 'you think it'll be a few hours at least? If it goes on longer than that, and we can't coordinate our efforts with the other forces, we could have problems by tonight.'

'You've already got people fighting because they can't buy food on plastic—'

'So what do you suggest, Jordan? Put them in jail?'

'What?' he said, momentarily lost for words. 'Because I'm a prison officer? Fucking stupid thing to say—'

'My point exactly,' the inspector growled, eyeballing him.

'Let's keep it calm,' the professor said. 'This kind of behaviour won't get us anywhere. We need to lead from the front, by example. Let's all think this through.' He perched on a corner of a vacant desk. 'You recall I told you that you'd be surprised if you knew what we academics used to talk about? Doomsday featured on the list. We'd often explore 'what if' scenarios, and in this case, after covering all logical steps, we realised there was one eventuality we'd really struggle with. What if communications were down, what then? The inevitable conclusion, you don't want to know.' Looking about the room, his eyes settled on the inspector. 'Do we have any portable loudhailers?'

Emerson's brow furrowed. 'I know we have at least one; could even be two here. Are you suggesting we take to the streets, making announcements?'

'Word of mouth is a great way to spread news and messages in the absence of anything else.'

Emerson nodded. 'Lara, see if you can locate them, will you?'

'Where do I start?' She shrugged, her hands palm-up in a silent appeal for guidance.

'I'll come with you,' Williams said. 'Help you carry them. I think they're in the spare office.'

She smiled as he held the door for her.

The old man continued. 'We haven't got the resources to impose strict regimes, but if we can get across that, orderly conduct and cooperation will get us back up and running sooner, and we might get somewhere.'

Emerson looked at his watch. 'You don't reckon those two have stopped off for a bit of nooky, do you?'

'I heard that,' Croft said, indignant, as she re-entered the room.

Williams walked in behind her, carrying a loudhailer in each hand, and protested. 'We've only been gone a minute, sir.'

'Never mind the bullshit, give me one of those.' Emerson took one and switched it on. 'Well, would you look at that? It works. Come on, let's get out there. We'll start with the people already here.'

'Everybody out. I'm going to make some important announcements.' Emerson shooed the people out of Reception. 'Come on. Out. I'm going to talk to you outside.'

The people were reluctant to leave, and a series of voices asked half-hearted questions. 'What's going on now?'

'When's the power coming back?'

Emerson held his hand held up and mimed a shoving gesture. 'Come on, let's go,' he said, waving the megaphone at them. 'I don't want to deafen us all by using this thing indoors.'

They retreated, lining up along the access ramp's safety handrails all the way back to the pavement.

Emerson checked over his shoulder; the professor was right behind him, Croft and the rest of the station staff stood under the canopy. Scanning the street, he noted there were more people making their way to the station, faces pale, etched with anxiety. Rosy pinks streaked the nebulous pale green sky. Emerson raised the cone of the speaker to his mouth and began to speak. 'Can I have your attention, please?'

His voice robotic, funnelled through the amplification system, echoed from nearby buildings and carried on the breeze. Passers-by over a hundred yards away turned to look in his direction, many deviating from their chosen courses, headed towards the sound, curiosity bringing them closer to hear better. 'That's right, gather round; move in. We will be making a series of announcements designed to keep you up-to-date with what we know at the moment, and to appeal for cooperation.' He paused, estimating there were perhaps upwards of two hundred people now congregated in his immediate vicinity.

'Before we go any further, let me introduce myself. I'm Inspector Tom Emerson. Most of you already know Professor Young. He's been working with us to formulate some plans, and I'm going to hand you over to him to explain what some of you already know. He'll do a far better job of it than I will.'

The professor stepped forward and took the megaphone.

After five minutes spent outlining the situation and answering questions, he handed the speaker back to Emerson.

'We need volunteers,' the inspector said. 'Those of you who are fit and able, start knocking on doors. Let's develop some community spirit. Look out for the vulnerable, the elderly as well as the very young. Appoint people capable of commanding respect.' Growing in confidence, he built on the foundations laid by the professor. 'Every street should have a leader. Once we've established who they will be, we'll reconvene here at noon.'

He broke off, amazed at the sea of different faces listening intently. At the crowd swarming in from all directions, a critical mass self-perpetuating, voices hushed, perhaps sensing they had become as one. A huge organism united in the face of a coming adversity.

'We're hoping we won't need to go this far, but we need to get organised, now.' The megaphone sweeping left and right, his voice growing louder, he said, 'We're going to talk to shopkeepers. Ask them to issue IOUs to people who can't pay for goods; it's better than having thieves helping themselves, and they will be reimbursed, we'll make sure of it. And let's start rationing, while we still have something to ration. If this stretches on for a couple of days, we'll be glad we took early action.' People exchanged looks. Heads bobbed, agreements were murmured, drowning out arguments against, creating a hubbub.

'Fuel,' he shouted, remembering more of what the professor had told him. 'If this drags on, we're going to need as much as we can lay our hands on. We need to conserve what we have. No travelling unless absolutely necessary. We're safer among people we know, if the worst comes to the worst. We're hoping we won't need to go that far, but we have to plan. We need to be ready. Now, I know I haven't covered everything, but it's a start.'

Professor Young laid a hand on his shoulder. 'Well done; you handled that well.'

Emerson smiled. For the first time since his promotion, he felt worthy.

Chapter 24

Copse Hall. 11:01 a.m.

In the absence of mechanical ventilation, Kotlas and Edwards sweated; the effort of carrying Brody downstairs and securing him in his basement cell had taken its toll. Fleur and Rubenstein remained unconscious. Edwards preserved her dignity by covering her with Rubenstein's jacket. 'It's so fucking warm, he don't need it,' he'd said.

Kotlas checked on them every time he and Edwards came back upstairs.

The guard worked like an automaton, devoid of any outward show of feelings.

'You okay?' Kotlas said.

His delicate veneer of control broken by the two simple words, Edwards exploded with rage. 'I'm fucking blinding, what do you think? I've just carted the bodies of six colleagues, most of them friends, and three outside contractors into a single cell and piled them in. Christ, Kotlas, you saw what those animals did to them.' He wiped a tear from his eye, fast, ashamed of his emotions. 'They looked like they'd been tortured by a third-world dictator and his cronies.'

'Come on, Edwards.' Kotlas laid a hand on his shoulder. 'We'll mourn the dead once we've attended to the living. Let's find something to put Fleur on so we can get her to the hospital wing.'

'I thought I was good at masking my feelings, but you – how do you do it?'

Kotlas contemplated the question. 'I learned from a master of disguise.' He stared into a horizon only he could see. 'I feel all that you do, believe me.'

Edwards took a deep breath, steeliness returning to his voice. 'There could be a gurney downstairs. I'll go and have a look. What about him?' Edwards said, jerking a thumb at Rubenstein.

'I don't need an x-ray to tell you his jaw's broken. The swelling between cheek and jowl is a giveaway, but I don't think he's so badly injured that he can't walk.' Kotlas shook Rubenstein's shoulder with gentle insistence. The doctor's eyelids fluttered. 'Good,' he said. 'He's coming round. By the time you get back I'll have him up on his feet ready to go.'

Edwards returned with a wheelchair. 'This'll do, won't it?'

Kotlas had Fleur's wrist in his hand, checking her pulse. 'It will have to. Bring it closer to the table.'

'How's she doing, doc?'

'Very weak. The sooner we get her treatment, the better.'

Together, the two men lifted the unconscious woman and secured her in place. Kotlas covered her again with Rubenstein's jacket. Fleur groaned and stirred, nestling into it. 'You're safe now. It's going to be all right; go back to sleep,' he said softly. Fat tears squeezed out from beneath her eyelids and rolled down her cheek.

Kotlas turned to Edwards. 'All right,' he said, 'let's go.'

'I've got a question for you,' Edwards said as he pushed Fleur down the corridor. 'What were those self-defence techniques you were using? Kung fu?'

Kotlas, lagging behind, shifted his shoulder underneath Rubenstein's armpit to lend the older man more support as they shuffled along. 'I need you get with it and walk a bit quicker,' he said to the injured man. Then to Edwards, 'Aikido.'

'You must have been doing it a long time.'

'I used to watch Steven Seagal movies a lot when I was a teenager. The moves fascinated me. I used to freeze-frame the film, and then hit the pause and play buttons, watch the sequences over and over so I could see exactly how he did what he did—'

'Seagal was only acting, though. How could you be sure what you were learning would really work?'

'You could *see* it would work.' Kotlas laughed. 'Besides, I practiced the techniques on friends at school so I knew. By the time I was fifteen years old, I thought, why not join a proper school for aikido? So I did.'

'I wondered why you were so calm, but why didn't you say you could do all that stuff?'

'It isn't something I like to talk about.'

'I think I'd have told you.'
'It's irrelevant now,' Kotlas said.

Edwards unlocked the door to the on-site hospital facility.
'It isn't manned at the moment,' Rubenstein said. His hand floated up to land gently on his swollen chin. 'All we can do is make her as comfortable as possible until we can summon outside help.'

'She's going to need a gynaecologist to look at her,' Kotlas said, 'judging from what she's got seeping out of her. And as soon as possible. She may need internal sutures.'

'Edwards, see if you can sort her out a gown,' Rubenstein said. 'Ah, look, she's coming to.'

The two doctors helped Fleur onto the nearest bed. 'At least it's made up and ready.' Kotlas peeled them back and together they manoeuvred her between the sheets, keeping the jacket over her to preserve her dignity. Once she was underneath the covers, Rubenstein retrieved it, placing it over the back of the chair next to her bed.

'That was some blow you took,' Kotlas said. 'That jaw is most likely broken. You could probably do with some painkillers. Any here we can give you?'

'The drugs cabinet is in the office, but I don't think there's anything stronger than paracetamol in there.' Rubenstein grimaced, the flash of pain bringing with it a crystal-clear vision of the carnage he'd witnessed. 'How many died?' His words, issued between unmoving lips, sounded metallic.

'Six staff, three contractors —'
'What about the patients, Kotlas?'
'All of them apart from Brody.'
'God, what a mess. There's going to be some explaining to do.'
'You're right, Rubenstein, but tell me, what else could we have done?'

''I saw what you did, you and Edwards. Those patients were carefully selected, irreplaceable. You never said you were a martial artist.'

'It's listed in my file under hobbies and interests,' Kotlas said. 'The people those patients killed were irreplaceable too.'

Rubenstein nodded. He moved his hand, the palm straddling the hollow between his cheek and jaw. The warmth offered him scant comfort. 'My opinion on your hobby? Seems at odds with your profession.'

'You think so?' Kotlas' eyes grew cold. 'I thought it complemented it.'

'Lucky for us it did,' Edwards said, returning from the stores. 'Or we'd be dead like everyone else down there. And as for Brody, I should have finished him while I had the chance. Might as well hang for a sheep as for a lamb.'

'Say that in the enquiry and they'll throw the book at you,' Rubenstein spat.

'Throw it at me?' Edwards snapped. 'I saw you with that pocketful of syringes sticking out of your jacket. You only came out of hiding when you knew it was safe. If you'd helped us earlier, a few more of your precious inmates might have survived.'

'The whole thing stemmed from an act of God,' Kotlas said. 'Where did you get all those syringes from, anyway?'

'After you'd gone, I went through Bales' pocket and found the keys he'd stolen. The controlled drugs cabinet in the dispensary was smashed open.' Rubenstein hung his head. 'You know the rest.'

Kotlas held his hand out to the guard. 'Pass me the gown; I'll leave it on the bed next to her. Meanwhile, can you rustle us up some food and drink from the kitchens? I'll come with you. Someone had best stay with her. You okay with that, Rubenstein?'

'Actually, no,' he said. 'Can you stay? I need to get some paperwork done; besides, I've got something stronger for the pain upstairs.' He grabbed his jacket from the back of the chair. A syringe clattered to the floor. He picked it up and put it back in his top pocket. 'Shit,' he said, grimacing. 'There's three missing. I must have dropped them back there. I'd best go and find them.'

'I'll be back in a few minutes,' Edwards said. He and Rubenstein left the hospital area together.

Kotlas sat by the bed, absently watching the even rise and fall of Fleur's chest. The movement lulled him, made him sleepy. He closed his eyes and drifted to a windswept beach where he walked among the dunes holding his mother's hand. It was his last clear memory of her.

A woman's voice floated in from the distance.

'I saw you fighting, helping the guard. I-I, don't know you, but would you please hold my hand?'

Kotlas shook himself awake. Fleur's head had turned towards him, her face contorted in agony, her eyes shot with pain. 'Did you speak to me?' he said.

'I asked you to hold my hand.' Her eyes met his, and she slid her hand across the sheet towards him. Kotlas took it, surprised at its softness, how cold it felt. He laid his other hand over it to provide warmth.

'What's your name?' she said.

After all she'd been through, she managed a smile, yet Kotlas detected an infinite sadness. She seemed remarkably calm. 'It's George. Help is on its way,' he lied.

'I'm beyond anything anyone can do,' she whispered. 'I've been gang-raped. Brutalised. My insides are on fire. There isn't an inch of me that doesn't hurt. And I've lost my child.' She closed her eyes and wept softly.

'You were pregnant?' Kotlas squeezed her hand. 'Oh, Fleur. I'm so sorry.' He bit his lip in anguish for her. 'I know you can't see it now, but we're going to get you through this.' Her hand relaxed in his. Lost its grip. He moved close to her face. She'd stopped breathing. 'Fleur? Fleur!' he cried. Yanking back the sheets to begin CPR, he saw three empty syringes tucked between her legs.

Oh, God, Fleur. No!

Chapter 25

Priestley police station. 11:25 a.m.

Trent walked through the open door into Emerson's office. 'Sir, someone else involved with that prison bus crash has just turned up.'

Jordan got up from the corner of the inspector's desk. 'Where is he?'

'In Reception—'

'Bring him in, Trent,' Emerson barked. 'This'll be interesting, Jordan. Oh, and Williams, get Lara to bring us some tea.'

Williams gave a tight smile as he replied, 'Sir, all that joking about Croft, calling her Lara, is getting her down. And even if there was a way to make tea—'

'I know there isn't, Williams,' Emerson said, red-faced. 'It was a joke. Some people around here need to get a sense of humour, Jesus.'

Williams bit his tongue. If all went to plan, he wouldn't be working with Emerson for much longer.

The group of men in the inspector's office listened intently as Styles paced the room, describing what he'd discovered at the scene of the accident.

'Are you absolutely sure he got away?' Jordan said, shaking his head.

Styles echoed his head movements. 'You never went down and checked, did you?'

'Christ, mate. You saw how far the drop was? We looked over the edge. The van was smashed to fuck and then it exploded—'

'Just say no,' Styles said. 'I'm not judging.' He looked to Emerson. 'I don't know how we do this without effective radio communications, but we have to warn people about Wolfe.'

Emerson held the other man's gaze. 'Don't you think it's bad enough without adding this news to the mix? People are barely coping with the effects of the power outage.'

Styles stood still for the first time since he'd entered the room. 'This man lives to kill. Unchecked, who knows how many will die.'

'We haven't got the manpower to organise a search,' Emerson said. 'He could be anywhere. Can you imagine what will happen if I announce there's a cannibal killer on the loose?'

'In the absence of TV or radio, you've no choice—'

'I know that. Jesus.' Emerson scrubbed his head with both hands. 'Any idea where he'd go? Relatives, friends?'

'There isn't anyone he'd go to,' Styles said. 'He's a lone wolf.' A half-grin acknowledged the irony of his observation. 'But let's see. There's ten in my detail. You've got four including you, Jordan. If we can get some strong men together, split into individual parties headed up by two guards in each group – You said not all vehicles are affected? If we can grab some transport, we can cover a fair bit of ground.'

'You had ten men to handle him,' Emerson said. 'That means you're looking for what, fifty-six people to join you for maximum effect, and they're not trained. Regardless of the situation we find ourselves in now, realistically, who do you think is going to leave their families to go and look for him?'

'He's got a point,' Jordan said.

'I agree, but at least people will see we're doing something.' Styles began walking the room again. 'If we can't make my proposal work, then at least tell residents to be on guard, lock their doors, that sort of thing.'

'Transportation is a big issue,' Williams said.

Emerson laughed drily, and said, 'Traffic Officer Williams reporting for duty.'

Williams tensed, but ignored the remark. 'So far, we've got a motorbike at our disposal and at least one car. The truth is, we haven't tried to, um, borrow any others yet.'

'I'd make that a priority,' Jordan said.

Emerson glared at him. 'I really wish you wouldn't try to steal my thunder at every opportunity, Jordan. I was about to say the same thing.'

Styles cut in. 'I don't care who suggests what to whom. I'm only interested in recapturing Wolfe. So, if I can put forward an idea? Let's get out there and appeal for volunteers to give up their vehicles for police duty.'

'That won't work,' Emerson said. 'Can you see anyone doing that?'

'The professor just did,' Williams said.

Emerson picked up a pencil. 'To get a posse together as Styles proposes, we'd need at least enough to carry seventy people. It won't work,' he said with a hint of one-upmanship.

Style stopped in front of the inspector's desk, and placing both hands on it, leant forwards. Close up, his bulk was intimidating. 'Then we'll just have to fucking commandeer them, won't we?'

Chapter 26

St Michael's Church. Midday.

The colours streaking the sky had made Timothy wary of going out. Concerned, he dressed in Father Raymond's hooded black habit, the one that the priest had always reserved for Easter weekend, to mark the three days that were so revered in the Christian calendar. Already warm, he considered removing his boiler-suit undergarment, but that meant he'd have no pocket in which to carry his sister's Bible. Wearing the priest's garments, Timothy was sure he had God more on his side. Otherwise, he reasoned, why did the holy men wear them?

It was a question he had scribbled on his pad and passed to Father Raymond one night. The priest put his whiskey down and squinted at the words in the dim light. 'What the devil does this say?'

Timothy shrugged, held his left hand out and stared at it while wiggling two fingers of his right over the top of his palm.

'I have fucking read it, Timothy; your punctuating is crap. Whoever taught you to write was useless.'

Timothy snatched his notebook from the startled priest and stormed out.

Later, Father Raymond knocked at his room. 'I'm sorry,' he said, speaking close to the wood. 'Can I come in?' A moment later a note appeared under the door.

'No!'

The priest shook his head. Walking away, he murmured. 'Nothing wrong with the punctuating there, boy.'

Timothy barely remembered the first few days spent with Megan, the woman who'd looked after him for ten years, but he did recall how she'd said to him, 'You can't talk, I accept that. I'll bet you can't write either. Well, I'm going to teach you. You know what writing is?'

He'd nodded.

She'd shoved a pencil and a piece of paper at him. 'Write your name down for me.'

He still sometimes stuck his tongue out when he wrote, and he had done so that day, almost chewing it off as if it would help control his shaking hand. Finally, he succeeded. *Timothy.*

Megan read it out loud. 'Tim-o-tee . . . see this?' She pointed to her nose and wrote a single word on a scrap of paper. 'Copy that down.'

Timothy painstakingly copied what she'd written. *Nose.*

Little by little, Megan taught him to write. Schooled him on everything she knew about life – why people often behaved the way they did, the order of things, and the beauty of nature. 'And there's symbolism to be seen everywhere if only you have an eye for it. You'll learn, as you grow older, that what goes on in the heavens affects us down here. As above, so below, Timo.' She smiled at his confusion. 'One day you'll understand.'

Over the years, what she'd taught him blended with Father Raymond's warped and drink-fuelled philosophical ramblings.

After Father Raymond had died, Timothy wore the Easter robes on his own special occasions. Deep in thought, he picked lint from the front of the gown. He was closer to God than the old drunk had ever been.

'It's a question of faith,' the priest had told him during another lecture.

It was why he carried the Bible close to his heart.

Timothy walked out into the churchyard and took a detour past his family's grave. He bent to pluck a blade of grass, the broadest stem he could find, and then made his way down through the woods towards the railway track.

Chapter 27

Hilltop Cottage. 12:07 p.m.

Anderson floated weightlessly in a world he'd never been to before. Disoriented, he spread his arms and legs like a spaceman tumbling through the infinity of space, the Earth disappearing below him, becoming no more than a dot.

'Not all behaviour is learned,' he heard Ryan say.
Anderson searched for the source of the voice. It was close. 'Where are you?'
'There's always a pattern if you know how to look.'
The book. *Problem Child.* Anderson recalled reading the words. Or did he?
'I'm talking about genetic blueprints,' Ryan said.
That wasn't in the book. The blackness of space and the stars all around him vanished, and he found himself sitting opposite Ryan, watching the light play along the length of the polished silver pencil the elderly psychiatrist held between the thumbs and forefingers of his hands. Anderson blinked.
'You're not with me, are you, Anderson? I'm talking about traits passed between identical twins, separated at birth, by accident or design, perhaps.'
'But Ryan, who would do that?'
'Twins, who despite being separated for twenty years, often discover once reunited that they share exactly the same traits.'
'Your point, Ryan?'
'It would seem our lives are mapped out for us from the start.'

Anderson felt as if he were stretched out at the limits of an elastic band. He could float no further. He experienced a brief moment suspended in time and then he was snatched back, hurtling through blackness, the Earth growing bigger and brighter. He smashed through the atmosphere, closer and closer, scattered houses and open fields, forest. He braced himself. He had to wake up. If he didn't, it would mean he had died.

His olfactory senses came alive. Dampness. The sweet, pungent odour of rotting leaves. Confused, Anderson struggled to remember where he was. The dream had turned into a nightmare. He woke, breathless and half-blinded by pain. *This can't go on.*
Insight settled on him. He knew what it was. Self-diagnosis to the nth degree. He knew beyond doubt. He felt it. Thousands of tiny eggs coursed through his bloodstream, log-jamming, clogging in the bends and bottlenecks of his veins. Soon they would be hatching.
Adrenaline surged. *Get to a doctor.*
But he couldn't rouse himself.

Chapter 28

Signal House, Churchend. 12:27 p.m.

Wolfe lumbered along the railway track, gauging the length of his step to fall on the evenly spaced sleepers. It had taken a few minutes to get accustomed to walking with shorter strides, but now that he was used to it, he had no need to watch where he placed his feet. *Where are the trains?* Still no sign of anyone. Apart from the people in the church, he hadn't seen a soul, hadn't heard any vehicles. Instinct told him it had something to do with the lights in the skies. They shimmered in ways he'd never seen before. Birds perched in the trees on either side of the track, shuffling nervously as he approached, seeming to be as wary of him as they were the shape-shifting lightshow playing out above them.

Distracted, he stumbled, cursing as one of his feet fell short and crunched heavy and hard, down onto the gravel bed of the track. Shockwaves sped through his aching body.

His focus shifted to watching the position of the sleepers. Counting with each step, he resumed his cadence. The rhythm lulled him. He lost all sense of time and his thoughts drifted back to his early interviews with his psychiatrist, Dr Kotlas.

'I have these recurring dreams, and in them, I'm seeing through the eyes of a killer.' Wolfe grinned at the irony. 'I know what you're thinking, doc, I *am* a killer, but this is someone else. And I think I know who it is.'

Kotlas stared. The patient, restrained in a straitjacket and flanked by guards, appeared sincere. The lengthy pause that had developed didn't encourage him to speak further. Wolfe, knowing silence was one of the tools the doctor used, kept a victorious grin locked deep inside.

Kotlas rolled his hand, gesturing for him to continue.

'I think it's Jack the Ripper,' he said. 'I know you'll think I'm crazier than you did before, but I've a psychic connection with him.'

The psychiatrist leaned forwards. Placing his elbows on the desk, he steepled his hands and rested his chin on his thumbs. 'Because you dream about him?'

'No, it's more than that. I feel it, here.' His arms jiggled beneath the heavy canvas. 'In my guts.'

'Tell me, what it is you think you see through this killer's eyes?'

'You don't believe me?'

'I'm just asking questions,' Kotlas said. 'Believing or not isn't relevant at this point. All right, let's try this. What do you think the dreams mean?'

Wolfe shrugged. 'I'm seeing through the eyes of the Ripper. I've told you all this before. The missing body parts. What do you think he did with them?'

The psychiatrist shook his head. 'No idea. Tell me.'

'He ate them, that's what he did. I knew he was related to me somehow – why do you think we share the same tastes? I told my last quack all this, but no one takes me seriously.'

The cables overhead hummed as the wind rose, drawing Wolfe back to the present. He glanced up. The sky had become predominantly pink, the atmosphere eerie. An unearthly screech cut across the tracks. It reminded him of how, when he was a child, he'd blown breath across a piece of grass held between his upright thumbs, his hands cupped to amplify the noise. Turning in the direction the sound had come from, he caught a glimpse of some indefinable shape, large and dark, moving among the shadows of the trees.

'You don't think making that stupid racket scares me, do you? Or is it you want to play games with me?' he shouted. 'Come on then, come over here.' Greeted with silence, and seeing no further movement, he dismissed what he'd seen as a trick of the light. The shriek? Just the wind. He strode on.

On the left-hand side of the track, two hundred yards ahead, a signal box. Would there be anyone in it? Would they have seen him? Wolfe cut down the steep bank, aiming to approach on the blindside. His lips were dry; he licked them. Maybe he could get something to drink from there.

The way ahead blocked by a level crossing, Wolfe clambered up the bank and crossed the railway lines.

There was no sign of life in the first-floor windows of the half-timbered building. Arranged under a slate roof, the upstairs was supported on a solid brickwork base, designed, he imagined, to elevate the structure for good visibility both ways down the track. He followed the footpath through a white gate, climbed a short flight of stairs, and tried the door. Locked. About to stove it in, someone yelled from inside, 'Who's there?'

'Couldn't get a train. I've walked up from the last station miles back,' Wolfe said, directing his voice at the door. 'I wondered if I could have a glass of water. Find out what's going on.'

'There's no trains. Power failure, I think,' a man shouted from inside the signal house. 'I can't let you in. Regulations. Sorry.'

Wolfe bent to look through the fish-eye lens of the door viewer. An eye stared back.

'Don't you trust me? Come on,' he pleaded. 'All I want is some water and somewhere to rest.'

'Okay, go around the trackside. I'll drop you a bottle out of the window, and then you can go. You can't rest here.'

'Just open the door.' Wolfe knocked on it gently. 'You're not scared, are you?'

'Scared? I'm seventeen stone. Why would I be?' the signalman said. 'Look, mate, I've been up all night, my shift is over, but I can't leave because the day-man hasn't shown up. There's no power. There's no phone or radio. In other words, I don't know what's happening.'

'Got anything I can eat in there?' Wolfe said, grinning. 'I'll bet you have.'

'No, I haven't. Now I told you, I'll drop a bottle of water down to you. Take it or leave it, but I want you to move on.'

Detecting anxiety in the occupant's voice, Wolfe's grin widened. He tested the door with his shoulder. Bump.

'I'm telling you. I've got a baseball bat in here. Now fuck off.'

Wolfe's voice lowered to a growl. 'You shouldn't have said that to me.' He stood back and kicked the door just below the lock. The timber frame split, but held. His foot poised to stamp down from a higher angle, he heard the tinkle of a bicycle bell coming from down the lane.

The signalman shouted from the window, 'Mum, don't stop! Turn around quick. Ride away. Don't argue. Just do it!'

Brakes squealed. An elderly woman came into view, slowed to a stop, and dismounting, called out, 'What did you say, Ronald?'

Wolfe thundered down the stairs.

'Mum! Run!'

She saw the hulking figure of the stranger bearing down on her, and desperately scooted the bike, trying to get back on.

Behind him, Wolfe heard the door unlock and the rumble of footsteps rattling the wooden framework of the stairs.

'Leave her alone,' Ronald cried. 'I'll swing for you, I swear, if you touch her.'

Panic-stricken, and unable to propel herself faster without remounting, the old lady shouted, 'Go back inside, Ronald, he won't catch me. I'll fetch the police!' She threw her leg over the bicycle. Her skirt caught on the saddle. She lost balance and hopped on one foot while disentangling herself. Lost precious seconds. A glance over her shoulder showed the giant was almost on her. She screamed.

Wolfe snatched at her hair. A handful grabbed, he dragged her from the bike. Aware of heavy footsteps and panting breath coming from behind, he swung round and saw her son.

The signalman raised his bat to strike. 'I fucking warned you,' he snarled, bringing the weapon down with all his might.

Wolfe, in a blur of movement, hoisted the old lady aloft, a rag doll in his hands, her body used as a shield.

The woman's son tried to divert the blow. It crashed home with sickening force, smashing her skull, cleaving her head open.

Face aghast, the man screamed, 'No!'

Wolfe let the corpse fall. Licking blood from both hands, he growled, 'I told you shouldn't have said that to me. All I wanted was a glass of water, and now look what you've done.'

Rage and grief contorted the man's face. He roared, raising the bat shoulder-high, as if about to score a home run.

Wolfe didn't move until the last moment. He leaned back out of range, the club missing by a hair's breadth, and whipped forwards from the waist to grab the man's throat. His fingers dug deep into flesh on either side of the larynx, and he yanked his second victim towards him. Ronald, captured in an unrelenting grasp, kicked and flailed, gurgled and choked, his eyes bulging from his head. Tighter. Tighter. Wolfe slowly crushed his windpipe, taking pleasure at the ineffectual taps of the bat on his back and buttocks. With frightening ease, he lifted the signalman up and held the lifeless body away to see the feet dancing, twitched by muscles yet to receive the message that life had gone. A moment later, Wolfe dropped him. The body thumped to the ground.

Wolfe carried the old woman upstairs last, along with her handbag, and dumped her on top of her son. After going back down to conceal the bicycle, he returned. 'Nice of you both to invite me for lunch.' Although he was famished, the choice between a broiler and lardy flesh didn't appeal. On a hunch, he searched her bag and retrieved a tin-foil package from it. 'How nice of her to bring us these,' he said, and then, swinging the armchair around, he unwrapped the sandwiches and ate them at the desk.

After he'd eaten, he toyed with the idea of arranging the pair into a compromising position. Although the idea amused him, tiredness took command of his eyelids. Pointless, he thought, to fight a losing battle against himself, so he settled comfortably, looking round his new lair at row upon row of colour-coded levers. If he wasn't so exhausted, he'd have had a play with them.

Heavy-lidded, his eyes closed, and not inclined to reopen them, Wolfe sank into the welcoming arms of soporific darkness, descending the worn and slippery steps into dank tunnels. The man he'd so often seen executing prostitutes and others down on their luck, exchanged the blood on his clothes and skin for the filth of sewer water. He beckoned him to follow. Wolfe grinned acceptance and together, they made their escape to dine on a choice cut taken from the man's latest victim.

Chapter 29

Copse Hall. Hospital wing. 12:30 p.m.

Edwards, letting himself through the door, wheeled in a trolley laden with food and drink. He saw Kotlas standing by the window staring out, hands clasped behind his back.

'You took your time,' the psychiatrist said without turning round.

'I've been over at Control. I told them what happened. They can't believe it. UPS – Uninterrupted Power Supply – never kicked in. No one knows why. Any investigation is going to pull this place apart.'

'You can say that again,' Kotlas said.

Edwards moved forward with the trolley. 'You must be starved.' He glanced at the privacy curtains pulled around Fleur's bed. 'Is she sleeping?'

Kotlas turned to face the guard. 'No, I'm afraid she isn't,' he said softly. 'She died.'

Edwards dashed to the curtains, and swishing them apart, froze. His fingers dug into the fabric, the truth sinking in at the sight of her. He stood, arms outstretched, as if crucified.

A few moments passed before, at last, Edwards spoke. 'What happened?'

'The syringes Rubenstein thought he lost in the fight – she'd taken them from his pocket.'

'Christ.' The guard sank to his haunches. 'I never gave them a thought when I wrapped the jacket round her—'

'Hey, you aren't to blame,' Kotlas said. 'She must have injected herself under the covers pretty much as soon as we got her into bed. Why didn't I think to watch her?'

'Fucking Rubenstein,' Edwards spat. 'If that coward had used them as he was supposed to, this wouldn't have happened.'

Kotlas approached the guard, dragging a chair behind him. 'If not now, she'd have done it anyway,' he said, gently taking the other man's arm. 'Come on, sit down.'

'She only started here a couple of weeks ago,' Edwards said ruefully.

'She asked me to hold her hand,' Kotlas said.

'And you had no idea?'

'None. I sat down next to the bed. Almost drifted off.' *Was that when she injected herself?* 'I held her hand like she wanted. We spoke. I told her we'd get her fixed up. She was out of it. I thought it was shock. Then she stopped breathing. I tried to resuscitate her. That's when I found the syringes under the covers.'

'Christ,' Edwards clasped his head in his hands between his knees. 'Why wasn't I there for her earlier? She's so young – what a waste of life.'

'There was something else,' Kotlas said. 'She told me she was pregnant.'

'How much worse is this day going to get?' Edwards said.

'Tomorrow it'll seem like it was a bad dream, only we'll know it wasn't. This is the start of a nightmare, and it's going to run for months before we even get to the inquest.' Kotlas strolled past the trolley and picked up a bottle of water. 'I don't know about you, Edwards, but I've a feeling we'd better go and find Rubenstein.'

The guard got to his feet. 'You don't think . . . ?'

'After all this, I wouldn't be surprised. He's facing ruin.'

Edwards locked the door on the second floor, securing the northern staircase. 'You know where Rubenstein went wrong, don't you?' the guard said.

'Enlighten me,' Kotlas replied.

'He rushed to get the place open, that's what he did.'

'Let's leave that for the enquiry.' Kotlas walked on a few paces. 'This is the way, isn't it? We came up from the other end.'

'Just down there,' Edwards said, catching him up. 'Turn right; his office is about halfway down. The thing is, you don't even work here.'

'Right now, Edwards, for entirely selfish reasons, I can't tell you how glad I am about that. When I woke up this morning, I was thrilled to be coming here, the prospects and everything,' Kotlas said. 'How all that changed. Tell me something. How did Fisher escape?'

They rounded the corner.

Edwards took a deep breath. 'In normal circumstances, he'd have been isolated from anyone else. I'm guessing the minute the circuits blew, the power switched to emergency generators. We can only speculate on the reasons why they didn't work. It's another failure for the investigation.

'Anyway, he must have been out of his cell – in transit – when it happened. Control would have lost touch with who was where and with whom, and he somehow ended up grabbing that fucking screwdriver from one of the contractors. They shouldn't have even been in the same corridor. Bang. Power out. No cameras. No personal attack alarms. Fisher would have been on it straight away.'

'And with everyone involved now dead.'

They stopped outside Rubenstein's office.

'I guess we'll never know,' the guard said.

'All those people. Poor Fleur,' Kotlas said, and rapped hard on the glass panel of the door. He listened, then knocked again. The men exchanged glances. Edwards pulled the keychain from his pocket, selected the correct key and unlocked the door.

Rubenstein looked up from his desk. He had written a note. In his hand he held a blue and white box. 'You took your time,' he said.

Kotlas walked around Bales' body. It had been turned over, face down. 'You were supposed to come back.' The younger man stared at the swelling on Rubenstein's face. 'They your painkillers?'

'I've taken some.'

'What are they?'

'Tramadol. Why are you looking at me like that?'

'The syringes – you never found them, did you?'

'No, I—'

'Well, we fucking did,' Edwards spat. 'Fleur killed herself with them.'

Rubenstein gawped in horror. His shoulders slumped. 'Leave me,' he whispered.

Edwards snatched the note from the desk, read it and then passed it to Kotlas. 'Give me the box.'

Rubenstein handed it over.

Kotlas opened it and counted the missing pills. 'You've only taken two.'

'I made my mind up just before you came in. I'm finished, Kotlas. Let me end it,' he implored.

'No, you fucking coward,' Kotlas said, putting the pills in his pocket. 'You're not getting off so easily. I'm going to sit here and watch you until the power comes back on.'

Chapter 30

Avon Gorge. 12:35 p.m.

Local news reporter Nick Summer, dashed to the scene of the prison bus accident on his vintage motorbike as soon as he heard what had happened. He parked the bike and padlocked it with the heavy chain he wore bandoliered over his shoulder. He climbed down to the crash site, the camera he'd borrowed from his grandfather swinging from his neck.

At the bottom, only human vultures remained, grouped together, picking over the story in hushed tones.

Summer approached a man whose blackened face, streaked with sweat, gave him the appearance of a commando on special operations. 'Excuse me,' Summer said, nodding towards the wreckage. 'Were you here when that came over the side?'

'Almost,' the man said. 'It was about four hours ago. Every time I think I'm going back up, someone else comes along asking questions.' He wiped a dewdrop of perspiration from the tip of his nose and studied Summer. 'Which lot are you with?'

'I'm a reporter. Nick, pleased to meet you.' He shoved his hand out.

The man ignored it. 'Can't tell you a lot, but what I do know is that whoever they had on board looks to have escaped. The officials are not saying much, though from rumours going round, I gather the prisoner was a psychiatric patient on the move under heavy guard.'

'Well, it was a prisoner transfer vehicle, so no surprise there,' Summer said.

'You think not?' The man looked around him cautiously and leant towards the reporter. 'He had at least ten of them guarding him.'

'Ten? No, you must have that wrong. There were other prisoners on board?'

'No, he was the only one. Six of the guards perished, plus the driver. You must have seen the mess on the bridge before you came down. The three surviving guards might still be up top.'

'I saw them,' Summer said, 'but I wanted to get a feel for what happened before I start asking questions. You got a name?' he asked.

'Of course I have,' the man said. 'But I don't want it in the papers.'

'Fine.' Summer popped the lens cap from the old Minolta and began taking photographs of the scene.

'I didn't tell you all of it, by the way. A couple of hours back, two more guards turned up asking questions. It was them who figured out how the prisoner had got away. Somehow, the guy in the wheelchair and the escapee survived the original crash. Got thrown clear, they reckon. I heard one of them say, 'There's only one man I know as big as Wolfe.' The man lowered his voice. 'Turns out it was the guy in the wheelchair. This Wolfe murdered him and stole his clothes.'

'Where did you say that was?' Summer said.

'Behind those rocks.' The man pointed to an outcrop further down the slope. 'There's a guard looking after the body until it can be recovered.'

'There?' Summer said as he wandered down. 'It's hard to imagine a formation like that occurred by accident. Looks like a corner of Stonehenge.' He made a mental note to ask his grandfather, Professor Young, if he knew anything about it. If he didn't, he'd surely be interested enough to take a look.

He rounded the corner of the largest stone, doing his best to look casual. He saw the guard perched on the smooth flat surface of a stone that looked like it was made for the purpose, smoking. 'Hi there. Nick Summer's the name.' He flashed an identity card. 'I'm a reporter.'

The man blew a plume of smoke in his direction and then, taking another drag, he stood, dropping his cigarette to the ground. 'No comment,' he said, and screwed the burning stub out with his boot.

Summer ignored the remark and moved closer. The body lay on its side, the top half concealed by a tartan picnic blanket. Rivulets of blood had dried on the exposed bare legs.

The guard stepped in to block his view.

'I'm not asking for a comment. I'm just making conversation. You're a big bloke, what, six foot four? Even covered up, I can see the dead man is bigger.' Summer gauged the guard's face for a reaction, a clue for how best to get him talking. The man's face was as hard as the limestone surrounding them.

'I don't know about you, but it seems odd that he survived the initial fall. As far as I know, only one other person has, and that was over a hundred years ago. Her skirts saved her, acted like a parachute.' Summer closed the gap between him and the guard. 'And here, there's not one, but two survivors. Incredible, don't you think?'

'Maybe,' the guard said.

'There's no maybe about it. Listen.' Summer reached into his back pocket and produced a fifty-pound note from the wad he'd won at the casino the night before. 'I'll make a bet with you.'

'I'm not a gambling man, but what's the bet?'

'The coroner says it's to do with how big they were.'

'That's bollocks and you know it.'

'Right now, I don't really know anything. I'll tell you what,' Summer said. 'You take that. Just give me a little something I can use. I won't write anything down, and I won't reveal the source of my information—'

'You think you can buy me for a fifty?' the guard said. 'Fuck off.'

'I only want some background,' Summer said, 'nothing anyone's going to get sensitive about.'

'Listen, pal, if I'm going to talk, I want double that.'

Summer took the roll from his back pocket, skinned another note from it and handed the money over.

'What do you want to know?'

'Why ten guards?'

'The patient has a history of flaring up. That's how many men it takes to subdue him.'

'What's he being treated for?'

'I can't answer that.'

'Okay,' Summer said. 'I understand some other guards showed up asking questions a while back. What happened to them?'

'One went to the police station. The other stayed behind.'

'I take it that isn't you. Where is he?'

'Up on the bridge, with the others,' the guard replied. 'How much money have you got there?'

'About five hundred. Why do you ask?'

'Because, for that, Summer, I can give you something really juicy.'

'Like what?'

'Wolfe's a cannibal. He has a habit of exposing himself to his victims before he kills them.'

'I'm sure I could dig back through old news reports and find that out.'

The guard laughed. 'Yeah, probably. Here's something that came out of studies on him. You cannot reveal your source, though. Right?'

'You have my word.'

'He orgasms as he gorges on flesh. No need for penetration.'

'What?' Summer said, incredulous. 'How come I've never heard of him before?'

'You won't have done. He's been in the system since he was fifteen. He murdered seven girls. Started when he was thirteen. Took the police a while to catch him because they were looking for someone much older. He had a knack of getting away undetected.' The guard scratched his chin. 'That's your lot. If you want any more, you need to give me the rest.'

Summer nodded. 'All right, but this had better be good.' He fished the roll of notes from his pocket, counted the money and handed it to the guard. 'I've heard of junkies getting an erection as they prepare for a fix, sometimes ejaculating as the needle pops a vein, but who comes when he takes a bite out of someone?' Summer said, his expression a mixture of puzzlement and disgust.

The guard glanced around him. 'The way I see it, it isn't any different to a boy getting a hard-on in anticipation of sex with his girlfriend. I heard his doctors discussing it once. They said it was like the experiment with dogs and bells done by some Russian. The dogs hear a bell. They associate it with food. They salivate.'

'You mean Pavlov. Are you sure he was Russian?'

'I don't give a fuck if he was or wasn't.'

'What else have you got?'

'I used to have a drink sometimes with one of the psychiatrists. I could have been a psychiatrist, if I'd wanted. I was bright enough. Just didn't have wealthy parents. I had to get out and work as soon as I left school. Anyway, that's another story. When he'd had a few, he used to spout on about all kinds of shit. He knew about my interests. We used to have some really heavy conversations. I remember him telling me one night how we understand the workings of the brain so much better now, and how much dopamine plays a part in addictions and perversions. There's no doubt killers get a high, and often, after a while, it simply isn't enough.

'Look at the American cannibal killer, Albert Fish; that bastard preyed on children, for God's sake. Self-mutilation. All stemmed from the beatings he got at an orphanage, and over time, the pervert acquired a liking for the punishment dished out to him.'

'You know that for a fact?'

'Fish said so himself. Of course, I don't know how much, if any, is true. The way I understand things, there isn't much doubt that often, the abused become abusers. Learned behaviour is passed on. The sins of the father and all that.'

'These your words or the doctor's?'

The guard grinned. 'It's an extract from a discussion we had.'

'So Wolfe was abused?'

'No. Something else happened. Wolfe told doctors he acquired a taste for blood just after his father died. He and a girl were playing, and there was an accident. She cut herself badly. Got glass in the wound. Wolfe sucked it out. My psychiatrist friend told me he thought it activated something that had lain dormant. The same as in children of drug addicts. If a mum uses while pregnant, the kids are far more likely to became addicts themselves.'

'Interesting,' Summer said. 'So it could be that bloodthirst is in everyone, but most people have learned it's bad for society.'

'No,' the guard said. 'I thought, and the doctor agreed, that some people are genetically predisposed to certain triggers.' The guard paused, slyness evident in his voice as he resumed talking. 'I saw you had another fifty. Add that to what you've already given and I'll tell you something better still.'

'You know,' Summer said, 'for all your intelligence, you're really just a con-man.'

'Take it or leave it. I'll tell you this for nothing, though. The doctor also mentioned a DNA link to Jack the Ripper.'

Summers' eyes lit with interest. 'Tell me about that.'

The guard stuck his hand out. 'The other fifty. Give, and then I'll tell you.'

The reporter pulled the note from his back pocket. 'This really is the last,' he said, and handed it over. 'Now, let's hear the rest of the story.'

'I was part of the team that looked after him when he was a kid.'

'You did?' Summer said, eager for more. 'I assume it was a special place for juveniles?'

'Yes,' the guard said. 'He was fifteen, though you wouldn't have known it from his size. Already six foot five, he was unmanageable. Couldn't move him without a four-man escort, and then only after making sure the rest of the kids in the home were put away.'

'He was that hostile?' Summer said.

'Not always, but you just couldn't trust him. At that time, despite his size, he was still just a child. I wanted to know what made him do the things he did. It's a natural curiosity. Nothing morbid about it. At times, I felt quite sorry for him walking alone in the yard.'

'You were going to tell me about the Ripper.'

'I still am, but all this is relevant.' The guard pulled a cigarette pack from his pocket, shook one out and lit it without asking Summer if he'd like one. 'The kids from the local housing estate used to play in the field the exercise yard looked out over. When they saw him out, they used to taunt him. When that happened you soon forgot how young he was. He'd go berserk, crashing into the wire trying to get to them. He'd damage himself, but he didn't care. The fence used to look like it had been charged by a rhinoceros. For those doing the teasing, it was just a game, but if he'd have got out, he'd have slaughtered them.'

Summer whistled low. 'I don't even want to imagine what he's capable of now. Did you talk to him?'

'Other than issue instructions, no.'

'No small talk at all?'

The guard shifted position.

'Come on,' Summer said, 'we'll keep it between you and me.'

'According to Kotlas – shit! Forget that I said that name.'

'Okay, I will, but who was he?'

'The psychiatrist I was telling you about. He said Wolfe was never really forthcoming in one-to-one sessions. I'm still not sure if I was somehow manipulated.'

'By whom?'

The prison officer chewed his lower lip, then took a deep pull on his smoke. 'I was on duty one night, and I heard Wolfe crying out in his sleep. I went down to his room to make sure he was all right and opened the hatch. Got the shock of my life. He was already standing on the other side, waiting for me.'

'Go on,' Kotlas said.

'He hadn't been sleeping, said he wanted to confide in someone other than a quack.'

The reporter squinted as a curl of smoke from the guard's cigarette found its way into his eye. 'So what was on his mind?'

'He said he kept having dreams that he was a murderer. I laughed and told him, "But you are." Now, what is all this bollocks?' The guard brushed the hot end of his cigarette against the rock he sat on, sharpening it to a conical shape. He took another drag.

'Well, what did he say to that?' Summer asked.

The guard shrugged. 'He said he thought Jack the Ripper had got inside his head.'

'What did you think? Did you tell Kotlas?'

'Not at first. Then Kotlas confessed he'd given Wolfe MDMA.'

Summer frowned. 'What is that?'

The guard scratched the back of his neck. 'Ecstasy.'

'How on earth was he able to get away with that?'

'Local authorities used to pay a fortune to get problem kids off their hands, ship them into another county if need be. Apart from a few cursory checks, they just assumed they'd left them in good hands. I think a few quacks took advantage of that to experiment with different things. They were able to get away with it at that time.'

'What was the purpose, though?'

'Kotlas was obsessed with regression techniques. He took Wolfe's claims seriously. Between you and me, I think he felt he might use Wolfe to discover who Jack the Ripper was.'

'That's crazy.' Summer shook his head. 'I thought you were going to give me something good.'

'Kotlas had his DNA tested. A sample of the Ripper's semen came to light on a piece of a victim's clothing. They compared the results. It was a match.'

'What happened then?'

'Wolfe got shipped out, much to Kotlas's dismay. Last I heard, he got a job in Ashmore, specifically to work with Wolfe so he could solve the mystery.'

'Does Kotlas still work at Ashmore?'

'Listen, Summer,' the guard said. 'Don't get any ideas. I don't want you talking to him about what I've just told you.'

'Don't worry.' The reporter unhitched the camera from around his neck. 'My word is my bond,' he said moving closer to the corpse. 'Now let me take a picture and then we'll talk about this guy.'

Chapter 31

Bell House, Churchend. 12:55 p.m.

Gloria Fallow hadn't touched a drink in weeks. Back living with her parents after years in the wilderness, a wilderness created by drugs, alcohol and prostitution, her mother and father had forgiven her everything. She owed it to them to at least try to stay clean.

When the power had shut down earlier and the skies changed, alternating between light, darkness and unnatural colours, her father had insisted on manning the bells in the dilapidated church, which stood beyond the field adjoining their garden. 'We have to warn people,' he said. 'It's a sign. The power of man is gone. Soon, the devil will walk among us.'

Her mother had looked at her and nodded. 'Bells are not just for celebration, child.'

Gloria smiled at their shared eccentricity. They'd chosen the house purely on the basis of its close proximity to a place of worship. By road, the church was three miles away, and yet across the garden shortcut, the distance was less than a mile.

She looked out from the window above the kitchen sink, and wondered where they were. The bells had stopped ringing some three hours ago. They'd tried to persuade her to accompany them, but she'd declined. Her father had insisted, but her mother put him off by suggesting their daughter might be better at peeling potatoes than bells. The two of them had laughed.

She surprised herself by preparing the vegetables in their absence. The last of them dropped into the saucepan, she filled it with water. Everything she did these days, it seemed, she carried out in a dream-like state. A sleepwalker, she'd lived her whole life divorced from the reality other people experienced.

Gloria wiped her hands. She licked her parched lips. *How much longer can I survive without a drink?* Her heart fluttered, coming alive at the re-emergence of some buried prospect. *No! Get thee gone, dark spirit.* She smiled faintly. She'd used the words her father had tried years before when he'd thought her possessed. She inhaled deeply. In a while, she'd walk across the field to meet her parents. They had to be on their way back. She lost herself in thought, staring out of the window.

The pub. The image popped into her brain unbidden. Everything was ready on the stove. It just needed lighting.

Just one glass won't hurt. Shit. Dad took my money. Resolve fell from her shoulders, discarded like a heavy gown as she ascended the stairs. Gloria walked over the landing and into her parents' room. The threshold crossed, she sat at the dressing table and gazed into the mirror her mother had stared into a thousand times. Turning her face left and right, not taking her eyes from her reflection, she pondered her mother's thoughts. *Did she think, when she looked at herself, the same as I am now, that she was a sham? Of course she didn't.*

Drawing the jewellery box towards her, Gloria opened the lid. The crown jewels she'd admired as a child now seemed lacklustre. She scooped up a bracelet filled with charms and examined each one. A little church, hinged at the back, submitted to her prising fingers and opened to reveal a bride and groom. She smiled, but the smile collapsed. Woeful inadequacy bubbled up. She'd never find happiness the way her parents had. She knew it. Tears clouded her vision. She wiped them away. Lifting the tray to get to the compartment beneath, she spotted a key. In her mind she telescoped from where she sat upstairs into the basement, to the racks and racks of wine. She wouldn't need money or the pub after all, not now. She had the key to where her father had locked away the booze when she'd arrived a few weeks ago.

With shaking hands, Gloria replaced the tray, closed the lid, and fondling the key, took it with her downstairs.

At the cellar door, her mouth flooded with saliva in anticipation. She fitted the key into the lock and turned it.

Chapter 32

Priestley police station. 1:00 p.m.

Williams took a break outside on the ramp. He leaned on the railings that faced the road. Three-quarters of the stationary cars were still occupied, as if the drivers expected the engines to splutter back to life at any moment. A man stood close to the back wing of his vehicle and urinated. It occurred to Williams to have a word, but he quickly dismissed it as a bad idea. He gazed at the sky. *Where are the birds?*

Most of the people outside had gone. Only a half-dozen remained. 'Where is everyone?' he asked the Italian he'd seen earlier.

'Those two big men, the prison officers. They came out,' he turned his wrist to look at a non-existent watch, 'oh, about an hour ago, and they say, go home. These police in there, they tell you nothing.'

Anderson watched the man's hands, fascinated; he seemed to carve his vocabulary from the air. The faster he spoke, the more his command of English deteriorated.

'This chief inside, he don't tell you there is very dangerous man on the loose. The big one, he say, soon we have team together for look this danger-man. He say, go home, lock doors is best thing. Police in there won't help you.'

'What are you still doing here?' Williams said.

'Me? I don't got nowhere to go.'

'What about the rest of you?' he said, addressing the others.

A middle-aged woman with squirrel teeth answered for them. 'It's better than staring at four walls on our own—'

'Yeah,' her slack-jawed male companion said. 'We've been having a game. Who can guess what crime the next person walking up is going to report?' His eyes lit up as a man entered the ramp at the bottom and began to trudge up the slope. 'Look at him – I wonder what's happened? He's got a face on him like a dog chewing a wasp.'

'Keep your voice down,' Williams cautioned. 'We don't want any trouble starting out here.'

A pinch-faced woman turned from the pavement and stormed towards them.

'Oh, and this one, look at her—'

'Right. All of you waiting to report an incident, queue up there. The rest of you,' Williams pushed his face close to slack-jaw, 'especially you.... Bugger off.'

The Italian spread his hands. 'What about me?' he said, dog-eyed.

'Anyone else starts playing games out here, I want to know. Got that?'

'You reckon I can cadge some water from you lot in there?'

Williams glanced at the Italian. 'I'm sure we can organise something,' he said. Then he turned to the man who had just walked up. 'Can I help you, sir?'

'I've had my motorbike stolen.'

Williams pointed him to the top of the ramp. 'Wait there. You'll be called in once they've dealt with the people already inside. 'And you, miss?' he enquired.

'I've had a break-in. I can't believe it. I'd just stocked up at the supermarket. People are panic-buying, fights breaking out. There's a sign on the door saying cash customers only, but people aren't taking any notice. I think someone followed me home from there.'

'What makes you say that?'

'All they took was food.'

'Join the queue.'

So, the prison officers had told the crowd. Emerson would be livid. They'd left over an hour ago, following a furious row. For once, Williams understood where the inspector was coming from. It was too soon for the police to start commandeering vehicles. The heavy-handed approach put forward by Styles was skewed towards him putting together a search party for Wolfe. Emerson had resisted.

'These are separate issues entirely,' Emerson said. 'There's a far greater danger from the public if we spook them. The way it is at the moment, although they're worried, we've had relatively few incidents. I want to keep it that way.'

Styles jabbed an accusing finger at him. 'You haven't listened to a word I've said, have you? How many fatalities did you have in the big Bristol riots at St Paul's?

'You're muddying the waters to suit your own ends, Styles—'

'No, not me.' Styles looked over to Jordan. 'If this lot won't back us up, we'll go it alone. You coming?'

Jordan slid from the corner of the desk. 'Okay, let's do it.'

'Styles,' Emerson said as the two men went through the door, 'I don't want to hear you've stolen any vehicles on my patch.'

The prison officer stopped, the doorway framing his huge stature. He turned to face the inspector. 'There comes a time when we have to do wrong to do right. I'd have thought, as a copper, you'd know that.'

Williams recalled his father had said something similar about war. He'd been a soldier. Killed on duty. When he was old enough, Williams had wanted to follow him into the army. He met strong resistance from his mother.

'It's too dangerous,' she wailed. 'If you must wear a uniform, why not be an ambulance man?'

Williams fought long and hard to persuade her, in the end settling for a career in the police force.

He'd been a constable at the station for five years, and now he couldn't wait to get away. When he heard who'd got the inspector's job, he knew Emerson would become even more intolerable. He made a decision. He'd apply for a job with Traffic.

He phoned his mother to tell her. She was over the moon for him. 'I can't tell you how happy I am, boy. The streets are so dangerous these days. I'm proud of you.' She paused. 'Your father would've been, too.'

There was something he didn't tell her because he knew she'd never accept it. He knew how she struggled on her widow's pension. When he got the new job, he would use the extra money to help her more. *I must pop in to see her.*

The next thing was to tell Sergeant Emerson.

'You, a traffic officer?' Emerson sneered. 'Good luck with that. When will you hear they've turned you down?'

'If they do, they do. I'll live with it. Unlike you, who never announced he'd gone for inspector. You kept it quiet in case you never got it.'

'It wasn't like that,' Emerson replied, 'not that it's any of your business. I was told to keep it quiet.' He pinned his subordinate with a glare. 'Traffic Officer Williams,' he mused. 'I'm going to start calling you that straightaway.'

'I don't know why you always have to try and belittle people, *Sarge?*' Williams said sarcastically. 'Is it to bring them down to your level so you can feel bigger?'

'Out, Williams, before I lose my temper—'

'I haven't finished yet. What about Croft? All this harmless calling her Lara while your eyes are stuck to her tits. That's the real implication, isn't it?'

'Your career is hanging in the balance, Williams.'

'Maybe I should just report you, then we'll see whose career is on the line.'

'No one likes a snitch, Williams. Whatever happens, it'll be a blot on your copybook. The trouble with you, and always has been, is you've got a chip the size of an oak beam on your shoulder.'

I don't have much more of you to put up with now, Emerson.
He wondered if he should tell Croft he'd stuck up for her.

The door opened behind him. Adams poked his head out. 'You're wanted.'

Williams groaned inwardly, and pushing himself away from the railings, turned to accompany the waiting sergeant.

Chapter 33

Priestley police station. 1:10 p.m.

Emerson turned away from the window as Williams knocked once on the open office door and walked in.

'I can't afford for you to be loafing around out there, Williams. I want you to make your way to Professor Young's house. Bring him back with you.'

Williams raised his eyebrows. 'I wasn't loafing, it was my break—'

'Your whole life is a break, Williams.'

'Sir, you said you were going to reconvene at noon—'

'For a half-dozen people?'

'Yes, they already think we don't talk to them.'

'I don't give a shit.' Emerson growled.

'I can't see why we don't try to hook-up with headquarters, sir.'

Emerson's voice took on a tone of infinite patience, as if he were speaking to a child. 'Because to do that, we'd have to go over there. I'm not abandoning my post or my people.' He dismissed Williams with a backhand gesture. 'And don't look at me like that. I'm the one who says what goes. Do as you're told. Adams will tell you where the old boy lives.'

Five minutes later, Williams started up the hill leading to the professor's house. A tall, grey-haired man laboured against the steep gradient a hundred yards ahead. *Is that the professor?* He didn't want to make a fool of himself calling out from so far back, so Williams jogged until the gap between them had narrowed to twenty yards. 'Professor?' he said in a loud voice.

The man stopped and turned round. 'Oh, it's you,' he said. 'How can I help you?'

'Emerson wants you back at the station.'

'Does he now?'

The deep-throated roar of a motorcycle coming around the corner at the bottom of the hill interrupted them.

'That's my grandson, unless I'm very much mistaken,' the old man said. He raised his hand in salutation. The bike accelerated towards them.

A few moments later, the rider pulled up, and raising his visor, said, 'Granddad. Officer. Is everything all right?'

'Of course, Nick. The constable has just passed on a request from the new inspector to attend the station.'

Summer regarded Williams with suspicion. 'What for?'

'I think the inspector needs the professor's advice,' Williams replied.

Summer looked at his grandfather. 'I have something I need to talk to you about first. In confidence.'

'Let's go to the house, Nick.' He motioned Williams with his eyes. 'You as well.'

Summer could barely contain his irritation. He throttled the bike, covering the last hundred yards and set about parking his machine.

'Shit,' Professor Young said, patting his pockets. 'I've locked myself out. Wait here.' He disappeared down the path leading to his back gate. Williams heard the hollow scrape of something dragged across concrete. A moment later, the professor returned with spare keys in his hand, and inserting one of them into the lock on his metal garage door, turned it. Twisting the handle, he heaved upwards. The ribbed sheet thundered as it tipped. Hidden wheels rolled back on overhead guides; a shaft of brightness moving with it penetrated deep into the gloom, revealing dustsheets covering what was clearly a car and two motorcycles. He flipped the light switch without thinking. 'How many more times will I do that before I finally get the idea there isn't any power?' He strode in and peeled the cream-coloured covers from the vehicles.

Summer and Williams followed the old man inside.

'These are the bikes I mentioned to you earlier, constable,' the old man said, admiring the classic lines and gleaming chromium parts. 'Thanks to Nick's attentions, they look like new.'

Williams nodded in approval. 'Professor Young, I can't keep calling you that. What's your first name?'

'It's Dai,' he said. 'And there's not a single joke I haven't heard about it.'

Williams grinned. 'Call me John.'

'John Williams?' the professor said, deadpan. 'What were your parents thinking?'

'John, can you give me a minute with him?' Summer said.

'Sure.' Williams backed away through the door. 'I'll wait outside.'

Summer steered his grandfather into the far right-hand corner of the garage and began speaking in hushed tones. Williams could tell by Young's body language that he wasn't comfortable with the conversation. *What are they talking about?*

Williams crept down the side of the garage. A high-level window was open a crack and he could just make out what they were saying.

'Granddad, Jack the Ripper is hot news, even now. There's always someone coming up with a new angle on it.'

'Yes,' the professor replied. 'What you have is an interesting story. An escaped psychiatric patient with a taste for blood would be enough for most people. Not for you, though. You have to go one better. I must admit, I'm somewhat intrigued. You're sure the patient confided to a guard that he had recurrent dreams about killing people, and he was convinced that it had something to do with Jack the Ripper?'

'That's what he told the guard, yes,' Summer said. 'What he didn't know is that the doctor treating him had collected a sample of his DNA. Here's the really interesting bit. The psychiatrist compared it to semen found on an article of clothing recovered from the scene a hundred and twenty-five years ago.'

The professor looked away.

'What's the matter, Granddad?'

'Isn't it obvious, Nick? How did the guard know this?'

'Apparently, the guard and the good doctor often had a drink together. It all came out during one drunken session.' Summer paused upon seeing his grandfather frown. 'You think it's far-fetched? What if I could give you the doctor's name? You could check it out when the power's back on.'

'To prove he worked with this patient?' The professor shook his head. 'It would still be hearsay.'

'Maybe, but it pushes the likelihood to a higher level. You want to know the results?'

'Well, don't keep me in suspense, boy.'

'It was a match.'

A few moments of silence followed, broken when Summer cleared his throat.

'Oh sorry,' Young said. 'I was just thinking. If that's true, it's an incredible coincidence. It presumably means we could track the patient's family tree—'

'Exactly, Granddad. We're on the threshold of discovering not only who the Ripper was, but whether or not his DNA carries a behavioural signature passed down on the father's side.'

'I think you may be getting ahead of yourself, Nick.'

'No, Grandad, I'm not. What if I told you the guard eventually let on that Wolfe's father was convicted of murder? What if I discover other murderers in the male lineage?'

'Nick, if you do, you'll have a fantastic scoop. It's a big if, though. And right now, you're stumped for further research.'

'No, Grandad. I'm not. If I can just borrow a tankful of petrol, I can access the libraries in London.'

'Even if you can verify your theory, the story won't count for anything until it can be printed and circulated. There's no point dashing off until the infrastructure is operational again. It seems that could happen in an hour or two. The engineers will be watching the sky before switching back on. They don't want to risk frying the circuits by doing it too early. Now, come on, let me deal with the officer and we can talk further.'

Williams scooted back to position himself adjacent to the garage door.

'Sorry to have taken so much of your time. Tell the inspector I'll be along as soon as I can. Meanwhile, perhaps he should take to the streets locally, and familiarise himself with people. They'll respect him for it, you know.'

'I'll be sure to pass that on, Dai,' Williams said. 'Oh and he's bound to ask, any idea when the power could be restored?'

'Keep watching the sky,' he said. 'When the lights disappear from it, there's a good chance there won't be much longer to wait.'

Chapter 34

Hilltop Cottage. 2:17 p.m.

Locked into a half-world from which there appeared to be no escape, Anderson ascended flight after flight of stairs. Thoughts raced like petals on a fast-flowing stream. *What is it I search for? What was it that attracted me to pick up that book?* He sensed he was changing, seeing in a different way and thus more connected with nature. Empathy. He felt at one with all beings. His mind shot through freeze-framed moments in a breathtaking display of photographic recall and stopped on the image of a heron. He knew it had stood for hours in cold water at the edge of a reed bed, unmoving. Then, without warning, the bird's head shot into the murky depths, the surface turbulent as it reappeared with a fish flapping in its bill. In three deft movements, the bird flipped its prey around, and tilting its head, swallowed everything. Skin, eyes, stomach contents, bowels.

A moment of epiphany followed.

The bite! He'd been injected. The saliva from the creature pumped in. It had in some way changed him, revolutionised his thought patterns. *Impossible.* Yet Ryan's voice whispered across the divide.

The two of them sat in his office, Anderson on the other side of his desk, in the days before his eye had become sightless. 'Such a thing happened to me once, Anderson, following a bite. I called it the Night of the Mosquito. It caused a reaction akin to a long, dark night of the soul. Tainted with the blood of the last person bitten, some religious zealot I would think.'

Anderson grinned. 'It isn't possible.'

'You believe that?' Ryan raised a single eyebrow and studied his friend's face. 'The theory isn't without merit. Consider how just one bite from a malaria-carrying mosquito can threaten your survival.'

'That's a parasite,' Anderson said. 'Something else entirely.'

'Is it?' The old man picked up his pencil and twirled it in his fingers. 'What is a disease if not a pathogen, a genetic mutation capable of causing devastating effects in human cells? Genetics is in its infancy. We're unlocking so many doors to understanding that were previously closed. We are what we eat, are we not? What if the genetic code in the saliva injected is so strong it infiltrates our own and takes over?'

'I can't say I've ever thought about it,' Anderson replied.

'You should. The world is changing. Here in England, malaria was eradicated in the fifties. The authorities are watching for its return.'

Further conversations resurrected themselves. They covered resistance syndrome – sufferers who obstructed all efforts to treat them, as though on a mission to punish themselves. Some of Ryan's child patients were addicted to chaos. Like black holes, they sucked others in. Followers. Leaders. Anderson followed the thought-train. His old friend was an accomplished hypnotist, and patients were often unaware he'd got them under his influence. Anderson shook his head slowly as his thoughts took on a life of their own. The medium, Vera Flynn. For him, Ryan's deviation into the paranormal had been the last straw. In his mind's eye, Ryan protested all over again. 'Using her was incredibly successful, I tell you. I drew the line, though, at experimenting on my patients with mind-altering drugs.'

Ryan had theories on everything. 'To ensure their survival, Anderson, plants evolved symbiotic relationships with birds, animals and insects. They found ways to interact with mankind. Through chemical experiences, they showed us that the whole world is one; we're all interconnected and capable of sharing profound experiences. Experiments with LSD and psilocybin have proven that.'

The bite. The mosquito's bloody saliva. Could it be possible? Couldn't be. He drifted, aware of a craving for salt and a raging thirst he needed to slake.

If the blood of a bad person was mixed with that of a good one, would the good prevail?

Chapter 35

Signal House, Churchend. 3:00 p.m.

Wolfe dug his heels into the floor of the signal house as he stretched out his legs and arms. The chair acting as a fulcrum, he held a plank-like pose while he yawned. At first, his long sleep had tricked him into thinking it was dawn and he'd slept the day away. *The last of that bloody cocktail Chisolm gave me.*

He took a bottle of water from the desktop, unscrewed the cap and drank. His eyes drawn to a large notebook, he leaned forward, and picking it up, opened the bookmarked pages, slicing them apart with the thin red ribbon attached to the spine. The day, the date, neatly written. The signalman had kept a note of the events of the day so far. Power failure. Telephone down. Visuals good. Clock stopped. Wolfe glanced at the wall where it hung. 8:44 a.m.

He rubbed his hands together. *No communications, eh, Wolfie?*

Outside, shimmering pinks and iridescent greens continued to marble the sky. It was near impossible to guess the time with accuracy. The old woman had been bringing sandwiches, but that didn't mean it was lunchtime. Though the sun wasn't clearly visible, from the brilliance in the southeastern sky, he imagined it to be midafternoon.

Wolfe pushed the chair back and half-rose. *Wait.* The remnants of a dream nagged at him and he sat back down, piecing together what he could remember.

Wolfe realised once again he'd been in the company of someone who'd lived a long time ago. Sometimes Wolfe rode in the stranger's head; others, they walked side by side. Snatches of conversation overheard while walking through the backstreets of London's East End filtered into his brain. He'd stopped at the mouth of an alleyway. Three men – toshers, scavengers of the sewers – huddled together in a doorway, drinking from a bottle they passed back and forth. Backtracking, he stood against a wall, hidden from view, listening.

'Rats bigger'n dogs, I seen. Hordes of 'em. Pick yer bones clean in about two minutes, so many of 'em.'

'Them's old wives' tales. Who told ya that?'

'Seen it wit' me own eyes.'

'If you was that close, how comes the rats left you alone?'

'They got me mate, the second he come off the ladder. I was still at the top. Jumping for me, they was. Nothing I could do, so I scarpered.'

Eyes narrowed, his companion said, 'Where was that then?'

Looking furtively about, his voice dropped to a whisper.

'That, my friend, was at the entrance to the richest pickings to be 'ad in all of London's sewers.'

The other man nodded. 'Oh, there,' he said. 'I know that place. It's true, bodies wash out the other end, picked clean by all the creatures in hell's creation. I know all the other tunnels like the back of me 'and. I've been everywhere, except there.'

Wolfe's companion moved to the side and stepped into view, scraping a heel deliberately on the cobbles. The men turned to face him. He towered over them, but despite his huge size, the biggest man stepped forward to intercept him. 'What the fuck do you want?'

A sovereign held out, glistening in the half-light, Wolfe heard the voice he'd become so familiar with speak. 'I'd like you to show me the entryways and exits into the sewers throughout the Whitechapel area. That's if you know your way around there.'

The tosher looked him up and down. 'I make that on a good day, and I'm not for sharing.'

'It isn't a share I want. Just a guide for a few days. A guinea a day.'

The man's eyes lit up. 'You're on,' he said, spitting into his palm and offering it to seal the deal, laughing. 'I bet you've never had dirty hands in your life, guvnor.'

Taking it, the stranger said, 'Dirtier than you could imagine.'

Dregs of other dreams came back to Wolfe and slotted into place. The errant jigsaw pieces finally made sense. When he was a boy, he'd been afraid of the dark streets and the stinking underground world he'd come to frequent. The closer he'd come to this devil, the more he sensed a connection. Way back, in his teens, he'd told doctors what he knew. They never laughed out loud, but they thought him mad; it showed in their eyes. Jesus, surely this was proof. In the moments before waking, Wolfe had floated out of his evil host, and looking back over his shoulder, had seen him under the glow of a street lamp, saw his face in detail for the first time. The eyes. Mismatched in colour. One blue, the other the colour of stormy waters.

He's got my eyes.

Time to get moving. He opened the fridge. Nothing but milk, a half-eaten bar of chocolate, and a shrink-wrapped pack of bottled water. His fingers dug into the plastic and forced a hole through it, making it wider. Removing one of the bottles, he slid it into his pocket, the cold not unpleasant against his thigh.

Wolfe let himself out and sauntered down the stairs. Going out of the gate into the lane, his inner compass pointed him up the hill the railway man's mother had cycled down. The sky had turned from pastel shades of green to a ghostly pink streaked with red. *What's with this strange light?*

Leaning into the steep gradient, Wolfe laboured towards the top at a steady pace. Fragments of his early treatment filtering into his mind, he recalled how he'd learned in therapy that his mother had been led astray by his father, something that came as no surprise. His parents freely admitted they'd taken LSD and magic mushrooms all the way through his mother's pregnancy with him. One line of questioning the doctors had taken, he recalled, seemed to focus on whether he saw unusual colours, or suffered flashbacks of any kind.

Maybe that's what's happening now?

Chapter 36

Priestley police station. 3:05 p.m.

'The way things are going, Lara,' Williams said mischievously as he looked at the trail of people queuing on the ramp, 'they'll be lining up on the pavement soon.'

'There's more and more people asking for toilets and drinks of water,' Croft said. She blew her fringe with a gust of breath, and fanned her pink cheeks with a flapping hand. 'John, we're just not geared up for this.'

'You're right,' Williams replied. 'In the absence of any leadership coming from inside, I'm going to nip round the corner and see if I can't get the churchwarden to open up the community centre. Can you hold the fort for five minutes?'

'Just don't get chatting while you're round there.' She smiled. 'In other words, hurry up.'

Adams finished taking the details of a street robbery from a previously well-manicured woman. 'Did you get a close look at him?'

'Yes,' she said. 'He had bright ginger hair and thick lips. Reminded me of an orangutan. I only just had my nails done last night, now look.' The false nail on her third finger was missing. 'I mean, can you believe it?'

'Well, there can't be too many people matching that description. There's a good chance we'll catch him once we get back to normal. We'll get back to you as soon as we hear anything,' he said. 'All right, who's next?'

Constable Fletcher let her out.

'Don't let anyone else in for a minute, Fletcher. We'll clear the public already in here, and then have a break, all right?' He shrugged apologetically at the remaining people at the counter. 'Sorry, but if I'd wanted to work on a conveyor belt, I'd have got a job in a factory. I've never known it like this before.'

Trent agreed. 'I haven't done this much writing since I was at school.' Then he volunteered. 'I'm busier than a one-armed man in a wallpaper-hanging contest.'

'Hey. That's my line,' Adams said. 'Wait here a minute; I'm going see the inspector. Before we get completely swamped.'

Emerson's door was closed. Adams frowned, then knocked before going in.

'What is it, Adams?'

'We could do with some help out there, sir.'

'What do you expect me to do? Wave a bloody magic wand and make it all go away?'

'Face it, sir. Public dissent is growing. There could be hours more of this. You need to do something.'

Emerson spun around on his chair to face the window. 'Where's Williams?'

'He's out there with Croft managing the crowd.'

'Williams couldn't manage a shit without someone to wipe his arse. Tell him to bring the professor down here and this time, he isn't to come back without him.'

'Williams said he'd gone out—'

'It isn't up for discussion,' Emerson barked. 'Send. Williams. Now. Adams.'

'I had an idea while I was round at the community centre,' Williams said, waving a book of raffle tickets at Croft. 'The warden said I could have them. We give these out to everybody in chronological order. It means they can leave the queue without losing their places. The community centre has agreed to donate tea and coffee for free, and allow the use of their toilets.'

'A bit like queuing for cooked chicken at the supermarket? John, that's brilliant,' she said. 'Give me those; I'll start handing them out right away.'

'That's not all. As you go round, tell people that if they'd prefer, they can write down their names and addresses, detail their complaints, and hand them over to Fletcher on the door. Then they can go home.' Williams winked. 'I'll just organise it with them in there, get paper and so on.'

'All right,' Croft said, and started to hand out the tickets.

Williams approached the door. The mood and tone of the crowd outside lifted perceptibly. He raised his eyebrows at Fletcher and pointed to the lock. He opened it just as Adams appeared. 'Emerson wants you to fetch the professor,' he said.

'Again? This is getting ridiculous.'

'I'm sorry, John, but you're to go right away.'

Williams knocked on the door, his signet ring producing a sharp rapping sound. Through the frosted glass, he watched as a figure ambled towards him. The door opened. 'John,' Professor Young smiled, 'so soon? Do come in.'

'I'm sorry to intrude on you like this, Dai, but Emerson has again asked if you can come to the station.'

'Is he suffering from agoraphobia? Tell him he's very welcome to come here. Second thoughts – I'm off out in a few minutes. I'll visit as soon as I can.' He looked at his watch. 'All right, come in and sit down for a while. Tell me, what's the problem?'

When Williams had finished briefing him, the professor pinched the loose flesh under his chin. 'It seems to me your inspector isn't very good in a crisis. Mind you, I would think there's been more than a few caught out by this solar storm. Throw into the mix a giant cannibal killer, and it's no wonder he's struggling. In normal circumstances, he could just pick up the phone and direct operations from there, even call in reinforcements from neighbouring counties. It's a wake-up call that may have come too late.'

A puzzled frown appeared on Williams' forehead. 'How do you mean?'

'You know the transformers they run the power grid through?'

'What about them?'

'I told a little white lie earlier, when I said the electricity companies had them stockpiled. They're made in Japan.'

Williams shrugged. 'What does that mean?'

'Apparently, John, the idea was to ship the parts around the world so they'd be ready for an emergency, but they never got around to it.'

'And?'

'Without communications, how is anyone going to order the parts? How will they transport them anyway? By sea? How will they refuel, with buckets?'

'Christ, it sounds like we've had it.

'It depends on whether they had time to switch the transformers off before the solar wind hit. If we're lucky, they did, or only the transformers at the edge of the grid have been damaged.'

'Dai, do you think the rest of the world is affected? I mean, we all club together and help one another in times like this, don't we?'

Professor Young considered the question. 'From the manifestations in the sky, I have to say it's possible the whole Northern Hemisphere is affected.'

'If that were the case, how long do you think it would take to sort out?'

The professor stood up. 'I'm afraid I have to go, John.'

Williams also got to his feet. 'You didn't answer my question.'

'No, I didn't.' The old man led him down the passageway to the front door. He opened it, his smile grim. 'Let's just pray that it is not the case, shall we?'

Chapter 37

Bell House. 5:35 p.m.

Drunk, Gloria staggered outside and onto the lane. She'd dismissed her parents from her thoughts when she took the first sip of wine. The afternoon had passed in a glorious blur. Two glasses taken in ten minutes, she'd laughed ecstatically. How could she have denied herself these feelings? *The potatoes. I've burnt the potatoes.* When she checked, she'd not put them on. She thought her sides would burst, she'd laughed so hard. And then, she cried. For her failure. For the disappointment certain to cloud her parents' faces. *Couldn't go look for them now. Where have they been all day, anyway?*

Twenty-seven years old, she'd returned to the family fold after her life had taken a dive. Her boyfriend had, without warning, committed suicide. She'd always thought they were close. If he had problems, he'd never spoken to her about them. Never even left a note. Selfish bastard. She'd taken to drinking – as if her life depended on it, one of her friends had said. And worse. In her brain, the pattern resumed as if it had never stopped. The drink led to cravings. Cigarettes first, and as each line was crossed, she'd go further. The vices born of insecurity bled into one another: drugs, sex and strangers. In her jumbled-up head, she knew all these things, but she didn't care. She swigged from the bottle of wine she had with her and headed for the pub. Someone would buy her a drink.

Gloria stumbled, almost fell. It started a chain reaction of clumsiness; tripping and lurching, she staggered from one side of the lane to the other until she reached a signpost. She leaned against it, and steadying herself, noticed a tall man in uniform striding up the hill towards her. Eyes struggling to focus, she was amazed at his height.
'Hello, handsome,' she slurred. 'You're a big boy.'

The stranger narrowed his eyes. *There's something not right about this one.*

Gloria emptied the bottle she carried and threw it in the bushes.

Drunk? He'd never seen a drunken woman before. He undid his flies and exposed his engorged penis. Gloria gasped and grabbed him, taking him in her mouth. Her sudden acquiescence took him by surprise.

'This uniform stinks,' she mumbled. Her lips around his cock, she made little mewing sounds as her head bobbed up and down his shaft. Already hard at the thought of what he planned to do, his stiffness reached another level. He felt something like gratitude. 'God,' he exclaimed. 'No one's ever done that to me before.'

'You have a beautiful dick,' she slurred. 'I can't imagine why.'

Afterwards, they lay down together. She caressed him, gently stroking his length. Semi-flaccid, it began inflating. Gloria glanced up at him, his eyes already locked onto hers. She smiled. 'Look who's coming back,' she said.

Chapter 38

Hilltop Cottage. 6:00 p.m.

At the edge of consciousness, listlessness held Anderson in its grip. Come on Michael, time to wake up. Fuzziness clouded his thinking. Nytol. At one time, he'd been used to them, taking them habitually, but he'd stopped. Smoking. Drinking. Using weed. All of his demons conquered in one fell swoop. He was unconvinced he really felt better, but kept with it. *Two bloody Nytol and I'm a zombie.*

He opened his eyes. The lights he'd turned on remained off. Still no power. *How long have I slept?* He checked his watch. Six o'clock. *Morning or night?* Could he have slept right through until the next day? The walls shimmered eerily green. Evening. The direction of the feeble light coming in through the window confirmed it. Soon it would be dark. He furrowed his brow. His eye felt bulbous, the skin tightest around the epicentre of the bite. Is it bigger? He traced its outline with a finger. It frightened him. He couldn't feel his face. The antihistamine in the Nytol hadn't worked. *Have the tablets reacted with the bite?* Anderson thought about looking in the mirror. *What good's that going to do, seeing something grotesque that I can't do anything about? I need a doctor.*

The CB radio. Maybe if I can raise someone, they'd be able to help me. To find the radio, I need a torch. There's one in the under stairs cupboard, next to the gun cabinet. He jackknifed in slow motion, swung his legs over the side of the bed, and pushing down with his hands on his knees, got up.

Snatches of dreams tumbled through his mind. Ryan had placed great value on dream analysis for assessing the depths of post-traumatic stress disorder.

A question came full-circle. *What is it you search for?* Heavy with a sense of déjà vu, he left his bedroom, walked unsteadily down the corridor to the head of the stairs, and began to descend them. At the last step, he stumbled. Unconvinced he was seeing out of both eyes, he felt curiously detached. *Not taking any more Nytol.* But he knew he would. He'd slept all day. How would he sleep without taking it?

He opened the cupboard door and felt around. *Got it.* His fingers closing around the barrel of the torch, he took it from the shelf and pressed the switch. *Not working.* Unscrewing the base, he tipped the batteries out. They dropped into his palm. Sticky. He'd had them so long they'd leaked. *Shit! Do I have any spares? Wait. Candles. I must have candles.* Navigating to the kitchen, he reached up to the corner wall unit. In there, he found an unopened pack of tea lights, and next to them, a box of matches he'd had the foresight to stow away alongside them. Splitting the pack, he lit the first candle. Holding it, he searched for something to put it in so he wouldn't burn himself. Hot wax tipped over the side of the foil casing, searing his fingers as he reached for a breakfast bowl. *Shit.* Now he had a means to carry light around with him. He repeated the process. More and more lit, he placed them in various rooms. One in the toilet. One in the lounge. Later, he'd put some upstairs if the electricity hadn't come back.

He hoped the radio still worked. There was a spare battery in the garage, which he kept charged. What was the point of a spare if, when needed, it was flat? He made his way to the front door, opened it, and cupping the candle, crossed the courtyard to the garage.

Anderson put everything he needed into a box and carried it inside the conservatory. Connecting it up was easy. He stood on a chair, raised up on tiptoes to hook the antenna on to the winding mechanism of a roof-light, and stepped down. The indicator on the handset glowed red when he switched it on. The radio crackled. *What are the chances anyone else is tuned in?* When he'd bought the unit years before, they were all the rage and he'd purchased it in the unlikely event of becoming cut off in his farmhouse. Although he'd played around with it, he'd not got into the lingo or protocol, and never had more than a five-minute conversation with anyone. Expectant, he scrolled the channels hoping to hear someone talking. He frowned. *Maybe I'm out of range. The emergency channel. Go to that.* Channel nine selected, he listened intently. No one was talking. He pushed the button on the microphone and spoke. 'This is Michael Anderson of Hilltop Cottage. Does anyone copy?' No response other than static. He repeated the call, adding, 'I've been bitten by a mosquito, and I think I'm in some kind of shock. I need medical assistance.' Still nothing. 'Can anybody tell me what's happening out there?' The electronic chatter intensified, the sound like a foaming wave rushing onto sand. A woman's voice came through. 'This is E.R. I hear you, Michael.'

'Thank God,' he whispered, and then raised the level of his voice over the distortion. 'E.R, this is going to sound ridiculous, but I'm having an adverse reaction to a mosquito bite.'

'Okay, Michael, take your time. What are your concerns?'

'I need a doctor.'

'I can't help you there, Michael,' she said. 'But I'm a nurse. Tell me what's going on. What symptoms do you have?'

If he'd lived in town, he could have just walked in to a surgery or a hospital. He silently cursed living in the countryside and being so far away from everyone. 'My eyelid is numb and swollen; so is half of my face. I can't think straight.'

'But in yourself, Michael, are you all right?' she said, her voice concerned. 'You don't *sound* all right.'

'I'm fine, really.'

'You seem a little drunk.'

He registered the suspicion in her voice and laughed. 'No, no.' Suddenly, he didn't want to burden her. 'I could do with a drink, though, I'm so thirsty.' He flicked the tip of his tongue over dry lips.

'Do you want me to hold on while you get something?'

'Honestly, I'm okay. I just need to wake up. I've been asleep all day, it seems.'

'Didn't you sleep last night? I sometimes get that. It makes you feel like a zombie, doesn't it?'

'No, it's not lack of sleep. I told you, I got bitten earlier today—'

'Not by a zombie, I hope?'

'Are you not taking me seriously?' he said, his voice almost drowned out by interference. 'I know it sounds daft, but it was definitely a mosquito.'

'They bite me all the time, the bloody things. You ask me, what value do they have? I'll tell you. None.'

'E.R.,' he said, 'I've had a reaction to it. My eye's come up. Didn't I tell you? I didn't have any antihistamine, so I took some Nytol.'

'Crikey, no wonder you slept all day. Look, switch to channel twenty-seven. We need to leave the emergency channel clear.'

Anderson clicked through the channels. 'You there?' he said.

'Course I am. Where are you? You not in town?'

'No, about nine miles out. I can't drive. My car's not working.'

'You haven't heard? There's been a solar storm. It's knocked out the electricity grid, communications, everything. I take it you don't have power?'

'No, I don't have anything,' he said. 'A solar storm? How did you hear that?'

She laughed. 'People have been talking about nothing else all day.'

'Any news on when we'll have electricity again?'

'We're reassured the authorities are working on it. Once darkness falls, though, I foresee problems.'

Anderson's mind traipsed through scenes of anarchy, riots, and fires burning. 'For some, any excuse will do for causing trouble, and then others join in like pack dogs. Once one city starts . . . Oh,' he said, 'I'm not thinking. If communications are lost there, too, they won't know about each other, will they?'

'So far, things haven't been too bad, considering.'

'E.R., I've got such a headache.'

'It could be dehydration. Are you going to get that glass of water?' She paused. 'I'll wait.'

Anderson took a long swig from the glass and placed it on the table. 'I'm back, E.R.' The set crackled. *She's gone.* A surge of disappointment rushed him. 'E.R.?'

'I'm here,' she said.

'I-I thought you'd gone. Is it normal to crave salt?'

'Don't have salt. It'll just make you thirstier,' she said. 'When did you last have something to eat?'

'I feel like I've swallowed a sponge.'

She giggled.

'What's so amusing?' he said dryly.

'I'm sorry, Michael. I heard a joke with that line in it once; always cracked me up, though none of my friends saw it.'

'I know it,' Anderson said, his mood lifting. 'About the German guy, Horst—'

'That's the one. Did you think it funny?'

'It was hilarious,' he said. 'I told it a few times, but my friends never got the joke either.'

'You know I can't get a doctor out to you, don't you?'

'That's all right. I just needed to talk to someone, I think. Yes, I feel better now,' he lied. 'I'll take a couple more Nytol in a bit; see if I can't sleep it off.'

'Don't do that,' she said.

'Why not?'

She hesitated. 'I want to be sure you're okay.'

'Don't worry about me – I'll be fine.'

Fearing he was about to sign off, she tried to keep him engaged. 'Michael, I can tell you aren't a CB enthusiast.'

'You can?'

'Of course I can.' She laughed. 'You haven't used one bit of jargon. So you bought your unit for practical purposes?'

'I tried to learn the lingo, but all that Good Buddy stuff drove me up the wall. And handles? I mean, what's it all about? Is E.R. your handle?'

'I only changed it today. It used to be Fabfoursong.'

'Why'd you change it today?'

'I had a feeling someone might need me. My initials are E.R. I'm monitoring the emergency channel. E.R. is short for emergency room; it just seemed appropriate.'

'Am I keeping you from what you should be doing?'

'This *is* what I should be doing,' she replied. A burst of static obscured her answer.

Oblivious to what she'd just said, he mumbled, 'I'd better go. Leave you to it.'

'Don't go,' she said, too quickly. 'I mean, there's no one else on. Why do you think that is?'

'You're not getting anyone even where you are? I thought because I'm out in the country, I'm out of range. No truckers come near where I live, unless GPS sends them. Apart from them, farmers, and die-hard enthusiasts, who uses CB radio these days? The Internet has taken over.'

'That's a good assessment. Still, I'd have thought I'd have picked up someone else calling in town, especially with the news a killer's on the loose.'

Anderson allowed her words to sink in. 'If no one's been online, how did you hear that?'

'A newspaper reporter lives in my street, Nick Summer. You might have heard of him; he works in London for one of the big daily papers. Can't remember which one, but anyway, he told me.'

'Thanks for that,' he said, with as much humour as he could muster in his voice. 'I've got no alarm system and I'm out here all alone.'

'Will you be all right? What will you do?' she asked.

'I've got a gun. And if the power's not up by tonight, I've got candles. I'll manage.'

'Make sure you lock your doors,' she said. 'What do you do for a living, by the way?'

Anderson pondered the question. If he answered truthfully, where would it lead? 'I was a hypnotherapist.'

'Was?' Her silence invited him to elaborate.

Should I tell her? 'It's a long story and I'm tired. What's your real handle, will you tell me?'

'It's Eleanor,' she said without hesitation.

'Eleanor? That's a pretty name.'

'My parents thought so, but they also had a weird sense of humour.'

'How so?'

'My surname is Rigby.'

'Eleanor Rigby? I know that name from somewhere.'

'Of course you do. My handle is Fabfoursong. Do you get it now?

Pain spread over Anderson's forehead. A gasp escaped him. He bit down on his lower lip.

'What's wrong?' she said. 'Are you still hurting?'

'I'm fine, I'm fine. Honestly.'

'Michael. Why won't you tell me? What's going on with you?'

'My head. It hurts.'

'You say you're thirsty? Is it a craving?'

'Yes,' he said. 'It's raging.'

'And the headache – is it blinding?'

'Yes,' he whispered.

'You need to watch that. Could be diabetes kicking in; it's one of the symptoms. How old are you?'

The lights flickered. Came on. Anderson shielded his eyes. 'I'm going to be all right, Eleanor, don't worry about me. The lights have just come back on.'

White noise roared over the channel. She shouted, 'Not here they haven't. But I'm pleased for you. Get something to eat, Michael, will you do that for me?'

'Not sure I've got the stomach for it—'

'The power's back on here as well!' she exclaimed.

His heart lifted. Things were going to be all right.

'Damn, it's gone off again,' she said. 'What's that beeping, is it your end?'

'I think we're about to be cut—'

The radio failed.

Eleanor Rigby. He wanted to tell her he had it now. *It's a song by the Beatles.* The lights flared and then went off. He sat in the dark, thinking about all she said, wondering if he'd speak with her again. Music wormed its way out of his subconscious. The song's chorus began playing in his head. *All the lonely people . . .*

He wondered if he'd ever get to meet her.

Chapter 39

Bristol Harbourside. 7:10 p.m.

'Mick? Come on, good buddy, answer me.' Eleanor stared at her radio's display. The problem wasn't her end. The beeping. They'd spoken for over an hour. *He's run out of battery, that's all it is.* A mantle of disappointment settled on her. In her head, she tracked the conversation back. He'd started off sounding desperate, and then miraculously seemed to recover. But he hadn't. She heard again his gasp of pain. His initial denials when she'd asked if he was all right, the eventual admission, the intensity of the headache. Blinding. No appetite. Why the reluctance to open up to her fully?

Deep concern took over her thoughts. She couldn't shake the feeling that her newfound friend was in trouble. Sitting alone, she turned the radio off to conserve what power might be left in the battery. In that moment, she made a decision. Go to him.

She set off on her bicycle, the full moon gilding her skin a mix of green and silver as she negotiated the lanes beyond the outskirts of town. On her way out of the city, she'd witnessed scenes of unrest, angry mobs, shop windows smashed, a motorcyclist torn from his bike, his vehicle stolen, cyclists pursued for their machines. Fires burned in the streets, but nobody bothered her. She had some antihistamine cream, aspirin and a tin of chicken soup with her. If necessary, she'd build a fire to heat it up. She'd make sure he ate something.

In a lifetime of cycling, Eleanor had never ridden on urban roads after dark before. The light of the full moon combined with the polarized energy traversing the sky, shape-shifting and ghost-like, the sea-green of clear shallow waters in warm climes, bathing the world below in a washed-out radioactive glow. She smiled at the hue. Green-silver. If an alien spaceship had arrived, she wouldn't have been surprised.

As a former schoolteacher, memorizing the route after years of class planning presented no problems, so she'd tucked the map into the rucksack before she'd hooked it over her shoulders. It bounced and chafed against the small of her back at every bump in the road. She passed an old church tower, the wash of colour rendering it majestic, the old louvres staring in silence like shuttered eyes following her progress. The sight of the graveyard sent a shiver through her. The crooked headstones seemed to lurch alongside, racing to keep up. She pedalled faster, not daring to look behind.

Chapter 40

Hilltop Cottage. 7:15 p.m.

Heavy-hearted, Anderson trudged up the stairs, gripping the balustrade. The candle carried in his right hand held the shadows that threatened to engulf him at bay. Who had he just met? Eleanor. No more than a disembodied voice from across the ether, and yet, she'd sparked a hope of something he thought he'd never hope for again.

He paused at the top step, his hand resting on a newel post. His mouth was dry. She'd suggested he eat, but he couldn't contemplate anything solid. The short climb had left him breathless. A moment passed. He frowned, confused at his lethargy, and then continued towards the bathroom. He caught a glimpse of his face, the swelling monstrous in the flickering light. *God, Michael, you look like you've just stepped out of a Stephen King novel.* He opened the cabinet and took four Nytol tablets from the pack. One by one, he pushed them between his lips and onto his tongue. Wincing at the sweet, sour taste, he turned the tap on and scooped a handful of water into his mouth. He swallowed the pills. He'd sleep through the pain. The lights had been on, albeit briefly, but it meant that the authorities were working on the problem. In the morning, the power would be up and running. He'd make his phone calls. Doctor, mechanic, electrician. In that order. He thought about Eleanor. Was there enough juice left in the car battery to reconnect, to try to get her back?

Anderson retraced his footsteps. The descent downstairs convinced him he wouldn't make it back up to his room to sleep. *The shotgun. I must have it with me.* He took the weapon from its secure cabinet, along with a pair of shells. About to load them, a vision of himself seated, gun between his legs, barrel pointing under his chin, flashed into his mind. He put the shells into his pocket. Then he shuffled along the corridor, through the lounge and into the back of the house.

Too weak to attempt resurrecting the CB, he lit sufficient candles to continue reading in the comfort of his conservatory, and lay on the sofa. Yellow flames licked the edges from the gloom as he continued with Ryan's book.

Fifteen minutes later, Anderson rubbed his eyes and realised he hadn't been reading at all; he had merely lounged while the book in his hands transported him to forgotten times. His head dipped. He drifted.

Once more, he was with Ryan, seated opposite him. The psychiatrist fixed him with his beady eye. 'Do you remember that boy, the one who watched from the sidelines while his friends drowned?'

Anderson nodded. 'How could I forget him? He refused to allow himself to be hypnotised. I told you it couldn't be done.'

Ryan's silver propelling pencil gleamed, the instrument held at an angle in such a way that the light shone into Anderson's eyes. He stared at Ryan's thumb, click, click, clicking the button at the top of it. The lead crept out notch by notch, over and over again. Twelve times before the doctor pushed the exposed graphite back in. Click, click, click . . . *What you were, you will be again.* Anderson tried to analyse this latest thought-dream. It meant something. He knew it. *You've been here before. Is this a genuine recollection? Yes, I've had this thought before. It definitely means something.* More of Ryan's words assembled in his head.

You know that eventually we'll part company because of the narrow-minded approach you have to things you don't understand. I hypnotised you without your knowledge on several occasions, Michael, and I did it to show you what it is you refuse to see. Margot died that you should live. Time to unlock yourself.

Velvet claws sank into Anderson's skin. Drowsiness dragged him down. Echoes of distant laughter reached his ears. A smile graced his lips. He'd been happy once. *What you were, you will be again.*

Anderson had never known Margot happier than she had been that first morning in Sorrento, Italy. They'd breakfasted overlooking the Bay of Naples, where Vesuvius squatted under a cape of snowy ermine beneath a crown of fluffy cloud. Chatty and lively, she'd rung around almost everyone she could think of, much to his irritation, to share the views. 'Did you know they believe the volcano was once as high as ten thousand metres?' She crinkled her nose and blew a kiss to Anderson. 'Yes, of course that's high. Over thirty thousand feet. Well, it's only three thousand metres now.' Margot paused, listening. 'What do you mean, what happened to the rest of it? Don't you know your history? It blew up all over Pompeii. Look, we're going there tomorrow. I'll send you some photographs. Yes, I will. Bye.' She double-checked the phone had disconnected. 'Can you believe that, Michael?' she giggled. 'Where did it go?'

The mirth on her face infected him and they burst into spontaneous laughter. When he'd gathered himself together sufficiently to speak, he said, 'Have you finished with the calls?'

'No, I've got a couple more to make,' she said. 'Don't worry, that's it then. I won't make another call for the rest of the holiday.'

Anderson raised his eyebrows. 'Really? Look, I'm going up to the room. I'll see you in a minute.'

Later, he would look back and wonder. Did she somehow know? A part of her alerting her to what was to come, compelling her to ring round and say her last goodbyes? And worse, had he had an inkling, too? To examine it afterwards in the sharpened focus of hindsight was to bring in small things that seemed so insignificant at the time. Could he even rely on the accuracy of his recollections? Had he tailored some evidence to fit, to justify his unawareness, his inaction?

If Ryan had planted this particular seed, why had it only begun to grow now? Was it because there wasn't anything anyone could have done? *She died that you should live.* The thought still nagged him. *Why am I thinking about all this now?*

They'd walked out of the hotel and strolled arm in arm down the cobbled side streets leading onto the teeming main square. Cars, taxis and scooters all vied for supremacy; men driving carts steered their horses around the periphery with seeming impunity. 'I'm so glad you didn't persuade me to drive,' he told Margot.

'But we'd have been in air-conditioned comfort,' she said with a sweet smile. 'Let's hope the bus doesn't get too crowded.'

Ten o'clock in the morning and already unbearable, the heat made Anderson irritable. 'Yes, all right. No need to rub it in.' He spied a stall selling ice cream. He jerked his thumb at it. 'You want one of those?'

'Michael Anderson,' she scolded, 'you've only just had breakfast.'

'Okay,' he said, shuffling his feet. He nodded. 'You're right.'

'Don't be silly,' she said. 'We're on holiday. If you want one, have one.'

A small voice inside him joined the debate. *Leave it, Michael.* 'Only if you have one,' he heard himself say.

'Come on,' she said, pulling him by the arm. 'I'm on a diet, but you can buy me a bottle of water.' She guided him over the busy road.

He'd only intended to purchase a small cone, but the vendor had piled three scoops on before he could stop him, making it difficult to take a bite without dislodging the ice cream. Margot carried her water, and engrossed in nibbling, he followed her blindly back over the street towards the bus stop. What happened next took place in a blur. From out of nowhere, a car screeched around the corner, its engine screaming. People to the left and right of him dashed to safety. About to take a bite of the ice cream, Anderson looked up too late. Margot shrieked a warning and shouldered him hard. He flailed instinctively at the falling scoop as he lurched forward, the speeding car clipping the back of his heel. BANG. For one crazy second, all he thought about was his ice cream. The car roared off. Someone screamed.

Ryan couldn't have known about Margot; he died well before she did. Yet he'd spoken of her death in the past tense. *Margot died that you should live.* And he couldn't have known the circumstances of her death.

It was a prediction.

The medium! Maybe she was for real after all. But why was she predicting for me, and why did Ryan pass the message on? It *had* to mean something.

Shit! What other messages had Ryan planted? Slack-jawed, Anderson's head bobbed, halting his slide into unconsciousness. *Got to fight this.* Unable to get up, he lolled over the arm of his seat and clumsily forced his fingers down his throat. The gag reflex almost pitched him to the floor, but he did not vomit. Fingers again. The reaction no less violent, he dropped to his knees and spread his hands onto the ground in front of him. String-like mucous trailed from his lips; rapid salivation followed. His shoulders bunched a split second before his stomach muscles contracted, painfully ejecting a gush of viscous liquid, which pooled, growing wider with each spasm.

Satisfied he'd finished, he rolled onto his back. The coolness of the ceramic tiles against his damp clothes refreshed him. He gazed out through the glass ceiling. The moon was full, silvery green. Bigger than he'd ever seen it before.

Anderson's eyes dropped away from the sky to follow the line where the white timbers of the conservatory roof, converging on a hipped corner, joined with the wooden mullioned windows just above the dwarf supporting wall opposite him, to settle on the twin blue-black gleam he realised had drawn him into looking there in the first place. His shotgun.

Oh, Margot. You deserved to live so much more than I.

Chapter 41

Churchend woods. 7:30 p.m.

A day spent down by the railway tracks. Every year, Timothy did the same thing, hoping to catch something of his sister's spirit. He wandered either side of the rails, calling to her by blowing through a selection of little green blades. Never one to give up hope, he rationalised he just hadn't found the right note. The stranger he'd seen along the tracks earlier had frightened him; he'd never seen such a big man before. He thought he was going to chase him. The years of trial and error had sharpened his memory, but the moment of fear had wiped his place in the mental catalogue of the sounds he'd already tried. He'd had to begin all over again.

In a couple of hours, he knew, in spite of the strange glow in the sky, darkness would fall.

Timothy thought about the lights. He'd learned most of what he knew of history from the pages of daily tear-off calendars. Megan, the woman who'd taken him in as a child, used to read them to him. There was a connection, he felt sure. Timothy raked back through the years as he strolled.

'What you get, Timo, when you study these,' she said, flicking through the stack, 'is words of wisdom at the bottom and a small bite of history at the top. Look at this one. August 10, 1519, Fer-din-and Mag-ell-an sets sail to cir-cum-navigate the world.' *That was it.* What had bothered him ever since he'd torn off this morning's date? *August 10, 1990, Magellan space probe reached Venus.* It was no coincidence that the probe had been named after him, but to arrive on the anniversary of the day Magellan had set off? They couldn't have planned it, could they? This day. The sky. The stranger. A sense of foreboding crept over him.

Coming out of the woods, he walked along the road. He crossed at the churchyard, taking his usual shortcut over the wall, and approached the dilapidated set of buildings he called home.

Timothy let himself in and immediately knew something was wrong. The door leading to the tower staircase was open. He listened to the low, mournful notes the pigeons cooed, and the incessant ship's-deck creaking coming from the bell loft.

He'd heard the bells earlier. He knew it could only have been the Fallows. He didn't bother to investigate. On this day of all days, he wanted to avoid them. A sense of guilt tugged at his conscience. He hadn't seen them in a long time. He should have come back. Then a thought occurred to him. Why hadn't they closed the door when they left? A feeling of uneasiness edged into him. Something was definitely wrong.

Timothy began to ascend the stairs. He gazed up. The birds were perched on the joists as usual, but had crowded together at one end. They queried each other like old women gossiping over a fence. Through the years, he'd become familiar with their behaviour, their language. Something had disturbed them. Step by squeaking step he climbed, turning around the winding stair, completely unprepared for the horror he was about to encounter.

Chapter 42

Yew Tree Cottage. 7:45 p.m.

David Hall took the last of the candles from the cupboard, and trudged upstairs to place it on top of the toilet cistern. He hesitated before lighting it. 'Molly,' he cried, 'are you sure we haven't got another box of these somewhere?'

'Candles?' she said, coming out of the bathroom onto the landing. 'That's all I could find.'

'Christ,' David said. 'I'd best not light this one then.'

'Why don't you nip to the church? I'm sure Timothy will lend us a few.'

'Molly,' he grinned. 'That's a great idea; he's bound to have some. Still, seems a waste to light it. I'll leave the matches next to it. Shall I ask him for some of those while I'm there?'

'David Hall,' she chided. 'You are tighter than a duck's arse.'

'I know,' he said, 'and that's water—'

A loud banging at the front door interrupted them.

Molly's eyes widened. 'Christ. Who on earth can that be?'

David took the stairs going down two at a time and rushed along the hall. 'All right, all right. I'm coming. You'll have the bloody door down in a minute!' He peered through the bull's-eye glass at the distorted shape of a black-robed and hooded man. 'Molly,' he yelled, wrenching the bolt back. 'I think it's Timothy.'

Wild-eyed and shaking, the unofficial caretaker of the church thrust a sheet of paper into David's hands.

'What's all this about, Timothy? Calm down, for God's sake. You nearly gave the pair of us a heart attack.'

Timothy jabbed a finger at the note.

The handwriting reflected Timothy's state of mind. David deciphered what it read. 'Oh, Lord, Molly,' he said as she appeared beside him. 'There's been a murder at the church.'

'Timothy,' she said calmly. 'Would you mind waiting outside?' She closed the door.

'What are you doing?' Colin whispered.

'How do we know he didn't do it?' she hissed.

'No, he didn't. Shame on you, Molly. Did you see how hurt he looked?'

She covered her mouth and then quickly shouted, 'We'll be right out, Tim, just getting our shoes on.'

David opened the door.

Timothy had gone.

Chapter 43

Churchend Road. 7:55 p.m.

Eleanor had ridden for three-quarters of an hour. *Can't be far now.* Heavy-limbed, she rested her legs, allowing the bike to coast on a downhill stretch. Instinctively applying the brakes at the bottom, she slowed to clatter over a railway crossing. Slumbering birds on either side of the road shuffled and cawed low, complaining at the disturbance. A light breeze tugged at the leaves, rattling them. She rose from the saddle and trod hard on the pedals, coaxing her cadence higher. Her thighs burned. The hair on the back of her neck bristled. She'd be glad to get away from this lane. *There should have been a turning. Am I lost?*

She stopped to check her bearings at a crossroads, looking left and right. From the corner of her eye, she caught a glimpse of something coming closer, before it moved out of sight. *It's only a rabbit.* Her heart, already pounding from the climb, stepped up a beat. A shriek, unearthly, wailing like the high-pitched trumpeting of an elephant, cut through the night. Whatever had made that sound was now crashing through the undergrowth towards her. Unnerved, she made a decision. Rising from the saddle, terrified, she turned right, not daring to look behind and pumped the pedals as hard as she could, listing first left, then right as she pushed herself to go faster. The sounds of pursuit faded, and after another good minute of hard pedal-pushing, she sat back in the saddle and glanced over her shoulder. Her front wheel struck something in the road. She lost balance and fell, hands out ready to break her fall. Eleanor landed heavily. Palms grazed and sore, she sat up, gathering her senses. *What tripped me?* Her eyes focused on two smooth branches. Waxen-looking in the pale glow, they disappeared into the ominous shade of the bushes by the side of the road. Then, she spotted a discarded shoe. She knew intuitively the limbs she'd mistaken for branches were a woman's legs. Suspended in disbelief, she was brought to her senses by a squeal of triumph. Whoever, or whatever, had killed her silent companion, was coming for her next.

Eleanor scrambled to her feet, grabbed her bike and mounted it, feet slipping from the pedals three times in her haste to get going before finally, legs working like pistons, she rode thinking her lungs would burst. She wanted to go home, but it couldn't be far to Michael's house and safety. *Where are you?*

Chapter 44

Churchend Road. 8:10 p.m.

Eleanor hadn't cycled for such an extended period since she was a teenager. Her efforts to escape her pursuer had robbed her legs of power. Afraid if she stopped to rest, she'd not summon the will to get going again, she put her head down and pressed on.

Five minutes later, she slowed and came to a halt. The stretch of road she'd taken seemed to lead her deeper into the countryside. Despite the luminosity of the night sky, she couldn't see any landmarks against which to plot her position. Her ears strained, listening for signs of her stalker. The silence reassuring her, she swung the rucksack from her back and removed the map from its pocket.

'Oh, hell,' she whispered, studying the location of the crossroads she'd passed a few minutes ago. 'I should have gone the other way.' To return in the direction she'd come raised the unwelcome prospect of a further encounter with whoever had just chased her. 'Eleanor, get real,' she muttered. 'I mean, logically, who in their right mind would be trumpeting around like that?' She laughed nervously. 'It's ridiculous.'

The dead woman's image crept into her mind. She shuddered. Could it be the killer Nick Summer had spoken about? No, he'd be long gone, putting distance between himself and the guards out searching for him. He wouldn't hang around looking for victims, would he? She couldn't be sure. Nick had said he was a madman. If possible, she needed to find an alternative route. Her position located, she traced the road with her fingertip to where she'd joined it, stopping on a line marked with a continuous series of dashes, which indicated a bridleway looping off in a wide arc. It would connect her to where she wanted to be, beyond the crossroads.

She couldn't recall seeing it on the way, but then she'd been distracted in her haste to get away and hadn't been looking. She returned the map to the rucksack, zipped up the pocket and slung it over her shoulder. Reversing the direction of the bike, she remounted and began to pedal, the mouse-squeaking spring in her saddle and the light whirr and occasional pop of the tyres through the gravel the only sounds disturbing the stillness.

Ten minutes later, she spotted the tell-tale horse-and-rider sign. She turned the bicycle and nudged it through the gap between two timber barriers flanked by bushes. The rough ground jolted the bike. In and out of ruts and over bumps she rode, the impact juddering through the handlebars into her wrists and arms. The bike's frame rattled. She gritted her teeth, praying no one was within earshot. The trees and bushes crowding the track were more densely packed than the lane she'd just left, allowing little light to filter through. She could barely see where she was going. How much longer?

After what seemed like an eternity, she cleared the bridle path and found herself on the smooth surface of the road. If she'd read the map correctly, she shouldn't be far from Anderson's house. Two or three hundred yards should do it.
Something whizzed through the air and dropped into the bushes behind her. Startled, she turned to look over her shoulder. A single, tremolo shriek blasted from the undergrowth. Dread sucked at her heart. Her blood stalled. She couldn't move. Dark and indistinct, a tall shape loomed among the leaves, triggering a wild thought. *Nosferatu?* Adrenaline surged. She tore herself free of inertia, and on legs rubberized by fear, hurtled downhill towards where Michael lived.

Chapter 45

Hilltop Cottage. 8:35 p.m.

Partly obscured by tall trees, the house sat back from the road, the pale weatherboarded frontage glowing in the semi-darkness. Eleanor made the turn into the drive too fast and lost control of front and back wheels. The bike slewed over. She got a foot down. Her ankle gave. She yelped in pain and fell. Breathing heavily, she scrambled to her feet and hobbled up the path towards the front door. There, looming in the shadows, she saw the figure of a man. He looked as if he were about to go inside.

'Michael?' she wheezed.

The figure turned towards her. His eyes lit up. 'Hello, sweetie.'

'Thank God it's you,' she blurted. 'There's someone following me.'

He looked over her shoulder. 'No one there now,' he said, drawing himself to his full height. He grinned like a shark. 'Whoever it was can see who the top dog is around here.'

Eleanor squinted into the darkness. Something about Michael's manner didn't gel with how she'd imagined him to be. 'My God,' she gulped. 'Is it really you? I wasn't expecting you to be so tall.'

The man stepped from the murk and moved towards her. Eleanor eyed him suspiciously. He had no swelling on his eye. 'You're not Michael, are you?'

A knowing look crept onto his face. He realised she'd never met Michael before. Here was a new game to play. He smiled easily. 'My dear, but of course, I am.'

Michael's radio voice played back in her head. Too tinny; it was impossible to match the tone. 'I thought you were sick. What are you doing outside?'

'I am sick.' His eyes glittered. 'I thought I'd get some air.'

Unconvinced, Eleanor said, 'Shouldn't we go in? I've brought you some medicine.'

He slapped a hand against his forehead. 'I've locked myself out,' he said, thin-lipped. 'I'm always doing that.'

Her gaze drifted over his crumpled clothes. Michael's voice crackled in her memory. *I was a hypnotherapist.* This man was wearing a uniform. The possibility he was the escaped killer, dawned on her. She laughed nervously, and took a step back, unable to believe it. 'Didn't you say you have a raging thirst and a craving for salt?'

'What?' he said, taken aback.

It isn't Michael. Now she knew for sure. If she were to have any chance of survival, she had to think fast. 'I've got supplies in my rucksack. It's just over there.' She smiled quickly, hoping she wouldn't betray that she knew who he was. 'I dropped it when I fell off my bike.' She limped towards it. 'I'll just pick it up, and then we can take a look at you.'

The killer's boots crunched on the path behind her. Could she scoop the bike up, leap on and bolt for it? Doubtful. Her heart sank. She'd come to save a man she'd never met, and would now most likely die with him. A light breeze rustled through the leaves at the edge of the driveway. She caught a glimpse of movement, which had nothing to do with the passage of air. Who, or whatever was stalking her, had moved into the bushes.

Eleanor stopped and turned to face the man masquerading as Michael. She took a gamble. 'L-look,' she stammered. 'I know you're not M-Michael. You're that escaped prisoner, aren't you?'

He held his hands up. 'Okay, I admit I'm not Michael, but I'm not Wolfe, either. You've seen the uniform. I'm his guard.' His smile of reassurance didn't quite reach his eyes. He stepped towards her. 'Been out looking for him since this morning. Soon as I saw you looking so terrified, I knew you'd be game for some fun – you know, break the day up for me.'

'It seems you're not the only one out playing games tonight,' she said, swaying as she focused on keeping her weight on her good leg.

His dark eyes bored into hers. 'What do you mean?'

She tilted her head and gazed at a point beyond where the bike had fallen. 'Someone's in those shadows over there, and he isn't impressed by your top-dog act.'

'You think it's an act?' Wolfe narrowed his eyes, squinting into the gloom behind her. 'Don't worry; I won't let anyone else hurt you.' His fist swung up from nowhere and drove into her forehead.

Eleanor crashed unconscious to the ground.

'Don't move – I'll be right back,' he said, and marched confidently into the shadows, out of sight.

Chapter 46

Hilltop Cottage. 8:40 p.m.

Unearthly screaming snapped Anderson out of his stupor. What was that? His eyes narrowed as the sound replayed in his mind. It was strangely familiar, yet, unable to identify the noise, he clambered to his feet. *Better have a look.* He peered through the window into the garden beyond. Nothing out of the ordinary. Without thinking, he wrapped a hand around the double barrel of his shotgun, hoisting it to his hip. On his third attempt, he mustered sufficient strength to operate the opening mechanism. He exposed the breech and fumbled in his pocket for the shells he'd put there earlier. His hands trembled as he fed them home, one by one, and then snapped the gun shut. His fingers turned the key in the door and unlocked it. A voice inside cautioned. *Don't go out there.* He didn't listen. On unsteady legs, he stumbled outside, jumping at the sudden close proximity of the sound he'd heard a few moments before. It came from over there. He had the distinct impression he was being watched. The hairs on his arms rose as he peered into the shadows.

Sweat streamed from Anderson's forehead, trickling through his brows and onto his eyelids. He wiped it away, blinking his good eye rapidly to clear the salty sting, but it left his vision blurred. The act of wiping his cheeks confirmed he'd lost the feeling down the side with the bite. Numb all the way to his lips, they tingled, raising concerns the poison would soon infiltrate them too. Aware his breathing had grown heavy, he tried to slow it. In. Out. In. Out.

His palms slick against the gun, he raised the barrel and moved forward, holding it at waist height. The moon's unnaturally green light dissipated as he squeezed past the outer conifers, which stood sentinel-like, guarding the deeper shade stretching from the back of the house to the front. Apprehensive, Anderson felt his senses heighten to compensate for his impaired vision and lack of mobility. His ears tuned in to the whine of a mosquito to his left. He shuddered. In the relative darkness, his good eye adjusted, drawn warily in the direction of the sound, seeking it out. He couldn't afford another bite. Frightened for a moment, he considered retreating inside. And then, he saw it, hovering ghost-like, almost transparent in a thin shaft of moonlight and behind the insect: a dark, familiar shape. The crescent end of an old-fashioned scythe, and below it, someone stood half-concealed behind the thick trunk of a Douglas fir.

Anderson eased the trigger back and took aim. About to call out a challenge, he registered a blur of movement to his right. Too late, he swung around.

Wolfe, plucking the gun from his hands, slammed the butt into his abdomen, and in the same fluid movement, jerked it up, striking him under the chin. Anderson cried out as his legs folded. He dropped to his knees, cradling his stomach, before falling forward onto his hands.

Wolfe administered a sharp kick to his victim's ribs. The air whooshed from Anderson's lungs. He curled into a ball, gulping for air like a landed fish on a trawler deck. His eye rolling, he desperately sought a way out of his predicament.

'Why were you following that lady?' Wolfe snarled.

The question unnerved him. Anderson hesitated and then wheezed. 'I'm not following anyone. I live here—'

'Mikey?' Wolfe grinned in the half-light. 'Well, I would say I'm pleased to meet you, but you were going to shoot me, weren't you? You know I can't let you get away with that.'

'I wouldn't have shot you,' Anderson gasped.

'Yeah, yeah, you say that now, but let me tell you, by the time I'm finished with you and your lady, you'll wish you had've done.'

'What lady?' Anderson said, his voice ragged.

'You don't know?' Wolfe said, 'Fuck me; this game just gets better and better. She came to join you for dinner.'

'Eleanor?' he croaked.

'This is just too sweet.' Wolfe laughed. 'Blind date, was it? It must have been. You are one ugly fuck.'

'A mosquito bit my eye,' Anderson groaned. 'I need help. It's infected me with something.'

'A mosquito did that?' Wolfe leaned closer, to examine the swollen, blackening flesh. 'You got some kind of blood poisoning. Tell you what you need for that: a leech. A nice, big, friendly bloodsucker, but you're out of luck on all counts.'

'Where's Eleanor?' Anderson said weakly.

'She's fine – just waiting on the drive where I left her.'

'You and your friend had better not hurt her,' Anderson said, raising his voice.

Wolfe's eyes narrowed. 'What friend?'

The tone of his assailant's voice told Anderson he was unaware of the third presence in the bushes. He rolled onto his back and stared into Wolfe's face.

The man in the black robe silently bent down, and picked up a pine cone. He threw it in a high arc. It crashed into the bushes twenty feet away.

Wolfe wheeled around in the direction of the noise. 'Who else lives here?' he demanded.

Anderson squinted to where he'd seen the figure by the tree trunk. Gone. 'No one else.'

Wolfe whirled through three hundred and sixty degrees. 'Come out. Show yourself. It's okay, I won't hurt you,' he said, almost softly.

Greeted with silence, Wolfe's head tilted, listening intently. He detected movement and fired without warning. The shot smashed through leaves, tainting the air with the smell of vapourised sap and cordite. 'You should've come out while you had the chance,' Wolfe growled. 'Because now, I'm going to kill you on sight.'

With the shotgun in one hand, he reached down, grabbed Anderson by the ankle, and dragged him through the vegetation, heading for the front of the house.

Chapter 47

Priestley police station. 8:45 p.m.

In the gloom within his office, Tom Emerson checked his watch, and standing up, moved away from the desk. Dusk seemed earlier and darker than usual. The murmur of voices coming from outside grew louder. People seeking the symbolic sanctuary the station offered had built up steadily as night had begun to fall, and with it, an increase in riots and looting. Emerson walked to the window and parted two vertical slats of the closed blinds. The line of cars that jammed Kings Head Lane remained as they had since the power failed, their occupants having long abandoned them in favour of walking. Leaning close, he looked both ways, catching the eye of an old man before retracting his fingers.

'Look at you, skulking in there while the streets aren't safe,' the man yelled. 'Where were you when they kicked in the shop windows down the road?'

Emerson returned to his desk, and about to sit down, jumped when someone banged on the window.

'Get out here, now!' a woman howled.

Emerson had wanted to keep his door closed all day, shut out the world and all its problems. *What a way to start your first week, Tom*, he said to himself.

Sergeant Adams appeared in the doorway. Emerson hadn't heard him approach. 'There are more and more people arriving outside, sir. Did you ever see that film *Assault on Precinct 13*?'

'Are you comparing our situation to a Hollywood movie?'

Adams shook his head. 'No, sir. I suppose I was trying to say it could be worse. We've heard the troublemakers have converged in the shopping areas. That lot out there seem to be seeking sanctuary from the violence. Look at them. They're scared. They've come here for protection, to feel safe.'

'I don't know what we can do about homes and businesses being ransacked. I'll go out and talk to them in a minute, but what can I tell them?' Emerson said, and slumped in his seat. 'If the authorities don't get the lights back on, and we don't get operational again tonight, this has the potential to escalate into the worst trouble we've ever known. Shit. We don't have enough personnel to do anything effective. If we try stopping the rioters, they'll string us up. We have no choice other than to sit tight and see how it plays out.'

'Seeing as you put it like that, sir, let's hope the ringleaders from rent-a-mob in the town centre don't get bored and decide to vent their fury on the station.'

The two men stared at each other, the possible consequences reflected in the grim looks on their faces. At the sound of approaching footsteps, Adams turned towards the doorway.

Williams strode into Emerson's office. 'It's anarchy out there,' he said. 'I hear the trouble has spread to every street containing shops. Stealing food, I can understand, but televisions and computers? People are going to get killed.'

Emerson removed the end of a chewed red biro from his mouth. 'People have already been killed. We've had a report from St Michael's in Churchend. A man and a woman were found dead in the bell tower, and another woman's body was discovered by the roadside, not a mile away. All three victims drained of blood, apparently.'

'What?' Williams' mouth hung open.

'The people who reported it said it looked like they'd been attacked by a wild animal. Isn't that right, Adams?'

'That's right, sir. Obviously none of us have seen the bodies for ourselves yet. All I can say is, if it is the killer, he's got to be a fucking maniac.'

'Wait a minute,' Williams said. 'How did we hear all this?'

'The mute,' Adams replied. 'Do you remember him?'

'I don't know any mute,' Williams said.

'No, you wouldn't, you bloody heathen, because you've never been to a church in your life,' Emerson said, fiddling with his pen. 'Timothy, someone or other. Used to help the old priest at St Michael's doing odd jobs when he was alive, in return for a place to doss down. He still lives rough there. Hasn't spoken since he witnessed his sister run over by a train. It happened down by the level crossing at Churchend when he was five years old. The two of them were runaway orphans. It's a long story.' He snapped his fingers. 'Father Raymond, that was his name. He died, and the authorities condemned the building not long after. Anyway, it was Timothy who raised the alarm. He dropped a note into a neighbour's cottage and then ran off in a terrible state.' Emerson paused, and laid the biro down on his desk. 'They, of course, went to investigate, then came down here to report it. Strange, but they said Timothy was dressed in a priest's gown.'

'Is he all the ticket?' Williams said. 'I suppose he could have dressed up as a clergyman to give them last rites?'

'As far as I know,' Emerson said, 'the only thing not right about him, is his refusal to speak.'

'Did he see Wolfe do it?'

'Not sure. The victims were the eccentric couple that lived in Bell House. Oddly enough, they were bell-ringers. David Hall and his wife cycled down about an hour ago. They looked dreadful, said both had had chunks bitten out of them.'

'So we think Wolfe's up there somewhere.'

'Could be.'

Williams shook his head slowly. 'Do we know if anyone else . . . ?'

'No, we don't. It's almost ten miles away, and we don't have the means to get up there. Too far to walk, and if we send a Bobby on a bike, he'd be in danger of being mugged for it.'

'Well, the Halls made it here all right.'

'And our Bobby might not. I'm in charge here and I'm not chancing it.'

'What happened to the guards?' Williams asked.

'Styles and company? They're allegedly looking for him.'

'Do they know about this development?'

'How could they? They're long gone.'

'The word's got about like wildfire around here, but if Wolfe is on the loose in Churchend, don't we think someone should at least warn the residents they should be on guard, for Christ's sake?' Williams gestured to the megaphone resting by Emerson's seat. 'Can I have that, sir?'

'They won't be able to hear you from here,' the inspector said, his tone dry. He leaned over and picked the instrument up, thumping it down onto the desk. 'All you'll do is cause more mayhem.'

'I can get up there,' Williams said. 'The professor has another motorbike.'

'Now you've mentioned him, where the hell is he?'

'I told you earlier on. He said had to go out, but he'd come down here to the station when he returned.'

'Christ,' Emerson said. 'That was ages ago. We're going to need his help before the night is out.'

'Sir,' Williams said, 'do I have your permission or not?'

'I can't spare you. Things are getting worse out there.'

'There's too few of us to make an impact if things do go tits up. We're not the Seven Samurai.'

'There's only six of us,' Emerson said, the sarcasm in his tone unmistakable.

'It's irrelevant; just a figure of speech. All I'm saying is if it goes pear-shaped, there's nothing we can do. So whether there's five, six or bloody seven of us, a man down for an hour won't hurt. Those people are isolated up there, they have a psychopathic killer in their midst, and he's already picked off three of them that we know of. Don't you think we owe it to them, if we can, to warn them?'

'You won't need this,' Emerson said, and put the loudhailer back onto the floor. 'Just call at each house. There's only half a dozen of them. Adams will give you the addresses and locations. Whether you think you can make a difference or not, I want you back in an hour, is that clear?'

'Yes, sir,' Williams said. 'Shall I tell the crowd you'll be out in a while?'

'Tell them *someone* will be out in a few minutes.' Emerson waved him off dismissively and glanced at his watch. 'No, on second thoughts, go out the back way.'

'Sir, they were all right with me coming through just now; besides, they'll see me when I go out of the gates.'

'You're downhill from the entrance. I doubt they can see over the hedge. I just don't want them asking questions.' Emerson picked up the loudhailer. 'All right, just in case, I'll go outside now. Give you a chance to slip away while I'm talking. You'll have to go down the hill and round the other way to get to the professor's.'

Adams unlocked the rear access door to the car park and service yard, and opened it. 'I've marked up a map with the locations of the properties,' Adams said, unfolding it. 'Just so you don't miss any. You know your way?'

Williams took the map and examined it briefly before folding it to fit in his pocket. 'Thanks, Mike. I've not been there for a while, but I don't think I'll have any trouble finding the houses with this.' He stepped outside. The sky shimmered, animating the windscreens of parked cars with a show of reflected green and pinkish light.

'Good luck, John,' Adams said, and closed the door behind him. Williams walked to the corner of the building and listened. The constant drone from the crowd rose in volume. Individual voices shouted, 'Someone's coming out!'

'Hallelujah.'

'About fucking time.'

Tom Emerson's metallic voice began his address. 'Good evening. For those of you who weren't here when I introduced myself earlier, I'm Inspector Tom Emerson and I'm in charge of this station.' He cleared his throat. 'First of all, I'd like to reassure everyone that the authorities are working hard to get the power back on, even as we speak. I understand how hard it is not knowing what's going on. As you know, communications are down and that's hampering all of us, but we're working closely with our colleagues at all the other police stations throughout the city,' he lied, 'to minimise disruption and enforce law and order. Sadly, as always, rent-a-mob turns up determined to cause as much havoc as possible. This situation is unprecedented. We've never faced a total meltdown in communications and power before. But we're going to pull through. To do that, we need the help of good citizens, not just here, but everywhere.'

'What about the escaped killer?' a man yelled. A chorus of other voices joined in. 'What are you doing about keeping us safe?' 'How do we call you lot if we can't use our phones?'

Emerson patted the air with his left hand. 'I know rumours have been circulating about an escaped killer.' The crowd hushed. 'We don't believe he's in the city. Reports suggest he's been active in an isolated community about ten miles from here. We don't think he's going to risk coming to town.'

'But isn't he a madman?' a woman cried.

'Yes, though he isn't stupid. He's extremely tall, almost seven feet; he knows he'll stand out, even in a crowd. Hard as it is, we have to try keeping our community intact. We can't control the rioters without a coordinated effort by the police, and we can't do that until communications and electricity are restored. At some point, if we have to, we'll get a message out to the army, call them in. In the meanwhile, we need to keep an eye on our kids, keep them off the streets. You should go home, stay safe indoors.'

'How many officers have you got in there?' a man shouted.

'This station has never been at full capacity, and today is no exception.'

'I've been around these parts all day and I've not counted more than six of you.'

'We've got more than that.' Emerson lied.

Williams sauntered away from the corner, moving in the opposite direction to the crowd, heading for the professor's house.

Chapter 48

Professor Young's house. 9:10 p.m.

Williams knocked on Professor Young's door, and getting no answer, strode down the side of the house towards the back gate, guessing he'd have replaced the spare keys. He searched for a likely candidate to match the scraping sound against concrete he'd heard when the old boy had retrieved them earlier. Nothing – apart from two terra-cotta flower pots. He dragged one back. Bingo. The professor wouldn't object to him borrowing the motorbike on police business. He looked around before returning to the front of the house to unlock the garage door handle, and turning it, he lifted the metal door as quietly as possible. A rectangular shaft of moonlight cut a wedge into the gloom as Williams' long-legged shadow stretched over it and disappeared into the darkness beyond.

He stepped inside, stopping to squeeze his eyes shut. When he reopened them, the shape of two vehicles had become visible. The professor had kept the car covered with a dustsheet, but he'd left the Triumph uncovered when he'd taken the Norton. Williams' eyes were drawn to the faint reflections, which outlined the polished chrome surfaces, lending them a ghostly green tinge, as if irradiated. He stretched out his hand, and inching forward, felt for the workbench. His knuckles bumping against it, he ran his fingers along the wall to where the professor had hung his keys.

Three hooks. Two lots of keys. One set would be for the car. He grabbed both sets and fumbled, turning the leather fobs towards the open door of the garage. The light caught shiny steel letters and revealed the car maker's name. Riley. Williams visualised his grandfather sitting proudly at the wheel of the one he'd owned. He smiled, hardly needing to check the other logo, but did anyway. It read Triumph.

Satisfied he had the correct key, he backtracked and replaced the car keys. Petrol. Williams could smell it. The professor had obviously topped up the Norton's tank before taking it. Locating where the fuel had been stored in the dark was easier than he'd imagined; he simply followed his nose. Coming across the five-gallon jerrycan, he discovered a funnel right next to it. He'd check the fuel level outside. Wheeling the bike out, he rested it on its kickstand and turned the ignition key. The indicator on the gauge swung to show the tank was full. He closed and re-secured the door before taking the map from his top pocket.

Adams had marked the locations of the properties with an X and scribbled the house names alongside. The first address was Hilltop Cottage. Williams folded the sheet and tucked it back inside his jacket. Rather than use the kick-start, he decided to bump the engine; he wanted to be rolling before alerting the neighbours. He reached under the tank, turned the petcock on and put the bike in second gear. Pulling back the clutch, he began to push the machine, and gaining momentum on the hill, he hopped his left foot onto the footrest and swung the other leg over the seat. He keyed the ignition and released the clutch. The engine spluttered before catching. Williams revved, and accelerating with a roar, rode the bike out of the cul-de-sac at speed.

The Bonneville was more responsive than he'd anticipated. Noisier, and with harder vibrations than Williams was used to, he settled down to enjoy the ride. The route out of the professor's road enabled him to cut through the backstreets and thus avoid those roads congested with broken-down vehicles. He'd heard the looters were largely confined to the shopping centre, though some were breaking into vehicles and houses looking for easy spoils. Transportation thieves had become commonplace.

Cars jammed the approach to the bridge at Clifton. At the scene of the prison bus crash, at least twenty vehicles had ploughed into one another in both directions. The pile-up and sudden loss of power had left the traffic dormant, haphazard and misaligned in a crazy herringbone arrangement on either side. Williams decelerated to a slow walking pace. Feet down, he steered left and right, picking his way past the point where the bus had gone over the edge. He shook his head in disbelief as he continued to weave in and out along the narrow corridor in the centre of the road.

Williams was amazed that some people had remained with their cars. He assumed that they were holding on in the hope that help would come soon, or perhaps they lived too far away to get out and walk. Through the open doors of a Transit van, he saw a couple vigorously enjoying intercourse. A small group huddled together nearby, gazing out over the gorge and smoking. They looked up at the sound of Williams' approach.

'Hey,' a young woman yelled, 'wait up. I want to ask you something.'

'I can't stop now. Police business,' Williams shouted, 'but if you're still here on the way back . . .' His voice trailed when he saw the V sign she threw his way.

At the other end of the bridge, in the middle of the road ahead, a girl stood in the gap between the abandoned cars with her thumb out. In her other hand, she held a square of cardboard with the destination, Portishead, written across it in capital red letters. Drawing closer to her, he accelerated, making it obvious he had no intention of stopping. She stepped into his path, flagging him down.

Williams screeched to a halt. 'Get out of the way!'

She grasped the handlebars, smiling seductively. 'Can you give me a ride?' she said. 'I know you're not supposed to, but I really need a lift.'

'I can't help you.' One of his hands released the clutch slowly, while the other increased the revs.

Her eyes attempted to hold him. 'Please,' she said, refusing to move. 'My grandma's all alone. I have to reach her.'

Do I tell her? Williams made the choice. He spoke rapidly. 'There's a killer on the loose. I have to warn the residents scattered around the lanes of Churchend. Keep your wits about you. Be careful who you hitch a ride with. Most people with vehicles have acquired them illegally, and therefore aren't going to be the most trustworthy of travel partners.'

Her eyes widened.

'Don't be scared.' He grinned reassurance. 'Just be careful. As for the killer,' Williams looked towards the forested hills, 'he's up there somewhere, possibly still in Churchend.'

She isn't scared! The realisation struck him a split second before his head exploded. The severity of the unexpected blow drove his chin down onto his chest. His crash helmet saved him.

Stunned, Williams turned from the waist, ears ringing, one arm instinctively raised against a further assault. The force he'd been struck with had cracked his visor open. Through the gap, he saw his attacker looked like an orangutan. Sparse ginger hair, thin on top, conspired with a wispy beard to contain a wide face. His eyes gleamed with animal cunning. He held a three-foot length of scaffold pole above his head ready to strike again. 'Off,' he said, jerking his head at the officer. 'Or I swear I'll break every bone in your body.'

Williams eased the bike onto its stand. He slipped one hand from the handlebars and rested it on the seat as he swung his leg over, the machine a barrier between him and his attacker.

'Move back, pigshit,' Orangutan snarled, brandishing his weapon. Williams stood clear.

'Tracey, get over here,' he said, eyes fixed on the officer. 'On the bike.'

The girl hopped onto the seat; her toes barely touched the ground. Her accomplice shifted his grip on the pole as he prepared to mount the Bonneville. Williams took something from his belt with his left hand, while the other reached for his extendable baton. He snapped it out, ready to fight. 'You,' he said, levelling the tip of the metal rod at the girl. 'Get off the bike.'

'What?' Ape-man said, incredulous. 'You think you can take me with that, against this?' Hefting the pole to rest against his shoulder, he marched towards the officer.

'It's not the size of your weapon, mate,' Williams said. 'It's knowing how to use it.' Without warning, he drove his heel hard into Tracey's upper thigh. She screamed pain and tilted her body, desperately trying to set a foot on the ground to keep the bike upright. She was too weak to hold it; the Bonneville tipped through its centre of balance and toppled over, trapping her. The engine stalled. 'Pig bastard!' she howled, pain choking her voice. 'You've broken my fucking leg!' She sat forwards, struggling in vain to extricate herself.

'I'll kill you for that,' Orangutan yelled and charged into range, the metal pole held aloft in two hands. Williams stepped back and pepper-sprayed him. His would-be assailant cursed, dropped the pole, and used the front of his T-shirt to try to wipe the chemical clear. Williams cracked him hard on the back of his head. The man's knees buckled. Already unconscious, he pitched forwards, striking his face on the tarmac.

'You dirty fucking pig!' Tracey shrieked. 'You didn't have to hit him.'

Williams leant over to lift the bike from her. 'No, you're right,' he said, spraying her. 'I didn't.'

Her hands flew to her face, rubbing her eyes. 'Filthy pig bastard,' she raged, writhing on the ground in agony.

Williams climbed on the bike, disengaged the stand, and stamped down on the kick-start. It caught first time. He revved the engine, engaged first gear, and releasing the clutch, continued on his way.

Chapter 49

Hilltop Cottage. 9:27 p.m.

Insects, attracted by the Bonneville's headlight, streamed into the beam like tracer bullets. Williams crested the hill, slowed for the crossroads and stopped. The map he'd memorised on leaving the professor's house confirmed that Hilltop Cottage was the next turning on the left. His helmet and visor splattered with dozens of tiny winged bodies, he drew a gloved hand across the Perspex to wipe it clean before accelerating away from the junction, heading downhill.

Eleanor jolted awake. Heavy-eyed, she stared at the sky, the ground beneath her hard and uneven. It no longer shimmered. The pale green hue had given way to the silvery glow of the moon. *Where am I? Why am I flat on my back? Has all this been a dream?* Her head pounded, signalling the restoration of her senses. Her memory returned. An image of the huge man she'd encountered filled her mind. *Where is he?* Panicked, she struggled to raise herself up on an elbow, and looked around to see where he could be. In the stillness, sounds reached her ears. Plodding footsteps. Her mouth went dry.

Something hefty was being dragged through stones and coming closer. *Oh, God. It wasn't a nightmare. The killer. He's still here!* Too weak to stand, she realised any attempt to run or hide would be futile. Her fingers explored the loose surface they rested on. Gravel? She scraped a few pebbles together, scooped them into her hand and allowed them to fall through her fingers, the sound like the first few splats of rain before a storm. And then she heard voices.

Wolfe glanced over his shoulder as he hauled Anderson around the corner of the house onto the driveway. 'There she is, Mikey. Looks like our dinner guest is just waking up.'

'For the love of God,' Anderson pleaded, his voice little more than a croak, 'let us go.'

'God?' Wolfe sneered. 'Surely you know by now, He means nothing?'

Her thoughts fogged by fear, Eleanor bit down on her lower lip, forcing herself to focus. *Mikey?* Rolling onto her side, she planted a hand firmly on the ground. Propped on one arm, she watched the giant approach, hauling his victim behind, his face hideously swollen.

'Oh, God,' she cried. 'Is that you, Michael?' Her teeth found her lip again; she grunted, and bending a knee, dragged a foot close to her bottom, preparing to get to her feet. 'What have you done to him?' she demanded.

'His face?' Wolfe laughed. 'Ugly fucker, isn't he? He was like that when I found him. Honest. Stay there, lady, I'm bringing him to you.' He manoeuvred Anderson alongside her, and let go of his leg. It dropped to the ground with a thump. 'Look who's here, Mikey,' he said, leering at Eleanor.

She slumped to the ground, hands flying up to cover her cheeks at the sight of Michael's face. 'For the love of God, he needs a doctor right away.'

'You've mentioned Him now three times between you. For the last time, He isn't going to help you.' Wolfe turned to Anderson and barked, 'Undress her.'

Anderson rolled onto his front, struggled to all fours, and then sat back onto his knees. 'No,' he said, shaking his head slowly. 'You've got this all wrong; we spoke once on a CB radio. We're not lovers. We've never even met before. I won't do it.'

'No, Mikey, it's you who's got it wrong. I'm giving you a chance to have some fun. Me, I don't give a fuck if you do or don't,' Wolfe said, pressing both barrels of the shotgun into the back of Anderson's head. 'You can have it whichever way you want.'

'Michael,' Eleanor said quietly. Locking her eyes on his, she pushed herself up, the strain showing on her face. She forced a smile. 'It's all right,' she said, and shrugged off the shoulder of her jacket.

For the first time since he'd been bitten, Anderson saw everything with clarity. It was the twenty-seventh anniversary of Margot's fatal accident. This Death had come for him slowly; he'd been allowed to reflect on his life throughout the long day. 'Why don't you just release us? Or at least let her go. She only came to help me.'

'Why would I want to do that?' Wolfe said, digging the cold metal harder against Anderson's skull. He cocked the trigger.

Eleanor reached for Anderson's hand. 'Michael, you mustn't blame yourself,' she said. 'It's my own fault for being such a nosey do-gooder.'

'Get on with it,' Wolfe snarled. 'You, woman, get him going. Get his dick out. Suck it as if it's your last day on earth. Do it!' The killer unzipped his own fly, exposing his massive cock. 'Then, you can have a go with this baby.' A rock struck him square in the back of his head and bounced off, skidding across the drive. Wolfe roared, 'What the fuck?' His face livid with fury, he swung around, gun up, ready.

Fifteen feet away, a figure stood black-clad and hooded. Hard, white knuckles, unmistakably those of a man, tightened around the shaft of the scythe he held onto. Above his head, hovering like a broken halo, the shallow crescent of a blackened blade, its cutting edge silver and sharp, gleamed in the moonlight.

'Fuck me, it's the grim reaper,' Wolfe snarled, raising the barrel of the gun. He took aim. 'Death becomes you, tosser.'

The man remained silent. The whites of his eyes, the only features visible in the darkness of the cowl, lowered. Slowly, the man raised his left hand, forefinger extended, and moved it in front of his unseen face, the gesture unmistakable.

Wolfe laughed at his audacity. 'You telling me to shush?'

The man sucked air noisily, his shoulders squaring as his chest inflated. And then he blew between his thumb and upright finger. The sound, a shriek, deafening at such close quarters, streamed from within the shadows of the hood.

'You!' Wolfe levelled the shotgun at the man's chest. 'It was you following me on the railway track. Fucking stupid noise. You think it scares me?'

The stranger stood firm. His right hand left the handle of the scythe, allowing it to rest briefly against his shoulder, before using his fingertips to make the sign of the cross.

Wolfe howled with laughter, rolling his eyes heavenward. 'Another believer,' he scoffed. 'Ready to meet your maker?'

Fearless, the man raised his weapon.

'Wait.' Wolfe held up a halting hand, his eyebrows knitted together, confused. 'How come you aren't begging for your life?' He heard the sound of scraping stones on the driveway behind him and wheeled around to look. The captives had gone. Wolfe's eyes narrowed. 'You bastard,' he growled. 'You helped them escape.'

The stranger brought the unlikely weapon down with all his might. The cutting edge swooshed through the air. Wolfe dodged. The blade nicked at the fabric of his shirtsleeve. He fired at point blank range. The blast caught the man full in the chest, knocking him off his feet, driving him through the air. He crashed down onto the drive and laid motionless, still gripping the scythe.

Wolfe knew the couple couldn't be far. The game had turned out so much better than planned. He frowned, and then grinned. *There's no way they'd even try to outrun me. They've gone inside the house.*

In the distance, the engine of a motorbike rumbled. Wolfe listened, gauging the direction of the noise. *Getting closer.* He stomped his foot hard against the front door, the lock held, but the frame splintered. The door swung open. He stepped into the hallway.

Eleanor picked up a poker from the fireside in the downstairs lounge. 'Haven't you got another gun?' she whispered.

'No, I haven't.' Anderson looked at the short metal rod in her hand. 'That's not going to do much. All we can do is hide.'

Terrified, they heard Wolfe shout, 'Get out here, now!' His footsteps thundered across the timber floors, while he systematically ransacked room after room in his search for them.

Eleanor's eyes searched the gloomy corners and deep shadowy recesses. 'Where?'

'Under this rug. There's a trap door leading to the cellar.'

'We'll never make it,' she said.

Anderson kicked the patterned rug out of the way. Stooping, his fingers probed for the recessed pull handle and finding it, he heaved the door open. 'Follow me.' Anderson descended half a dozen steps into the dark pit below. 'And pull the rug over the trap, or he'll find it straight away.'

Eleanor followed. Poised on the second step, she leaned to snatch at the decorative mat Anderson had moved, and eased it over the front of the access flap. Her fingers clamped the woollen pile in position. The palm of her other hand, used to keep the door steady, she backed onto the next step, and the next, slowly closing the hatch, in the hope that, once shut, their hiding place would be concealed. Footsteps clomped in the hall outside. Eleanor panicked, and lost her grip on the rectangular piece of carpeting. She ducked below the level of the floor as Wolfe flung the door open. Had he seen her?

On the threshold of the room, Wolfe saw the raised lid of the hatch. His eyes lit with manic glee. He cleared the space in a single bound. Wrenching the door from the woman's grasp, he fell to his knees and seized a handful of her hair. He wrapped it around his fist and jerked her upwards. 'Got you.'

She screamed.

'Stop that fucking screaming, bitch,' he yelled. 'Now, Mikey-boy, up you come. You, your girl and me have a date to finish.'

Anderson stumbled from the cellar, tripping over the rucked-up carpet, and fell to the floor.

Wolfe's head shot up, instantly alert. The motorbike he'd heard earlier seemed to roar up the passageway; for the briefest moment the headlights penetrated into the room before swinging away. The sound of the engine cut. 'Move,' he warned Anderson, 'and I kill her right now.' He ran, dragging Eleanor behind him, to the nearest window overlooking the drive. *Shit! A policeman.* He raced back to where he'd left Anderson. 'Give me another shell, Mikey,' he said.

'I haven't got any more.'

'Give.' Wolfe stomped on his victim's chest; raising his foot, he brought it down again. 'Now!'

'Leave him alone,' Eleanor screamed, her fingernails raking at his wrists and forearms as she twisted frantically, trying to release herself from his grip. 'You're nothing but a cold-blooded murderer.'

'I am,' Wolfe said, 'and I ain't finished yet.'

Williams knelt by the body of the robed man he'd seen in the Bonneville's headlight. From the blood and the gaping hole in the fabric over the victim's heart, he knew he was dead. It wasn't the killer. Not tall enough. *The robes. Christ! It's the mute, Timothy.* He drew his baton and stood. Creeping towards the broken door, he hesitated before going in. With his heart hammering, he took the torch from his utility belt and flashed the beam over floors and walls, searching out the deepest shadows, alert for ambush. He made his way down the hall, checking the rooms either side, noting the devastation and sacked furniture. *Wolfe's been here. Might even still be here, looking for someone.* At the end of the passage, he entered a room. The beam picked out a man and a woman on the floor. *Where's the killer?*

Wolfe launched at him from out of the gloom, the shotgun held like a double-ended paddle cradled between his elbows.

Williams instinctively jumped back. From the way the killer held the gun, he guessed it was empty. His thoughts raced. He wanted to run, but he couldn't leave the victims to their fate. He tightened his grip on the baton, and dropping the torch, snatched the pepper spray from its holster on his belt. *Lure him outside,* he told himself. *If you spray him in here and he charges . . . No, you'll have more chance to circle him and fight out in the open.* He began to walk steadily backwards, towards the front door.

Wolfe followed. 'What are you going to do, cane me with that?' he said, taking two swift strides. Williams panicked, and half-turning to run, lurched through the front door, across the step, and staggered at the change in level outside. He dropped his pepper spray. Shit! Regaining his balance, he had no time to move before Wolfe was on him. Williams thrashed the killer with the baton, twisting his ankle as he sought to get away. Wolfe leapt on him. The smaller man fought back, as ineffectual as a gazelle in the grip of a lion.

'Let's see what you're made of,' Wolfe said, wrenching Williams' head back, exposing his throat.

'In the name of God,' Eleanor screamed, running out of the house. 'Leave him alone, you devil!'

Wolfe paused, torn between powerful desires, his cock bursting against the fabric of his trousers.

Williams thrashed, pinned beneath a weight he couldn't shift. 'Run!' he screamed.

Wolfe sank his teeth into the policeman's throat.

'Michael, come on!' Eleanor screamed.

Wolfe got to his feet and stood erect. Blood ran from his mouth and down his chin. 'Oh, no you don't. You and me, lady, have a date,' he said, holding the thick rod of throbbing flesh that protruded from his fly. 'And if I have to chase after you again, I'll kill Mikey without another thought. Please me, and I might let you both live. Get out here, Mikey, or I'll kill her!' he bellowed.

Chapter 50

Priestley. 9:47 p.m.

Emerson stood by the window in his office and stared out through the open slats at the moon, awestruck by its sheer size. 'Have you seen this, Adams?'

'What's that, sir?'

'The moon. I don't think I've ever seen it so big and bright before.'

'There was an article about it in the papers yesterday. They call it a supermoon,' Adams said, his serious expression giving way to a grin.

Emerson turned to face him. 'What's so funny?' he said.

'I was just thinking.' His smile grew wider. 'I know why you never noticed it before.'

'Why's that?'

'Because most of the time you've got your head up your arse.'

Emerson scowled. 'Is that any way to address your senior officer?'

'The way things are going out there, *sir*, it'll be every man, woman and child for themselves in a couple of days. Maybe even tomorrow, so I don't think it matters much. Do you?'

Emerson nodded. 'I'm in two minds about what I should be doing. Just sitting, waiting doesn't seem right.'

'I know what you mean, but me, I'm retiring soon. I'm up for the easy life. You'll get no heroics from me.'

'You think I should be doing more, Adams?'

'I do. I'm not sure what exactly. Maybe you should have been out there pounding the streets, talking to people, giving advice.'

'It wouldn't have made any difference.'

'I know, but you'd have felt better about yourself.'

'There are less than three thousand officers in the whole of Avon and Somerset. Even if we could have put out a call, pulled them all in here at once, we'd have been outnumbered in the town centre alone. We couldn't have responded with anything effective. No helicopters, no transport. What really crippled us is no communication.'

'Then that's your answer,' Adams said.

'I wish Williams would hurry up. 'And where's the professor?' Emerson returned to gazing through the window. 'Speaking of heads up arses, Adams, you never noticed this, did you?'

Adams joined him looking out. 'What are we looking at?'

'The sky,' Emerson said. 'It isn't green anymore.'

Chapter 51

Hilltop Cottage. 9:59 p.m.

Wolfe slapped Anderson hard, knocking him down. He fell into the flower bed. 'Don't fucking move,' he growled. 'You like watching, Mikey? I guess you must do, because you had a chance to have some fun and you didn't want to know.' He grabbed Eleanor. 'Well, watch this, see how it's done.'

The colour drained from Eleanor's face. She had the appearance of a hostage caught in some far-flung place. A missionary for good in the hands of evil, condemned to die.

Wolfe ripped her blouse open. His massive hand crawled under the cup of her bra and tugged her breast from it.

She cried out, indignant and in pain. 'No. Don't do that!'

The giant moistened his lips. He pinched her nipple, and pulling it towards his mouth, licked it. 'See how hard it's gone, Mikey? She loves it.' His fingers, deceptively nimble, popped the button open at the top of her jeans. 'Get them off, bitch.'

Unable to watch, Anderson turned his face away. He mouthed a prayer. Not the Lord's Prayer or a Hail Mary, but a prayer he hadn't used since he was a child, lying in bed, afraid of the dark. The terror he'd known then was nothing to how he felt now. A tear rolled down his cheek. His swollen eye felt like it would burst. All his life he'd lacked faith. Until today. Reading about Ryan had re-established a tenuous connection with the old psychiatrist. For a short while, he'd drawn comfort from the illusion that had led him to believe there was a deeper meaning to life. The realisation it was, at best, just a fancy, some wild notion, left him crestfallen. Yet, still he prayed. The words were more fervent with every mewl of pain, at every ripping sound he heard. Anderson squeezed his eye shut. An image came to mind. He was with Margot in Italy, crossing the road, engrossed, eating an ice cream. A squeal of tyres. She shouldered him hard. He watched as a scoop fell from his cone to the ground. He grabbed for it. Time stood still. His mind roared. *You coward! How will you live with yourself for even a minute more if you do nothing? Look at her. See what she's going through, and all because she tried to help you.* His eye snapped open. Eleanor was pinned beneath Wolfe, as helpless as a butterfly trapped by a spider.

A little girl emerged from around the corner of the house. Anderson did a double-take. *What in the world?* He yelled with all his might, 'Run! Get away!'

'Too late for running,' Wolfe said, drunk with anticipation of what he was about to do. He glanced in the direction of Anderson's gaze, turned and looked over his shoulder. 'What are you fucking looking at, Mikey?'

How had he not seen her? Anderson breathed a huge sigh of relief. In desperation, he shooed her away. The child shimmered pale in the silvery light, and at that moment, Anderson realised he was hallucinating.

The girl placed a blade of grass between her thumb and forefinger and raised them to her lips. She smiled.

Impossible. She's interacting with me. Anderson pushed himself up. In the flower bed, left there from days ago, standing upright in the soil, he saw a garden fork. He sensed the little girl's eyes on him, saw her draw a deep breath and blow. The resulting shriek was ear-piercing.

Wolfe's cookie-cutter teeth hovered above Eleanor's nipple, his huge shaft poised to enter her. 'What the fuck?' The question froze on his face.

Anderson staggered towards the fork.

Wolfe, taken over by animal instinct, turned, and rolling to one side, scrambled to his feet in almost the same movement. 'Oh, no you don't, Mikey-boy,' he yelled, charging to intercept him.

Anderson grasped the handle and yanked it. The effort of wresting the tool from the ground threw him off-balance. His leg gave way. His hands still grasping the handle, he crumpled to the floor. His backside landed first. He hadn't the strength to prevent himself falling backwards. He ended up flat on his back, his arm outstretched as if glued there, and looked up as the giant loomed over him. Wolfe's leg bent at the knee and rose into the air, foot poised to stamp down on him again. 'You know what, Mikey? I don't know why I didn't do this earlier.'

The fork. It came loose as I fell. I'm still holding it. Anderson's hand slid halfway down the handle. He jerked. His elbow cranked, bringing the four-pronged implement up the moment Wolfe's foot crashed down. Too late, Wolfe saw what Anderson intended. He tried to pivot on his other leg to get clear, but failed. 'No!' He screamed in agony, his lower thigh impaled. Wolfe hopped, grabbing for the handle of the tool that had spiked him. Anderson held on doggedly. Wolfe snarled and pitched himself forward, aiming to land on top of the older man. The fork caused his body to twist as he fell. He landed beside Anderson. His eyes ablaze with fury, the big man grabbed Anderson's arm and wrenched it with such force, it snapped at the wrist. Anderson cried out. The giant gripped the top of his head, and pulling it backwards, exposed his throat. Wolfe hesitated. He switched tack. Wrapping a hand around his victim's throat, he crushed his larynx. 'That was close,' he jeered. 'I nearly took a taste of the shit you've got in your blood, Mikey.'

Anderson's eyes bulged. He thrashed from side to side, unable to break free. Tiny rainbow-coloured flecks of light danced before him, the periphery of his vision totally black. A tunnel opened up before him and in it, the shape of a woman. She hovered above him. He couldn't make out her face.

Whumph. Wolfe's head crashed forward. Shards of terracotta and earth rained down on him. *Eleanor.*

Dazed, Wolfe lashed out. His hand cut through the air and caught her ankle, sweeping her from her feet. He bit hard on his lip and wrenched the fork out of his leg, yowling pain. 'Get up here, you fucking bitch,' he said, his voice guttural. Eleanor yelped as he scraped her half-naked body through the gravel towards him.

Released momentarily, Anderson choked, inhaling deeply. *What next, Mikey-boy?* He shuddered. Thinking of himself in Wolfe's derogatory terms triggered a spurt of bile. It rose, burning his throat. *What next?* What could he do against a man who, though badly injured, was still more than capable of completing his murderous aims? *If their roles had been reversed, what would Wolfe do?* He had his answer: *Bite him.* Anderson chomped down on the giant's thumb.

Taken by surprise, Wolfe, cried out, and letting Eleanor go, rolled on top of Anderson, forcibly shoving the fingers of his other hand into the older man's mouth in an attempt to relieve the pressure on his thumb.

Anderson's lips tore at one corner; the saline taste of Wolfe's blood mingled with his own. He bit down harder, determined not to let go.

Eleanor grabbed at the fork. Wolfe, seeing it sliding towards her, snatched it, his hand around the collar that secured the metal spikes to the wooden handle. Eleanor held on in a vain attempt to wrestle it from his grasp.

The angle of Wolfe's grip and her weight slowed the metal tips in their inexorable progress towards Anderson's throat.

'Michael,' she cried, 'I can't hold on much longer.'

Ignoring the pain in his leg, Wolfe slid higher against the other man's body. Anderson recoiled at the first touch of the cold steel points, but with nowhere to go and completely helpless, he finally bit Wolfe's thumb off. The giant roared; the remaining four fingers freed, he stared fierce-eyed at the bloody stump. He didn't say a word as he used his free hand to pull Anderson's head up from the ground, forcing the fork deeper into the skin of his throat.

'No!' Eleanor cried, her face inches from Wolfe's crotch. Amazed his penis was still erect, she took a deep breath and bit it.

A sound popped, something akin to the cleaving of a melon in two. Wolfe's expression froze, agonised, uncomprehending. He threw Eleanor off and began to stand, a bloody curtain descending over his face, and then he fell forwards. Wolfe's head rocked violently from side to side. Squelching, like the noise of a boot being extricated from mud, reached Anderson's ears.

Eleanor screamed.

In the half light, Anderson registered the horror on her face, the flecks of blood that had sprayed over it, and close to her feet, standing beside the stricken giant, a dark hooded figure wrenching on the shaft of a sickle. Standing beside the mysterious person, the little girl smiled down at him.

The light above the porch flickered. The house flashed as if it were transmitting messages to another world, a beacon of hope, the only light visible for miles.

Surrounded by carnage, Eleanor sobbed, her hands trembling as she adjusted her bra and pulled the tattered remnants of the blouse around her. She buttoned a seam that hung ribbon-like, detached from the rest of the fabric. She couldn't find her panties and suddenly it seemed the most important thing in the world.

The robed man sunk to his knees, leaning for support on the handle of the scythe.

Anderson, shell-shocked and with his arm broken, hadn't moved. He watched Eleanor circle around on all fours looking for something. He almost asked if she were all right, but dismissed the question as ridiculous. Although he was indifferent to her nakedness, he thought she should cover up. He rose to his feet in painfully slow stages, conscious of further injury to his arm should he fall. Once upright, he arched to ease the kink in his back, and walked over to retrieve her discarded jeans. He returned, holding them out to her.
'Eleanor. Here.'

She stopped circling, hesitated, and then reached up and took the clothes. Relieved to see her undergarments rolled up inside, she fished them out, shivering as she began to dress.

Anderson turned away and looked for the jacket she'd taken off earlier. Locating it, he staggered over to pick it up. 'Put this on,' he said, draping it around her shoulders.

Eleanor lifted the front corner of it and used it like a flannel, but only succeeded in spreading congealed blood across more of her face. She eyed the killer nervously. 'Is he dead?' she said, her voice tremulous.

'I think so.' Anderson squatted next to Wolfe. The white pieces of bone clearly visible amidst the blood and gore in the gaping wound confirmed he didn't need to examine the giant's skull further. 'No one could survive an injury like that.' He turned to face her. 'Eleanor,' he said. 'I'm so sorry for what you went through.'

A ragged gasp drew their attention.

'Oh, God,' she cried, 'how could we have just left him like that?'

Together, they rushed to the stranger, taking positions kneeling at either side of him.

'Come on,' Eleanor reassured him. 'You don't need that anymore.' After prising his fingers from the scythe, she allowed his weight to rest on her. 'Take this, Michael,' she said handing him the sickle. 'And help lay him down.'

Anderson grabbed the scythe with one hand and threw it down. 'I think my arm's broken,' he said, placing his good hand on the man's shoulder. 'You'll have to get the other one.'

'Oh, Michael.' She smiled thinly. 'What a disastrous first meeting this has been.'

Together they lowered him, the size of the bloodstained hole over the man's left breast now clearly visible. 'I don't know how you survived that,' Anderson said, peeling the hood back. 'But we owe you our lives.'

The stranger stared at Anderson, tight-lipped. Deep-set and dark-rimmed, his brown eyes spoke of a suffering beyond anything he felt now.

'What's your name?' Anderson said.

The man remained silent. He turned his face toward the corner of the house.

Eleanor tore away the shredded front of the black habit. 'Michael, have you got a clean towel? We need to stop the bleeding.'

'I'll get one. We really need an ambulance.'

'Towel first. If we don't staunch the blood flow, he'll die before it gets here.'

Anderson left her to go inside the house.

The man's chest rose and fell quickly as he struggled for breath. Eleanor's fingers worked furiously, ripping the stranger's outer clothing to get to the wound. Beneath the outer garment, he was dressed in a blue boiler suit. The canvas-like material wouldn't tear. Re-adjusting her grip, she said, 'Please forgive me if I hurt you.' Her fingertips hooked into his chest pocket. They brushed against something hard. She reached in to pull it out, and as she did, her eyes filled with wonder.

Anderson returned. 'Here's the towel. I've brought my mobile, too, now the lights are on.' He caught the look in her eyes. 'What is it?'

'You won't believe this, Michael,' she said and held up the book she'd taken from the man's pocket. 'His life was saved by this Bible.'

'Yes,' Anderson said. A moment of enlightenment brightened his expression. 'Saved by a bible and that little girl blowing on a blade of grass.'

Eleanor frowned. 'What little girl?'

Chapter 52

Priestley. 9:59 p.m.

Along the street, lampposts lit like electric daffodils. The crowd who had gathered outside the police station gawped in jubilant surprise. The lights inside the station flared, flickered and stayed alight. Someone started to cheer, a single voice which, in moments, turned into a tumultuous racket.

Emerson got up from his desk. Striding to the window, he opened the Venetian blinds and watched as people began to disperse. He stared at his reflection, turning his face to examine his profile. Inspector Emerson. In a couple of hours, the job title would become official. *We'll see some changes around here.* He wondered how Williams had got on. Soon he'd be with Traffic, no doubt about that. In a crisis, he had what it takes. *What about you, Tom?* He straightened himself up. *I wasn't ready. The situation caught me out.* Doubt nagged at him. He shrugged at his image and muttered, 'Tomorrow's another day.'

A sharp knock at the door drew his attention. He half-turned his head, but remained at the window. 'Come in,' he yelled.

The door clicked open.

'Looks like you didn't need me after all,' Professor Young said.

Emerson returned to his desk. 'Better late than never,' he said, sitting. 'Have a seat.'

'No, thank you,' the old man said. 'I prefer to stand.'

'Does this mean it's over, professor?'

'I don't think so,' he said, approaching the window. He cupped his hands onto the glass and peered between them at the sky. 'But it is the start of another chance.'

Emerson thought he understood. *It was indeed.*

The professor continued to talk. 'This was a short, sharp shock. A warning. If the governments of the world have any sense, they'll heed it. It could be we won't see quite such a storm again, although I suspect that someone, somewhere in the future will. I just hope they'll be better prepared than we were.'

Emerson lifted the telephone receiver and listened. 'Still not working,' he said. 'Any idea when?'

Young shrugged. 'Depends on a lot of things. If we're lucky, we may have some communications working by morning.'

'You didn't bump into Williams on your travels, did you?'

'No, though I did see him a couple of times today.' Professor Young read concern in the lines on Emerson's face. 'Why do you ask?'

'It's just that he said he was going to borrow one of your motorbikes to ride up to the village at Churchend—'

The old man frowned. 'Churchend? When was this?'

'Well over an hour ago.'

'How strange,' the old man said. 'Nick dropped by to borrow some petrol to refill his tank. He mentioned he'd bumped into a prison officer who'd been here earlier, driving a builder's crew bus they'd borrowed. Nick had been talking to one of them at the crash site, apparently. Anyway, a rumour had gone round saying the escapee had murdered at least three people in the village—'

'All true, I'm afraid,' Emerson said.

'Really? Anyway, Nick filled up and dashed off to go there right away. He's hoping to get a story.'

'The killer,' Emerson said, 'if he had any sense, would be long gone.'

'From what I gathered from talking to Nick earlier, this is the first taste of freedom the killer has had in years. He's a psychopath. Untreatable. I'm not sure sense comes into it.'

Emerson chewed his lower lip. 'Christ alive, let's hope they caught up with him.'

The roar of a motorcycle at full throttle rumbled into the office, the sound coming closer by the second.

Emerson stood up. 'Is that Williams racing up like a maniac?'

'No. It's Nick. He's coming in.' Professor Young turned away from the window, and grimaced. 'And from the look on his face, something is badly wrong.'

Emerson shoved back in his chair and stood. 'Let's go and see what's going on.'

The two men opened the door and sped down the corridor. Seconds later, Croft's anguished scream pierced the air as simultaneously, Adams, cried, 'No!' Footfall sounded from all directions, converging on reception.

Emerson drew his hands from the back of his neck over the top of his head and covered his face. 'You're sure it's Williams?'

Summer nodded. 'One of the officers, Jordan, met him earlier in the day.'

The inspector's legs buckled and he swayed.

'Tom,' Professor Young said, 'why don't you sit down?'

Emerson sat at his desk.

Seven people had crammed into his office in stunned silence. A minute was spent trying to make sense of it all. Questions flew. Accusations followed. Bitter tears fell. Emerson felt as though his head was stuck in a fishbowl. He slammed the palm of his hand against the desktop. 'I take full responsibility for what happened to John. When he asked if he could go into Churchend to warn people that a lunatic was on the loose, I said no. He was persuasive. I changed my mind.'

Emerson eyed them all in turn. Croft's lips quivered, her face screwed and tear-stained. Adams glared, red-faced, angry. Not at him; he sensed that. The two young constables appeared dazed, their expressions blank. Professor Young looked on, filled with sympathy, while Summer scribbled notes. 'Now, God help me,' Emerson sighed, 'I have to tell his mother what happened. What can I say? Bristol has lost one of its best young policemen. He'd put in for Traffic.' He paused. 'He would have done a great job. Back to police business. What happened to the injured?'

Summer cleared his throat. 'The prison officers helped them into their van and ran them down to the hospital. They left a couple of their number at the scene. The others were going to continue back to where they'd come from.'

'I'm going to need a statement from you, Summer,' Emerson said.

'Of course,' the reporter replied. 'I'll come back in the morning, if I may. I've got a job to do.'

'We've all got jobs to do,' the inspector said. 'Not much more we can do tonight. Come on, everybody out.'

Chapter 53

Professor Young's house. Monday, August 11, 1:07 a.m.

'All right, Granddad, how about this one?' Summer held up a sheet of A3 paper with a mock headline scrawled across it in black felt pen.

Cannibal Killer Murder Spree in Sleepy Village. Four Dead.

'Nick, that headline isn't right either. I'm going to bed. I've a feeling tomorrow is going to be filled with challenges.'

Summer flipped the sheet over and dashed off another. 'This one?'

Ripper Rampage Stopped by Tragic Orphan.

'Better.' The old man smiled. 'How's the article going?'

Summer grinned. 'Sensational. I haven't quite finished it yet. Obviously, this is my lead into the scoop I was telling you about, but first I need to talk to Kotlas.'

'I wouldn't hold out any hope of him talking to you.'

'Why not? I know where he works. I can but try.' Summer's grin ignited into a smile. 'And if that doesn't get me what I want, I've an ace up my sleeve.'

The professor hauled himself from his armchair. 'Needs to be a good one.'

The two men faced each other. 'Why are you grinning like a ninny?' Professor Young asked, his eyes gleaming as the penny dropped. 'That's exactly what you have, isn't it?'

'Yes, I think so. I managed to get some research in at Bristol Library earlier. Some interesting aspects to the case. The Ripper lived in a world where people hardly ever locked their doors. I find that amazing. Also, many people came forward claiming psychic links to the killer. All debunked as far as I know. If only the police had had DNA testing in those days.'

'Yes, but then the world would have been deprived of one of its great mysteries.'

'Granddad, did you know it's thought the Ripper claimed seven victims?'

'I thought it was five.'

'I thought that, too. I know you'll mock this as nonsense, but Wolfe killed seven girls before they caught him.'

'Mere coincidence, Nick. In your investigations, beware the experimenter effect.'

Summer laughed. 'Funny you should say that, because that's the thing I have on Kotlas.'

'Oh?'

'Yes. What else would you call it when someone uses an unlicensed drug on a patient in their care?'

'You've lost me, Nick.'

'I'm assuming Kotlas had no authorisation to use ecstasy on Wolfe. It's my ace. I think it might open him up somewhat when I mention what I know.'

'You know what, Nick, you cunning devil, I've a feeling you might just pull this off.'

Chapter 54

Ashmore. Monday, August 11, 10:29 a.m.

From the moment Rachel Grimes arrived for work in the high-security psychiatric hospital's reception department, she knew it would be a long day. Transport being an issue, she was fortunate to live only three miles away. Now seated at her desk, she cursed her choice of shoes. One call after another came in, mainly visitors cancelling visits because they had no means to travel. Her head ached. She glanced up at the clock. Only another six and a half hours to go. She sighed as she picked up the phone to speak to the next caller.

'Is that you, Rachel?'

'It is. George?' She laughed. 'Give me a chance to introduce myself, why don't you? Let me guess. You're phoning to tell me you can't get in because your car won't start. Seriously, the phones have only just come back on, and they're going crazy. You okay? Were you very much affected by the power cut?'

'I'm going to be tied up for a day or two. It's a long story. I'll tell you all about it when I get in. How did you all cope yesterday?'

'Backup power took over seamlessly. Apart from losing everything signal-related, apparently, we carried on as normal. Some of the inmates kicked off about having no TV or radio. I dread to think what would have happened if we'd had a total blackout. Oh, and there was a telephone call from someone called Nick Summer. He was trying to get your mobile number. You know him?'

'Never heard of him. Did he say what was it about?'

'No, he didn't, but he left a number. I have it here. Would you like me to read it out to you?'

'No, that's all right. If it's important he'll ring me again. Is the boss there?'

Rachel laughed. 'Mike's here. You want a word?'

'Yes, please,' he hesitated, unsure of when to tell her he'd be back. 'I'll see you soon.'

She frowned at his hesitancy. 'I'll put you through, George. Hope everything's okay.' Rachel pressed the speed-dial button for the extension number she wanted. 'Mike, I've got George Kotlas for you. Will you take it?'

'Where are you, George? I'm guessing that, like half the population, you've got no transport. Do you want me to arrange a car for you?'

'I don't know, Mike. I've heard about the way the solar storm affected newer vehicles, though I haven't tried mine since yesterday. Look, I can't explain over the phone, but trust me, I can't wait to get back to a normal environment.'

'Were you badly affected by the cut?'

'You could say that. I'm in a lockdown situation at a private facility. I'll fill you in with the gory details as soon as I can. It's going to be a day or two.'

'It's fine, see you then.'

'Tell Wolfe to behave himself. I'll see him soon.'

A moment passed before Mike replied. 'By the way, George, when you do get in, you'll find a couple of changes.'

'Oh?'

'Yes, on Sunday they ghosted Wolfe out.'

'I heard.'

Mike hesitated again. 'How did you hear? Even I didn't know until afterwards.'

'I just heard, that's all,' Kotlas said. 'We'll talk when I come in. You mentioned a couple of things. What else?'

'You've been assigned a new inmate.'

'One out, one in,' Kotlas said philosophically.

'Yes, you can say that again. An interesting patient. He's tailor-made for you, George. I had his details here just now.' The sound of papers shuffling came down the line. 'Where have I put them?'

'Don't worry about the details now, Mike,' Kotlas said. 'What's his name?'

'Here they are,' Mike said. 'His name? It's Brody.'

Epilogue

Churchend. Six months later.

Anderson crunched across the gravel driveway and out onto the lane, pausing to look back towards the house. The February air seared his nostrils. Inhaling deeply, he jettisoned a plume of smoke-like vapour and watched it hang with some satisfaction. He turned left, walking slowly up the hill toward the crossroads, where he took a right in the direction of the church.

The demolition order which had been fixed to the graveyard wall the last time he'd visited had gone. Four circular nail-holes in the mortar joints were the only evidence it was ever there. Anderson stared at the bell tower. Magnificent, still gleaming frost on its cracked, north-facing wall. The reasons for its demise were blamed on the Church's abandonment, first of the orphanage, and then later, the house of God itself. All true, he'd later discovered while researching the backstory of the tragic siblings. They'd escaped the evil clutches of child abuse, only for their lives to end. For, in a sense, Timothy Salter's life had ended too that early August morning in 1987, as surely as if he'd died along with his sister.

Anderson backed up to the wall and pushed down with his gloved hands while lifting his backside onto the top of it. He swung a leg over and straddled the stone coping, the coldness penetrating the fabric of his jeans. He lowered himself down the other side.
The windows on the ground floor remained fully boarded.
Except one.
He'd heard Timothy had come back some time ago. He hadn't visited before, but it had prompted him to take action. He wouldn't have come if he didn't have something positive to say.

Deep in thought, Anderson meandered among the graves. Eleanor had stayed away. He'd expected that. The shock of the night that Wolfe came to his house had affected both their lives in ways they couldn't have imagined.

In the aftermath, the full story had emerged. Anderson couldn't help but wonder how Dr Ryan would have approached Timothy's trauma if he'd been able to treat the boy twenty-seven years ago. As far as Anderson was concerned, there were only two possibilities. Ryan would have unlocked him using stealth hypnotherapy, something he'd excelled at, and if that hadn't worked, there was always Vera, the medium. When Anderson had at last finished the book by Stella Bird, he made a mental note to trace her, to drop her a line thanking her. A smile crossed his face as he imagined her surprise at being told she'd inadvertently helped an old man get his life back on track by releasing Ryan's words, and that he'd read them at a time when he needed them most, the night of the mosquito, as Ryan had so eloquently put it. What followed could have happened to anyone. The convergence of Anderson's life with that of Wolfe, Eleanor, Constable Williams and Timothy, had perhaps been set in motion at the exact moment a coronal mass ejection exploded across the divide. Had that event drawn him to focus on significant moments and breathe new life into them? Anderson's prolonged epiphany didn't provide him with all the answers. What it did, though, was to narrow the field of questions.

Anderson trod the last few yards of turf, and then he was onto the shingle path leading up to the side door, the entrance to the priest's quarters.

Timothy Salter's eyes snapped open, grasping desperately and wordlessly for a hand he hadn't felt for over twenty-seven years. He winced at the pain in his chest and gazed at the photograph by his bed. The calendar displayed February 9, 2015. Removing the old page, he looked at the new one and read the wisdom quote by the light coming in through the slats. "In three words I can sum up everything I've learned about life: it goes on." Robert Frost. Catching movement from the corner of his eye, Timothy stooped and stared between the gaps in the boarded-up window. He watched Anderson approach and set the calendar down. A hooded robe selected, Timothy pulled it on.

Anderson noted that the doors had been left unsecured. He took a key from his pocket and checked it in the padlock. It didn't fit. Someone had changed it. He hadn't been inside the church for years. He entered. The air was colder than it was outside, but despite that, the scents of long gone masses teased his memories. Margot's funeral. The coffin bedecked, the aisles overflowing with flowers from well-wishers who'd ignored his requests to make charity donations instead. The eulogy he'd blustered his way through. The sympathetic looks, intended to be supportive, had torn him up inside. On the way in through the churchyard, he'd avoided her grave. Anderson lingered. He'd visit his wife on the way out, once the final arrangements had been made.

His footsteps echoed off of the flag-paved floors as he noted the tombs of the great and good, the ancient acoustics, leaning walls and high, pitched roofs set the sounds swirling at each subsequent step and created the impression that he walked in the presence of someone higher, someone greater.

At the altar, under the streaming array of colours from the one uncovered window, a hooded figure knelt in prayer. If he'd heard Anderson come in, he didn't acknowledge it.
Anderson stopped next to him, noting the battered Bible he had beside him. 'Can I join you?' he said.

There was room for a half-dozen other people on the kneeler. The hooded man needlessly shuffled six inches to the left. Anderson assumed his request had been accepted. Lowering himself to his knees, he propped his elbows on the shelf in front of him, bent his head and then closed his eyes.

Anderson wondered, what qualifications did a man need to become a priest? Goodness and humility? All the virtues of a saint? Surely the man dressed in robes next to him was a holy man, his devotion deserving of some recognition.

When Anderson had heard of the deconsecration proposals for the building, and that the Church had won its appeal to demolish it, he knew he couldn't have that. Not with Margot buried in the graveyard. They'd married here. She'd been christened here. Anderson intended to be buried in the same plot with her.

His understanding was that whatever happened, the cemetery would remain untouched, but with the building gone, for how long?

His investigations into Timothy's background had led him to Sarah Salter's grave. The best-tended of all the plots. Anderson couldn't see the man who'd saved him without a roof over his head. He considered offering him the use of an outbuilding he'd converted into living accommodations, but knew Timothy wouldn't take it.

When Timothy had concluded his prayers, he crossed himself, and getting to his feet, turned to Anderson, his gaze cast in the direction of the floor.

'I heard you were back here, Timothy, and I'm glad you've made a good recovery.' Anderson allowed a moment to pass before continuing. 'Your place here is neither safe, nor secure. You can't stay.'

Timothy's head lifted, his eyes darting from side to side.

'Don't worry,' Anderson said. 'The Church sold the building to me. I'm having it repaired. Of course, you'll have to move out while the work's done. But you're welcome to come and stay with me until that happens. What do you say?'

The mute shook his head.

'It's for a few weeks. Okay, longer than that, but listen, Sarah wouldn't have wanted this, living how you do. Your quarters are not fit for kennels.'

Timothy's pressed-lip, blazing-eyed refusal conveyed his response without the need of words. 'What you did, you and Williams, saved our lives. Come and stay. I've an outbuilding that's perfect for you.'

Timothy picked up his Bible, genuflected and crossed himself, and then, turning his back on Anderson, walked away.

'I have some work needs doing in my garden, Timothy,' Anderson said. 'Interested?'

Timothy's step faltered, but he kept walking.

'Well, you know where I am.'

Outside in the graveyard, strolling down the path, Anderson counted the rows of gravestones. He stopped, and leaving the shingle, made his way over the rough grass, checking his coordinates against the oak tree in the far corner and the bell tower behind. 'Well, I'll be,' he muttered. He visited very little. Margot owned a place in his heart. That was where he carried her, there and in his head. Today was different. He'd come to tell her something, and though it wasn't face-to-face, he felt it was the closest thing. Someone had cleaned her headstone, tidied the plot and put down fresh snowdrops. Some instinct urged Anderson to look in the direction of the presbytery. A shadow moved behind the slats covering the window. *Timothy.*

Anderson rested a hand on the shoulder of her headstone and knelt as he took her into his confidence.

A week later, Anderson went out through the conservatory into his garden. Timothy was on his knees, dressed in a new boiler suit. The mute saw him approach. He stood, wiped his hands on his thighs and waited for Anderson to speak.

'Good morning, Timothy. I've got something I'd like to tell you.'

The mute raised his eyebrows.

'Eleanor and I have decided to marry.' Anderson detected no reaction save for a gleam in Timothy's eye. 'We'd like you to be best man.'

Timothy lowered his gaze, slowly shaking his head.

'You know, I've been thinking ever since that night. I want to help you. This penitent life you lead, you punish yourself for something that wasn't your fault.'

Timothy turned away, sank to his knees by the flower bed and resumed plucking out weeds. There was anger in his movements; he pulled them up with more vigour than he had when Anderson had initially approached.

'Your sister wouldn't have wanted this life for you,' Anderson said.

Timothy stopped pulling. A fresh breeze whispered through the leaves. Timothy swayed. Anderson spoke, but he said what he thought Ryan would have. 'God moves in mysterious ways, Timothy. If you hadn't followed the path you took, if you hadn't put that Bible in your pocket – you'd have died, followed by me and Eleanor. All of us were saved for a reason.' Ryan's words tripped from Anderson's tongue. 'Sarah died that you should live.' He laid a hand on Timothy's shoulder. 'Can you not see that it's your time now?'

A small sob escaped the mute's lips. He sucked in air, struggling to contain his emotions.

'Think about it. We'd love you to do it. If you don't want to talk, I'll read your speech out for you. What do you say?'

Panic seized control of Timothy's movements. His hands flapped, fanning his face, eyes bulging as he sought to bring his breathing under control.

'Hey, fella,' Anderson said. 'It's all right. No one will ask you to do anything you aren't comfortable with. Let me get you a glass of water.' He strolled towards the conservatory. Reflected in the double glazing, he saw Timothy get to his feet, and pick up his scythe. He hurried towards him, a determined look on his face.

The older man's heart picked up a beat. He lengthened his stride. He'd almost reached the door when a strange resonance stopped him in his tracks. A spluttering, like the first turning of a long abandoned motor vehicle. He began to swivel around. 'Timothy?'

The noise repeated, the sound now like gravel dredged up from a long-dried riverbed, struggling for explication. 'M-M-Mic-h-ael?'

Anderson's face lit.

A message from Max

Thank you for reading *The Night of the Mosquito*. I hope you enjoyed it, and if you did, I'd be extremely grateful if you'd write a review, and possibly recommend it to friends and family.

Please check out my other books (available on Amazon):

The Sister
The Life and Times of William Boule
Don't turn on the Light (Release date: December 2015)

For news of upcoming releases, follow me on links below:
Amazon http://amazon.com/author/maxchina (follow for updates via Amazon)
Facebook https://www.facebook.com/max.china.1
Twitter @maxchina3

Website http://www.maxchina.co.uk or http://www.skinnybirdproductions.com

To contact me via email: Max@skinnybirdproductions.com

Thanks again for your support.

Max.

Printed in Great Britain
by Amazon